TRANSFORMATIONS

Ann Halam

PUFFIN BOOKS

PUFFIN BOOKS

Published by the Penguin Group
27 Wrights Lane, London W8 5TZ, England
Viking Penguin Inc., 40 West 23rd Street, New York, New York 10010, USA
Penguin Books Australia Ltd, Ringwood, Victoria, Australia
Penguin Books Canada Ltd, 2801 John Street, Markham, Ontario, Canada L3R 1B4
Penguin Books (NZ) Ltd, 182–190 Wairau Road, Auckland 10, New Zealand

Penguin Books Ltd, Registered Offices: Harmondsworth, Middlesex, England

First published by Orchard Books 1988
Published in Puffin Books 1990
1 3 5 7 9 10 8 6 4 2

Puffin Books 1990

Made and printed in Great Britain by
Richard Clay Ltd, Bungay, Suffolk

PROLOGUE

ONCE, LONG AGO, *the land had been different. The towers of light marched across its little hills and valleys, almost without a break: trees of light stood outside every door and lined every road. There need be no night, it could be daytime always. In those days the human world was served by the strange unnatural tools the scholars of the new land called "machines", and ordinary people knew as "makers". One maker would do the work of a hundred hands, but greatest of all were the Daymakers, the centres from which power flowed to all the lesser kind.*

Then daytime passed and night-time came. That is to say, night and day continued in their succession as always, but the country now called Inland was remade: and in the new world the shadowy night-time power that people have always called "magic" replaced the power of the machines. The new magic was rooted in an agreement they called the Covenant: the bond of cooperation, of giving and taking, between all things, living and non-living. Little children learned in tiny village schools "to say the Covenant", to remind them always of the truth that they must live by: The Covenant is in the mind and heart of every individual who lives by free will in What Is and with What Is ... *And as long as this free willed consent to the nature of things was maintained, the unconscious world was obedient to its human caretakers.*

Each small community called itself a "meeting" of the Covenant. Every so often the meeting would gather under the direction of a woman talented in magic, and trained to use her mind as the channel and connection between the wills and hearts of her people and the physical world. Together they would decide on the magical shifts and holdings they needed to bring about. The covener was the centre of a community's life. She was the only one entitled to kill a warmblooded animal for food; and the one who would be called on to bless the harvest, or decide on land use, or judge how far it was proper to change the natural pattern of the weather. The "land of the towers of light" had been rich and crowded, teeming with people and their works. Inland was young and poor, a place struggling to live and grow out of the ruins of the past. Resources that the past had squandered were in short supply — there was not enough magic yet to repair all the damage — but the Inlanders' fields were fertile, the weather was kindly, their animals healthy and docile: the tools of their crafts obedient and cunning.

Inlanders were mainly content with their lot. They looked on the lost time, with its glittering towers and its wealth of shining metal, with fear and disgust: whenever some strange survival was discovered it was destroyed with horror. But there still remained the Daymakers, the centres of power. At Hillen, the school of magic and centre of the land, the thirteen members of Hillen Coven, guardians of all Inland, believed they knew the location of every remaining ancient powerhouse. But these women, skilled and talented as they were, did not dare to touch the great Makers. They knew that the hatred and fear they felt would infect their work of destruction, generating only more evil.

Then came Zanne of Garth. The child of a simple country covener, she astonished everyone with her natural talent and her effortless control of Covenant magic. But the prodigy had a fatal flaw. Her first teacher, who loved her, called her "a child of Day". It was all too true. Zanne secretly loved the old times, and longed to see the world as it had been, with its countless miracles: and most of all those glorious creatures of singing metal — the makers. It should have been impossible. A child who loved machines could not be talented in natural magic. But Zanne was different. She saw beneath the forms, to where the "alien" makers and the natural world were one: and there, in that deepest truth, she found her magic.

At the end of her training at the Covenant school, Zanne set out on a quest to find the great Daymaker of the Outlands, the old powerhouse that had served her native Mid-Inland. She meant to use her magic to waken it again, in defiance of her teachers and all the people. But there were things that Zanne the self-confident child had failed to understand about magic and the Covenant, and the nature of Inland. She learned the truth about herself and her world at a cruel cost: and instead of wakening the Daymaker, though she loved it she killed it — with the same humble words her mother would have used to slaughter a sheep for a country feast day ... sister, don't blame me. I will die too, and be eaten ...

There was no way back to the towers of light. The only way was forward, to a different beauty; a different accomplishment. Zanne accepted this truth, and accepted the work she seemed to have been born for — to give a good and natural death to the great undead relics that haunted her world. But however Inlanders disapproved or called her crazy, she would never give up her love; or her awed wonder, before the perilous marvels of the past.

Zanne slept on the bare mountainside. It was early summer and the night was quite warm. The hard rock with its thin quilt of turf and flowers had been an uncomfortable couch when she lay down, but now it seemed as soft as a feather bed. She dreamed that she was sinking into the rock. The centre of her being was pulled inwards, as if she was diving into a deep blue pool. Down, down into the mountain. She began to feel herself coming apart, breaking into a stream of bright fragments, flowing through the solid stone...

A shadow crossed the moon. A wild creature howled, desolately.

Zanne woke up sweating, gasping in fear. She grabbed her staff in one hand and her pack in the other, and stared about. There was nothing to be seen, only the moonlight and bleak steep slopes rising all around the little hollow where she had made her camp.

She dropped the staff and rubbed her eyes. She must have been having a bad dream to wake up in such a panic but she couldn't remember it. The cry she had heard still seemed to linger: but after all this was wilderness. It would be odd if there weren't any strange noises on a night like this. Hunters or hunted — under the Covenant they were no threat to a human traveller.

Her waggon cloak had sneaked away from under her, collecting in an awkward bundle behind her knees. Perhaps the discomfort had contributed to her dream. She picked it up and climbed to the rim of the hollow, stretching her arms and legs. The whole landscape was clearly visible under a white half moon: not a house or a tree to be seen, only dim moorland sliced by sudden inky valleys.

Zanne knew that this appearance was deceptive. There were homesteads hidden in every steep valley, and almost under her feet lay the largest settlement in the mountains. Still she shivered a little even in the soft summery air. This was an inhuman sort of country compared with the little green fields and woodlands that she had known as a child. It was comforting to remember that it was still Inland. The people of these mountains lived by the power and under the protection of the Covenant just like Zanne herself. She could not really be a stranger here.

Zanne sighed. She'd been born with a longing for adventure, but now that she had her wish she often longed to be home again in the little village of Garth, and never leave it.

"Of course, of course," she muttered to herself, huddling her cloak around her. "And if you were in Garth, you'd long to be on the road."

She went back to her bed, which was no more than a fairly flat piece of turf, and tried to thump her pack into a kinder sort of pillow. She was chilly now, but there was no fuel for what Inlanders called "wildfire" so she didn't bother to get out her tinderbox. She would not make a fire by magic. She was too close to the settlements: any small shift or holding she made here might alter the balance carefully worked out by the covener of the mountain meeting.

Cold and wide awake, she sat up in the silvery dark, reflecting.

It was four years since Zanne had been made a covener: four years since she had destroyed the great Daymaker in the Outlands. She had spent the time between partly at Hillen school and at the college of Kor continuing her studies in magic. The other part had been spent in desolate ruined places all around the margins of Inland, following up stories of relics of the past and giving them good death. Now for the first time Hillen Coven had sent her to disarm another great Maker.

The name of this country was Minith. Somewhere in these mountains a centre of power survived. The Thirteen guardians at Hillen could not tell Zanne the exact location. For that she'd have to rely on local knowledge.

The mountain people were an independent lot. On some level, naturally, they were intimately part of the web of magic: giving their consent or refusal to any major shift or holding that were proposed by the meetings of all Inland. But on a day to day basis they had little to do with outsiders, apart from some necessary trade. That was their right. Inland was a country made up of many little lands, each holding firmly to its separate ways. Besides, it was from the mines of Minith that Inland got most of its precious small harvest of metal. And though some people believed that excessive use of metal was downright unconvenanted — because of the wicked metal makers of the past — life would be very difficult without the stuff. The Minithers deserved respect. If they chose to take it in the form of isolation, nobody was going to argue.

So it came about that even Hillen Coven could tell Zanne very little of what she would find here. All she had were some enigmatic warnings. *Be diplomatic*, she had been told. *Walk carefully. Don't make hasty judgements, and don't tell everyone your business all at once . . .*

Zanne laughed and shook her head. A few years ago she had been a schoolgirl in awe of Hillen Coven. Now those women were more like friends. They knew their emissary's faults. It was their tact that made her chuckle. She could translate that warning, easily, *Zanne, please don't start laying down the law in your usual manner. Try not to offend anyone, or to pick any fights. If that is possible!*

Well, she would try not to get into any trouble this time. She had no inclination to lay down the law or to pick fights. It would be a sad and lonely job, that was all: to kill the great marvellous creature that must not be, that could only live in Inland as a sickness and a curse. She wondered what the Maker would be like. She knew more than most scholars about the lost past by now, and she'd learned the powerhouses could take many forms. For the first time she reached out cautiously, deliberately studying this mountain land with her mind. *Where are you?* she asked, thinking of the great masses of stone, the unknown crags and peaks stretching all around: and then remembered her dream, of diving into blue granite like a pool.

It wasn't a bad dream at all, she thought. How strange. I wonder why I woke so frightened.

She was settling to sleep again, when she heard movement. Soft feet trotted round the rim of her hollow. Zanne sat up. The shadowy form was indistinct: a wolf or a wild cat. Something panted. It was not a pleasant sound, but Zanne was ashamed of her earlier panic. She reached into her pack and brought out a sweet biscuit.

"Hello cousin, wild cousin. Do you want to be friends?"

Another long, shuddering cry. The creature was gone.

She was glad she'd seen the four-legged shape and heard its breathing. Otherwise she'd have thought she'd been visited by a ghost. Zanne had met many kinds of wild beast before, but never one that made such a miserable noise: like a human voice robbed of words, crying out in hopeless fear and pain...

Oh Zanne, stop being such a baby. Shut up and go to sleep. She pulled the cloak over her head and did her best to obey her own instructions. She would need to have her wits about her tomorrow, for her first meeting with the Minithers.

CHAPTER ONE

AUNT LECTE

THE SLACK YARD was an unattractive place, at least Sirato always thought so. It stood on the mountain side of the farm, walled in on three sides with brick pressed from grey tailings. The fourth wall was the back of the brickyards. Opposite that was the open gap where the sled track came down from the mine workings, a mountain vale away straight above Sirato's home. The burnished cobbles of the track glistened violently in all weathers, sometimes they seemed to shine in the dark. Sirato used to think it was like the tongue of an enormous fierce animal stretching down to lick her up.

As she crept in through the wicket gate from the farmyard the little girl dropped on her knees and covered her face, and gabbled the Covenant promise in a rapid mumble. *The Covenantisinthemindsandheart* ... Under the Covenant, she finished fervently, Mountain forgive me...

The gritty refuse of the mines, the "slack" or tailings, were poisonous in their raw state. Minith people used them, because everything must be used: making them into hard-wearing brick. Every house in Minith was built of the same glittering grey blocks and they were traded all over Inland. But it was only the strength of Minith's Covenant that stopped the people who worked in the dust from getting ill. And Sirato didn't have that protection, because she wasn't supposed to come here. She sneaked along the wall, half deafened by the noise of the brickyard at work; and into a shed by the sled track gap. This was a big place with a floor of packed rock dust and a high airy roof. It was dark inside when she carefully shut the doors behind her, but she didn't falter as she slipped between trestles and stacks of old tools. Still, her heart was beating very hard by the time she reached her secret place. There were watchers in the dark. They tormented Siri everywhere, even when she was in her own bed at night. It was worse when she was doing something forbidden.

There was a big stack of lumber in front of her corner, a pile of old pit props that hadn't been used for years and years. The timber was velvety when you touched it, with a coating of dust and cobwebs. Siri brushed by with a murmur of gratitude: she was safe. She crouched on the ground and her fingers found by touch the loose brick in the corner. When she pulled it inwards, a little dust fell down with a tiny sound. Light came after the dust so that Siri's hands suddenly appeared, small and workhard and glinting with silver. She scraped away a patch of dirt at the base of the wall. There was a cavity underneath. It must have had some purpose once but now it belonged to Siri. She pulled out a parcel of dark oiled cloth, an odd-shaped and awkward bundle longer than her arm. Underneath it there was a little wooden box. She took that out too. Inside the box there was a mirror, not a magical one but a simple piece of tradecraft glass with a silvered back. It might well be the only such mirror in Minith. Siri propped it against the timber stack and looked at her own face. She was eleven years old, she was pretty sure of that though nobody at Slack Road paid much attention to frivolities like birthdays. She had dark brown hair that grew down in a peak in the middle of her forehead, dark eyebrows in perfect semicircles that gave her face a surprised look; and clear brown eyes, the colour of mountain water. Her chin was rather pointed, her skin naturally pale with red cheeks that showed through the tan of outdoor work.

Siri pulled down her hair, which was kept severely tucked behind her ears. She pulled it forward around her cheeks and then scraped it back. She didn't know which was right, no one would tell her.

"Mother?" she whispered.

It was the face of her mother that she saw in the glass. Her father had told her so. He had probably forgotten, but she always remembered. He hardly ever talked about mother. Aunt Lecte didn't like it. When someone dies, the Covenant has taken them. To go on talking about them was like saying the Covenant did wrong. What's gone's gone, it must not be called back ... Sirato wished that was the only reason that mother must be forgotten. She was afraid there was more. Mother had been ill for a long time, and people don't get ill unless the Covenant is angry with them. Frightening, terrible things happen to people who defy the Covenant. She tried not to think about it. In a way she was glad no one would talk. As long as she didn't know, she didn't have to hate mother. She touched the glass that held her only friend very gently. Sometimes when she came here she cried and poured out storms of bitterness, but this wasn't one of those days. It was a day for silently telling mother things and imagining that she listened, gave you a hug and good advice for how to deal with a hard world.

After a while she put the mirror away, feeling quiet and comforted. She unwrapped the oilcloth parcel. Inside there was a violin and a bow. It was a full-sized instrument, rather large for an eleven-year-old. Sirato sat up straight, cross-legged, and settled the violin in the hollow of her shoulder with an automatic gesture: which she might have seen perhaps when she was a very small child. There was just enough room in the corner for her to move the bow. She tried the strings and twisted the pegs one by one. She didn't know that she was tuning her instrument, she didn't even know the names of the notes. She had found the treasure here years ago, and realised that mother must have hidden it before she was so ill she had to stay in her room. Everyone knew Rian Mountainside used to have a fiddle. She had it from her grandmother. The Mountainsides were very wild and shocking people, and therefore of course they didn't prosper. Rian had been the last of her kind when she came to Slack Road, the Mountainside farm didn't exist anymore. No one who belonged to Slack Road would play "unnatural" music. *Leave it to the wind and the water and the birds in the sky. That's where What Is put music, and anything else is wicked imitation* ... That was what Aunt Lecte had told her niece, when she asked for music lessons. Luckily she had managed to do so without revealing that she had found her mother's fiddle.

The mirror she hadn't found. She had stolen it, creeping one day into the room that had been mother's sickroom and was always shut up now. Sirato was a bad girl. She wished she wasn't, but there was no denying it. She could scarcely remember a day in her life when she hadn't been in serious trouble over something or other, or else waiting guiltily for some crime to be found out. And here she was right now, defying the Covenant again. It was a shame, a wicked shame, to do things that gave people a chance to say: *there goes Rian's daughter, as bad as the one that's gone* ... But she couldn't help herself. However she struggled she would still come back here, sneaking and hiding. She sighed, and lifted the bow.

Sing — sing lovely wooden shell. Like the wind and like the water, like the wild birds crying on the mountain. Once long ago a roadwalker had come by Slack Road: a young man with a flute and a little drum and a memory full of songs. The Minithers fed him cold charity and sent him on his way. They never welcomed strangers, not even the decent kind. But Sirato remembered. She played all those tunes now, and others that had no names, which she had heard perhaps when she was a tiny baby. And others still which were hardly tunes at all, that she had made up herself. Time slipped away, her fingers grew cramped on the strings: she didn't notice.

The noise of the brickyard covered Sirato's music and almost stopped her from hearing herself. But as always there came a moment when she knew that the song had collapsed and she was just making the most awful noises. The fiddle lay disconsolately across her lap. Really, she wasn't breaking the Covenant at all, she thought sourly. No one could call that disgusting row music — natural or unnatural.

The light from the hole in the wall went out. Sirato stopped breathing. Part of the light came back. She could see what was blocking the space. It was an eye, a round gleaming eye: the same peat water colour as her own and fringed in curling dark lashes. She gasped. The fiddle and bow were already behind her back. She had jerked them there instantly. Had the eye seen? It vanished, as silently as it had come. Sirato's breath hissed like an angry little snake. She shoved the loose brick back into place violently. In pitch darkness with desperate speed and care she wrapped up the precious guilty things, pushed them into the cavity and scooped dirt over them. Frantically her hands smoothed the place, feeling to make sure no fold of oilcloth showed above the ground. She scrambled from behind her lumber stack backwards, her heart thumping in panic and rage.

He wasn't in the shed. She brushed her clothes down, smoothed her hair and came out into the sunlight with her chin up. The owner of the spying eye was leaning against a pile of empty sleds, smiling infuriatingly. It was her brother Holne. He had the same dark hair and bright eyes but she was absolutely certain he looked *nothing* like mother. She glared at him."Sneak!"

Holne grinned. He was sixteen, not a child anymore but a flores, as people called half-grown young adults in Inland. He ought to have been Siri's protector and her ally but he wasn't. He was always teasing and spying and telling tales, and there was no one to stop him. He was Aunt Lecte's pet.

"Sneak yourself," he responded cheerfully. "You know this yard's not meant for little girls."

Holne laughed, showing a lot of bright white teeth. It was easy enough for him. He was never in trouble, no matter how many chores he missed. He never needed a place to hide.

"I hate you."

She clenched her fists. If she had any magic in her, she would give him a festering rash over his handsome face. She would make him see monsters following him about.

But he only laughed again at her helpless fury. "You ungrateful little Rat. I thought you might like to know: Aunt's looking for you. She was just about to launch a search. I decided you might even prefer me to find you first."

Sirato's face went white under the brown.

"Don't call me that. If you can't say my whole name call me 'Siri' — like m-mother used to."

"Oh, what nonsense. You don't remember mother at all. And if you did you'd know she used to call you her little Rat. It suits you."

Sirato glared. It was true, Siri was a name she'd made up for herself. But mother had never called her Rat. That was a foul lie. Without a word she began to hurry to the wicket gate.

Holne easily kept pace. "What do you get up to in there, Rat?" he asked curiously. "Are you nursing a sick cat?"

She felt sick herself. Did he hear? Did he know? He was horribly good at finding out her secrets. The worst thing about Holne was that you could never tell what he would do. Sometimes he seemed to be kind: like now, warning her that Aunt Lecte was coming. But the next moment he would be telling tales again. It was all a game to him. He was like a cat, and Sirato the helpless little furred creature caught in his claws. This time it was more serious than ever. If she lost mother's violin, she didn't know what she would do. She tried not to show any sign that she was more frightened than usual.

"None of your business," she snapped. "I don't have to tell you anything."

Holne laughed again as he strolled away. "Silly little Rat, I'm only trying to help. Keep away from the slack yard for a while, that's all. She's getting suspicious."

Aunt Lecte was in the kitchen. She was standing watching the door as her niece hurried in, there was no chance to get by. Lecte Slack Road didn't look in the least like her niece and nephew. She was one of those people they called "the black Minithers". Her brother, the children's father, was of the same type but his looks weren't so pronounced. It was a strain that came and went in certain Minith families. In other parts of Inland it would have been called unusual beauty, but Minith people did not talk like that. Lecte was tall and slender, her skin blue dark, her features clear cut as if carved out of gemstone. There were silver threads now in her crisp black hair, but that only made her more handsome.

Sirato knew that her aunt was beautiful. She cared far too much about things like that, it was part of her wickedness. But it was a hard, cold beauty, unyielding as the mountain. She stopped on the threshold. She longed to keep her head up and face Aunt proudly but it was always the same. What sneaked into the kitchen was not a brave victim of persecution. It was a cringing, wincing creature, that twisted its hands and kept its eyes on the ground.

"You were not at pensioner school."

Down in the town there was a school, run by people who had retired from their trades to live in the little row of pensioner cottages. She was supposed to join the other children there if ever she had no chores. Someone must have betrayed her, probably Holne. But Aunt never explained where her information came from. She rarely asked questions either. As she often said — that was only encouraging the bad girl to tell lies.

"I went for a walk."

She forced herself to look up. She was hoping to get by by confessing to a lesser crime — in Minith people didn't just go out walking for no reason, especially not children.

Lecte was smiling unkindly. "And where did you walk?"

"On the mountain," gasped Sirato, flustered.

They both knew that had to be a lie. Every Minith child was afraid of the huge grey bulk that leaned over Slack Road farm: and Sirato was more imaginative than most. She felt her face going red and couldn't stop it.

"Well, Rat, if you don't choose to learn your lessons you will never have a trade, that's all. Get out to the roadshed and help them pack bricks. The Covenant hates to see a child idle."

In the roadshed bricks bound out of the valleys were wrapped and sacked up ready to be carted off to the waggon road. The two farmworkers Truc and Mab were already there, baling up; and Danno, her father's apprentice. He came from a neighbouring valley, but lived at Slack Road while he was learning to be a brickmaker. Sirato walked in and pulled on a pair of heavy work gloves, giving the others bitter looks. Many Minithers came to work in Slack Road's brickyard at busy times, but Mab and Truc had lived and worked at the farm all Sirato's life. They were Aunt Lecte's people, not to be trusted: and Danno was just as bad; a proper meek Minither boy. Sullenly she took her place at the bench, picking bricks off the stack, folding each in a wisp of straw and passing them to Mab.

"Did you just come up from the town, Truc?"

"Yes, Rat, I did," answered the old man solemnly.

"Did you speak with Anarad Pensioner as you went by?"

Anarad, a retired miner, was in charge at the pensioner school.

He nodded. Getting information out of Truc was like panning for gold.

"Was it you who told Aunt Lecte I wasn't in school?"

Truc faced her accusing eyes without a trace of guilt. "Yes indeed, Rat my dear, I told your aunt. It was my duty, wasn't it. And for your good that she should know."

Danno gave Siri a worried glance. He was afraid of her, thought Siri: afraid that the wickedness was infectious. But there was no point in expecting sympathy from anyone here. Much less support. Anarad Pensioner used to say at school: "If you are unhappy, if you want advice or help, you should tell the covener." The covener was an outsider — someone sent by Hillen Coven, the thirteen wise women who were in charge of all Inland, to look after the people of Minith and lead the meetings in the big meeting house down in Minith town. But the idea of going to her for help was ridiculous. Children weren't even allowed into the meeting house. And if they were neither the covener nor anyone else would take Sirato's part. Lecte Slack Road was an elder of the meeting: everyone looked up to her. As far as Sirato could tell, Aunt Lecte was in the right. She was a good Covenant-fearing woman and little Rat was just born bad.

She set to work mechanically: lifting bricks and wrapping them and passing them until her back ached. She bit the inside of her lip until it bled to stop herself from shouting at old Truc for telling tales. He would only report that too, and make things worse. Her gloves were soon full of grit, they hurt her hands. She was eleven years old already and it was true, no one was ever going to offer her a trade. She would have to stay at Slack Road all her life, obeying Aunt Lecte. Everyone thought Sirato was just lazy and stupid. If only she had the courage to tell them — she did have a calling. She would work all the hours of day and night if they would let her learn music. One day she would take her mother's violin and run away, far away out of Minith ... Sirato had never heard any tales of other parts of Inland. The mountain country was isolated both naturally and by choice: Minithers didn't leave and strangers didn't stay. She had never even been as far from home as the waggon road. But she would just run and keep on running...

It was no use. Even in her imagination Siri couldn't believe it. The Covenant was everywhere. If she should succeed in getting away from Minith, there would be another meeting wherever she looked for shelter. There would still be people like Aunt Lecte and life would be just the same, hard and confined and dreary. That was the Covenant: that was right. And besides, Siri didn't have the courage. She knew that if she tried to escape, the mountain would know it and somehow stop her. That great fierce animal glowering down on the roofs of Slack Road was watching now, listening to her thoughts. It would punish her. Aunt Lecte and the mountain: they would punish —

"Sirato!"

She looked down in astonishment. It hardly seemed possible that a moment's inattention could have caused such damage. She had dropped one brick and the whole front of her stack was scattered on the floor. Several bricks were chipped, a few had actually broken in half. Now the waggon load would be short, the kiln have to be stoked again, hand work and magic taken away from other tasks to make up the loss. Minith never sent out imperfect goods or short measure, that was unthinkable. Poor Rat! She must have been thinking bad thoughts, or else she must have been doing something wicked today. Under the Covenant, there are no accidents. No one suffers unless they deserve it.

Sirato stood crimson faced, trying to stop the tears. If she cried or showed temper that would be another crime. She knew what the others were thinking. And of course they were right, quite right. She had spent hours this afternoon, secretly and deliberately doing wrong.

Truc and Danno began to clear up the mess, quietly and calmly like good Minithers. Mab sighed over Sirato. She was not angry. Her kind honest face, with its crown of rough dusty red curls, was full of real pity.

"Ah, dear. The one who's gone had just your temper, poor little Rat."

In the farmhouse kitchen Aunt Lecte presided over the evening meal. Gwil Slack Road and his two children, Danno, Mab and Truc sat around the white scrubbed table in silence. As it was nearly summer they had no lamp, only a pair of tallow dips. Lecte was very strict about wicked waste. She hated to see her household use anything it did not need. Sirato was in disgrace. She was so accustomed to this state that she barely noticed it. She had been sent to the far end of the table and must eat standing. Resignedly, she ate up her bowl of bean porridge. There was a platter of oatcake as well but she was to have no butter on her share so she had decided to do without. She had had no midday bite because she hadn't been at school: probably Aunt had forgotten that, but Sirato wasn't going to remind her. She would rather starve.

There was no idle chatter while they were eating. Sirato's eyes passed wearily from face to face. There was kind Mab, with her red curls and her freckles and her big hard work-worn hands. Mab had always worked at Slack Road. She had given Sirato all the gentleness and mothering she had ever known, when she was a little girl. Mab was almost a gossip by Minith standards: even now, she would sometimes forget herself and tell stories about the past. But as Sirato got older Mab had somehow slipped away. She couldn't be persuaded anymore to wink at Sirato's misdeeds, or help her out of trouble. She was afraid of Aunt Lecte of course. And of the Covenant.

Truc, the old shepherd, was different. He had big bushy grey eyebrows and a long face that always looked miserable: being sober and solemn came naturally to him. No one would ever dream of asking him to do anything against the Covenant.

It was strange to think that once Mab and Truc had been young. Mab came from a mining family, Truc had been the youngest child on another small Minith farm. They might have wanted to take up their own trades, have their own lives. But the meeting had decided they were needed at Slack Road, because it was a big holding and the family was small. So here they stayed like good Minithers.

And there was her father, Gwil Slack Road the brick-maker. How sad his face always was. He must have had some fight in him once, or he would never have married Rian Mountainside, the wild one. But he had lost the battle long ago. In those days, before Sirato was born, Aunt Lecte had gone away from Minith to learn a trade. When Sirato's mother got so ill, she had to come home to run the farm, that was the story that Mab told. Sirato wondered sometimes whether that was why Aunt Lecte hated her: because she had had a chance to get away but had to give it up. But that didn't make sense — for she didn't hate Holne. And she couldn't really imagine Lecte wanting to leave Minith. Probably she had been glad of the chance to take over, thought Sirato vindictively, so that she could bully her brother, and rule everything.

Beside Gwil was Holne, looking all handsome and rosy in his deep rust coloured smock with the embroidered sleeves. He was the only one at table wearing any decoration. He did that stitching himself, but Aunt Lecte allowed it. Siri was never permitted to dress up like that. She scowled, and looked away before he could see her "pulling faces" — and tell tales.

Silently, slowly, Gwil Slack Road ate his dinner. He was a good Minither now: never raising his voice, never moving quickly. Sometimes he looked as if the mountain had got into his blood and was slowly changing him from the inside, into stone.

Siri began to have one of her imaginings. Outside the sunny day had faded into a dull evening: although it was Old Spring very little evening light came in through the small paned windows. The kitchen was so big and dark. Its bare walls were not limewashed or painted, the grey brick showed everywhere behind the dressers and hanging kitchen tools. It was like being in a cave, as if the mountain had quietly opened its mouth and swallowed Slack Road whole. Sirato felt she could see herself and the others crouched around a lump of rock that they wrongly believed to be a table. The hunched little bodies seemed to be wearing fur, not clothes. If the dim tallow flared it would be quite clear: underground things, munching and peering at each other and planning ugly mischief...

She woke with a start to find that Danno was shyly offering her one of his buttered oatcakes. She stared at it, astonished.

Holne chuckled. "Grab it quick," he whispered, "quickly, you silly little Rat." And of course Aunt Lecte heard him and saw what was going on. She stared down the table, frowning. But she was not displeased with Danno.

"All things are bound together, even the smallest. That is what Rat must learn, Danno. But you are a good boy to think of her."

"No thanks," snapped Sirato. "I'm not hungry."

Danno sighed and calmly went back to his supper. If only she could be like that, like a proper Minither child. I've done it again, thought Sirato miserably. She was a bad girl, and it was her own fault she had no friends. Under her eyelashes she looked daggers at Holne. It wasn't fair. He ought to have been reproved for whispering. If it was right for Aunt Lecte to be so hard on Siri, why did no one ever notice that she was too soft on Holne? Because she was. Everyone was soft on him. He was always hanging around idle, when he wasn't off wandering on the mountain. But it didn't seem to make any difference. Sirato could sneak and spy too. She knew that recently Holne had been up to things even worse than wandering and idling in the daytime. She wished she dared to tell. But she was afraid of her brother's revenge —

She was so busy thinking bitter thoughts that she forgot herself, and her small hungry hand reached out towards the buttered oatcake which Danno had left on the side of his plate.

Aunt's stern glance fell on the hand so it felt as if someone had trodden on it.

"You did refuse before, child, and said you were not hungry. You must not make yourself a liar."

At the end of the meal Sirato cleared the plates into the scullery, and the daytelling began. Aunt Lecte folded her hands and began to speak, recounting everything that had been done that day by the household at Slack Road; and everything that was planned for tomorow. Of course Sirato's "accident" was discussed at length: its probable causes and the trouble that would follow after it. Any bad action, any lack of restraint, was an injury to the whole of Minith...

At every pause the household intoned together: "under the Covenant" or "within What Is". The daytelling was a Minith custom. Every evening, every household would sit together like this and go over the day carefully, almost moment by moment, to make sure the Covenant had been properly kept to Minith standards. The ceremony meant more to the mountain people than the covener meetings down in the town: and even the smallest children were expected to sit quietly and attend, though the daytelling might go on for two hours or more.

Under the Covenant! cried Truc and Danno and Mab, with real enthusiasm. *Under the Covenant* mumbled Siri, who felt as if she was being tortured. Holne was trying to catch her eye, he was giving her secret little winks. But she refused to notice. She could see nothing amusing in the hateful fuss they were all making over a few chipped bricks. She'd have liked to report the winking. After all, everyone was supposed to tell tales on everyone else. You were supposed to like it when people announced your faults in public. But she dared not. He knew too much.

The household meeting was bad. But as it came to an end Sirato remembered that there were worse things. She twisted her hands and chewed her lip, willing Aunt Lecte's voice to go on and on. But the moment had to come.

"Bed time, child," said her aunt.

The girl got up, She smoothed her dun smock and pulled at the knees of her coarse grey knitted leggings, in a hopeless attempt to put off the evil for a little longer. She walked slowly round the table and pecked at her brother's cheek perfunctorily, her eyes looking somewhere beyond his left ear. She brushed her lips against her father's cool cheek: and he smiled sadly and murmured as always "Good night, little one. Sleep sound and don't dream." She kissed Aunt Lecte, as she must. It was like kissing a rock. Unusually, her aunt put a hand on her arm.

"You are a hard child to teach. Try to learn restraint, Rat: and remember, all I do is for your own good."

"Yes, Aunt Lecte," answered Sirato bleakly.

She washed herself at the scullery pump. She could not linger, everyone could hear her. She passed through the kitchen again and shut the door behind her quietly. And now that shadowy cave seemed like a warm and glowing refuge. She was in the dark. She walked the windowless passage beside the kitchen and climbed a short flight of stairs. It was easy in the light to be angry and proud. But every night she was a little girl again. The Covenant loves the dark and hates the light. She had been taught that, and she believed it. She could feel it here. The Covenant and the mountain: they were one and the same, crushing her beneath their lightless weight. She had to pass her mother's room, and now even her dead mother whom she loved had become a thing of terror. Sirato scurried by with her eyes tight closed, praying that that door would not open...

She climbed another flight of steps, steep and long, that creaked underfoot and told all the monsters she was coming, and then she was in the loft. Her bed was separated from the rest of the big shadowy room by a makeshift partition that didn't reach up to the roof. In dark weather you couldn't see the gap but in summer or on bright nights in winter Sirato had to try and go to sleep watching that grey empty space, and the dim faces that came and peered there.

She took off her clothes and got into her nightsmock in a rush. The sheets on her hard little bed were good linen, the quilt serviceable: everything was scrupulously clean. There was no colour, nothing beautiful, but it was wrong of Sirato to care about things like that — another of her endless crimes.

She lay staring up at the space above the partition. Today had been a bad day. She would not dare to close her eyes, not for a long time.

The summer of Sirato's eleventh year was shaping up to be a long hot one, said those who knew the signs. The mountain country could be cold and dreary, with hardly any difference between Midsummer and Year's End. But occasionally one of these hot seasons would come, when the heather burned like purple fire and the sky became a blue white furnace over the crags. Then the miners were glad to get underground, and the shepherds watched the parched high pasture anxiously for devastating outbreaks of wildfire. When their shift was done in the brick kilns or the smelting furnace the tradespeople went soberly down to the cold pools of the Burnhouse stream and bathed, for their health's sake. But even in the height of one of these summers, which would have driven any other Inland people to wild water parties and complete idleness, the Minithers did not relax their stern rule of life. The harvest of metal from the rock was a doubtful business, almost unconvenanted. Everybody understood that, and knew that strict observance of the Covenant in all other ways, to accept What Is in all things; was essential, or else the getting of metal would be even more dangerous. But the mining people were not resentful of others who lived easier lives. They pitied the outsiders who would never know the true Covenant, the hard, real Covenant of Minith. Sometimes Hillen sent a covener who tried to interfere. However the elders of the meeting soon taught her that she couldn't bring frivolous outside ways to the mountain. The woman learned restraint, or else she didn't stay long.

Sirato did her chores grudgingly and went to school when she couldn't avoid it. In this she wasn't so different from many Inland girls and boys, in the rebellious years between childhood and flores. But nowhere else would she have been afraid, so afraid of her own naughtiness. She did not dare go back to her secret place after Holne's teasing. She lived in dread of the moment when he would decide to tell. But she found that she did not get any better, for giving up the forbidden music. She only felt more wicked and more miserable than ever. She had always been told that frightening, horrible things happened to bad children: now she discovered that it was true.

She began to dream.

It started very quietly. She would wake up in the night to find herself listening to a little squeaking, scrabbling sound. There were no rats or mice at Slack Road. She lay there terrified and not knowing why, until she realised that the little sounds were coming from herself. Then she was more frightened than ever. The dream came every night and gradually she remembered more, or else it grew. She left her bed and crept along tunnels no bigger than her body. She scrabbled and scratched her way into hateful places: she gnawed on foul refuse and bit at her own scaly tail. The furry body hurt her, it smelled bad, she hated it. And yet she could not help herself. She must be this creature ... not Sirato anymore.

One night she woke so frightened she simply could not make herself stay in bed. It must be quite late because the room was completely dark, but she could hear movement in the house below. She pattered down the loft stairs, past her mother's room to the top of the small flight above the kitchen passage. Aunt Lecte was at the yard door with Holne. She was holding a rush taper in her hand. Sirato hissed in surprise. She thought she was the only one who knew that Holne sneaked out like this. She couldn't imagine what he was up to, going out in the dark when all good Minithers were in bed — except that obviously it must be something wicked. But here was Aunt Lecte patting him on the shoulder, stroking his hair ... It was so long since anyone had touched Sirato like that. She didn't want Aunt Lecte's caresses, she'd rather die than beg for them. But she felt so lonely suddenly, that a loud gasping sob escaped from her.

Aunt Lecte shut the door behind Holne and turned. Her face was grey in the taper light, her eyes were like big black holes.

"What are you doing out of bed, child?"

Sirato knew somehow she must not mention her brother. "I had a dream—" she quavered. Aunt Lecte's voice sounded almost gentle. She took courage and burst out. "I wish people wouldn't call me 'Rat'. It gives me bad dreams—" She burst into tears and began to tell the horrors, about scrabbling in the dirt, about the tunnels and the gnawing of rubbish. But Aunt Lecte's gentle moment was over.

"That is not a bad dream," she said coldly. "That is a good dream, sent by the Covenant to warn you. And we call you Rat for your own good, as a warning too. You mind your ways and learn not to deserve that name, and then you'll be in no danger."

Sirato's tears stopped. Her face was pinched and small with anger. She bobbed her head like a good Minith girl.

"Thank you for reproving me, Aunt."

With one irrepressible glance of hatred, she ran off back to bed.

Lecte Slack Road was left alone. She blew out her taper and stood in the dark. "I have lost one," she murmured. "I will not lose both. I will not."

There was a note in her voice that sounded almost like defiance. She heard it herself, and frowned. "Always under the Covenant," she added firmly. "If it is the will of the Covenant, I will save the other."

CHAPTER TWO

THE ROADWALKER

SIRATO WAS AT the intakes haymaking when the stranger came down from the mountain. High above Minith town, on these sunny sheltered terraces, the early summer grass had grown long and sweet. Sheep were pastured just above but they couldn't touch the hay. It was protected by magic; more secure than any wall or hedge. All spring the flocks came and bumped their noses against the warding but could not break through. Now the same sheep, insatiably curious, gathered in groups to watch the humans at work; and half grown lambs danced and butted playfully at the invisible fencing. The ewes' dark fleeces showed pull lines and were coming away at the throat: it was nearly harvest time for them too. Sirato, trudging with her rake in line with the other children, eyed the beasts warily. In Minith shepherding was not children's work. She had very little to do with animals except for Slack Road's hens, and was slightly afraid of anything bigger.

Carad Breakwater, an elder of the meeting and a friend of Aunt Lecte's, was keeping a close eye on her charges. She did not see the small moving figure on the horizon. Neither did the other children, working away with their heads down. The rest of the adults were at the other end of the field. Sirato watched, squinting up her eyes against the noon sun. Who could that be, up in the middle of nowhere? She could make out a staff, and a gleam of bright colour. The person seemed to be wearing a shiny yellow sunhat. Sirato almost dropped her rake in excitement. She suddenly knew that this couldn't be anything but a stranger. A real live stranger.

"Lay your rakes, now — " shouted Carad. "Lay your rakes, into the shade and take your bite. No taking off of hats! No running about!"

Sirato let herself be edged to the back of the hungry crowd around the midday baskets. She dropped behind a tall boulder, slipped through the intakes' warding and raced away, her bare feet pounding on the hard footpath, green heather whipping by and scouring her ankles. Even in her excitement she kept to the path: children were strictly forbidden to "wander" on the hillsides. But she didn't consider for a moment how wicked it was to run away alone, or think what would happen to her if (when) news of this truancy reached her aunt. The person walking down out of nowhere must be heading for Minith town. Whoever it was, they must pass by Slack Road's gate. This was the first outsider Sirato had seen (except for the covener, who didn't count), since the young roadwalker with his flute had passed through Minith years ago, and set free her dreams of music. Minith meeting kept all strangers at bay, like the sheep from the intakes. The grown ups were proud of it. No one leaves, no one comes in: that was their idea of perfection.

Sirato was not the only one to have spotted something unusual. By the time that figure had reached the bend in the track above Slack Road, Aunt Lecte was at the farm gate by the roadshed, waiting. The stranger came up and stood, leaning on her staff. She seemed to be looking over the wall and assessing the neat yards with approval. Lecte Slack Road smiled thinly. Approval from a vagrant was something she didn't need.

"Good day — " Lecte's cold smile was returned cheerfully. "Lovely weather for the hay, isn't it."

Sirato, still out of breath, had scrambled the yard wall and was keeping out of sight behind a shed. It was yellow hair, not a hat: yellow hair in a wild unruly tangle. The stranger's skin was burnt brown, her clothes looked as if she had been sleeping in them.

Lecte nodded. "We don't often see outsiders on our roads. What's your business in Minith, young woman?"

"I — " The yellow-haired girl seemed to hesitate. She looked older than Holne, thought Sirato, but not quite grown up. She looked nicer than Holne, too.

"I suppose you want work."

Sirato winced. It was the only kind of welcome a stranger could expect in Minith, but this girl wouldn't know that. She would walk on looking for a friendlier house, and Sirato's chance would be lost. She did not know what kind of chance. She only knew that she wanted to jump out from behind the shed right now crying — take me with you! Take me away!

When the stranger didn't reply, Lecte explained more forcefully. "Either you work or you don't eat at any table in Minith. That's our rule. Maybe you'd better go back the way you came."

There were a few vagrants in Minith: born Minithers who moved from farm to farm dayworking, never wanted or needed enough to settle down. Aunt Lecte wouldn't tolerate that sort except when she was desperate for extra labour. She wouldn't let anyone starve, but she'd give a dole and turn them off down the track, like the poor flute player. The yellow-haired girl looked at the ground, and her own dusty bare feet, and the head of her staff.

"I need somewhere to stay in Minith," she agreed at last. "And of course I'll help with the farm work while I'm here. It's haymaking, isn't it; and I saw your sheep are nearly ready to drop the fleece — "

"You are unskilled then? You don't carry a trade?

Weaver, thatcher, tailor, tinker? — we've no use for tinkers, we mend our own metal."

"None of those — "

"I hope you're not a music-maker or a play actor."

The other laughed. "No — nor a horsethief either!"

Sirato's heart sank. No music then, and no useful trade. No one in Minith could respect an idle vagrant, not even Sirato herself. The great chance seemed to shrink and fade: but hope still held her in her hiding place. She noticed suddenly that Holne too had been drawn to see who had come. He was watching what was happening at the gate with a curious expression. He looked almost frightened, thought Sirato. Perhaps he was afraid of a rival for the place of favourite, though that seemed unlikely. But now, to Sirato's surprise, Aunt Lecte was opening the gate partway, with a sour face. She must have decided it was her duty to take the vagrant in.

She looked her new dayworker over sternly, paying particular attention to that mop of yellow hair, then pointed to the tall staff.

"Is that a weapon, young woman?" she asked forbiddingly.

It was smooth and weathered ash wood, with a hole bored in the top which had a loop of good stout cord threaded through it.

"I suppose it might be," admitted the stranger, without shame. "Not often, I hope. I thought I might have needed it last night, up on the mountain. Some of your neighbours made an awful racket near my camp. But there was no harm done."

Lecte stared.

"No neighbours of mine," she said sharply, after a moment. "Minith people don't wander about up there."

"Oh, I didn't mean humans. Just some wild beasts, howling. I didn't see what kind."

Lecte frowned. "It's better not to interfere with the wild creatures on our mountain. You should have stayed on the road."

"Should I? Well, never mind. As I said, there was no harm done."

This person had a kind of light, cheerful assurance which Aunt Lecte was bound to dislike: as if she didn't take herself or anybody else completely seriously. Sirato couldn't imagine her ever saying "thank you for reproving me — ". She studied the outsider's appearance, hoping to notice something exotic and exciting. It didn't seem likely there was anything of value in that lean and battered pack. And yet there must be something to explain the fearless smile. The stranger took up too much space for her size, she seemed to spread herself about even as she stood looking round the farmyard. No one in Minith looks like that, thought Sirato. Unrestrained, that's what it is. She's unrestrained.

She'll have to change if she wants to stay here.

At that moment, something happened. Holne was by the kitchen door, leaning there casually as if he didn't want to be noticed. Lecte was standing with her arms folded. Still frowning at that tall staff. The stranger was in the act of passing through the gate when she stopped, letting her pack slip from her shoulder to the ground. Her smile was gone. Sirato noticed that the sky above the yard was a deep and brilliant blue. The sharp-cut face of the mountain seemed to lean out of it, peering down at the little humans. Nothing stirred, there was no sound . . . Sirato felt that moment, when everything was more intense, when the stones and the sky seemed full of meaning, pass through her like invisible lightning. Then it was over.

"Is there someone with magic talent here?" asked the stranger.

Aunt Lecte drew in her breath sharply. She looked her new

dayworker sharply in the face, and seemed to see something there that she had missed before.

"You are a covener! Why did you not say so at once?"

The girl looked embarrassed, for the first time.

"Ah, nobody asked me—"

Sirato didn't understand, except that her aunt must have felt the lightning too; and she didn't like it. It was a strange thing, but though Aunt Lecte was very keen on the Covenant, she often talked as if Covenant magic itself was something like wicked waste: at best a necessary evil.

"If you are a covener, what are you doing away from your meeting? We have our own Hillen woman, we don't require another."

"I have no meeting yet," answered the traveller calmly, though she looked a little astonished at Aunt Lecte's accusing tone. "I'm a covener of the roads and the wild world — "

"Ah, I see. A Hillen student on a choice journey, that's what we have here."

Now Siri understood. She had heard of Hillen School, the place far away in the north of Inland where coveners were trained in magic. And she knew what a choice journey was. It was the time when a flores, someone about the age of her brother, would be deciding whether or not to go on training for a particular trade and would leave home for a while to think about it. In Minith no sane young person would expect to do more than maybe spend a night with a neighbour. How long does it take after all, to choose between one dull life and another? Perhaps in other parts of Inland the "journey" might be a little longer. But Aunt Lecte was being sarcastic. This person was older than Holne, and far too travel worn. She couldn't still be choosing: and as far as Siri knew there was no such thing as a covener without a meeting. The vagrant must be one of those shameless people who wandered about the roads of Inland trading in magic — even worse than a flute player.

It seemed to Sirato that there had been a kind of fight going on. Now Lecte was winning. She had forced the other to confess her guilty secret: that was how it appeared. Next, obviously, this covener who wasn't really a covener would be sent on her way. But to her astonishment Aunt Lecte was shutting the gate, with the stranger on the inside.

"Magic talent?" she remarked, as if just remembering the covener girl's question. "As you see, there's no one here but myself and my young nephew. And I assure you he doesn't meddle in women's business."

She nodded towards Holne at the kitchen door, and then briskly got down to business.

"We'll need to know your name, young covener without a meeting."

The sarcasm was plain now. The yellow-haired girl almost lost her determinedly friendly expression for a moment. But she controlled herself.

"I don't want to tell you that," she said coolly. "Name me as you please, for as long as I stay. I'll answer to most things."

Aunt Lecte laughed.

"We'll call you 'Sunny'," she declared. "That seems to suit you."

It was rather an insulting nickname, clearly referring to that shock of gaudy hair. But the vagrant accepted it meekly.

"Thank you. That will do very well."

"Good. Now take your pack and staff and leave them over by the scullery." She pointed ungraciously. "When you've done that I will direct you to the intakes. You can join the haymakers: ask for Carad Breakwater, tell her you're at Slack Road and she'll set you to work. My niece is up there, she'll bring you down again for supper.

Aunt Lecte went indoors. Holne had vanished inside already.

The stranger picked up her pack: turned and looked directly at Sirato, who was still crouched in her hiding place. She didn't wink as Holne would have done: but Sirato knew at once that this girl had seen her there all the time, and that she guessed that Sirato was the niece who was supposed to be up at the intakes. The yellow-haired girl smiled a little and headed off calmly towards the scullery door.

Sirato ran, as fast up the hill as she had come down. There was still a chance to get back before she was missed. It was all very odd. Why did Aunt Lecte want to take in a wandering magic-maker? But still — someone from outside! She wanted to shout and dance.

Something must happen. Surely, things would change now.

Zanne of Garth stood in the farmyard, noting the clean sturdy state of everything. There were a good many grey sheds huddled under a pall of dust behind the house, which gave the place a grim look. But there were also chickens scratching in a run beside the barn, and the corner of a kitchen garden showed beyond. She went and looked at it over the inner wall: as she had guessed there were no flowers, only useful rows of vegetables. She smiled. Zanne came from plain, Covenant-fearing farm people herself. She wished she had made a better start with the Minith farmer — but after all it was a trying time of year and perhaps the woman had reason to be short-tempered and suspicious. *We have our own Hillen woman here, we don't require another* ... It sounded as if Hillen Coven wasn't very highly regarded in Minith. The Thirteen had probably been hinting at that when they told her to "walk carefully" and make no hasty judgements. Zanne grimaced: from her welcome so far she wasn't looking forward to explaining her real business in the mountains. She knew from experience that Covenant-fearing farmers hate all mention of the dead past.

She wondered about that feeling of someone with magical talent. Had she really been challenged at the gate, or was that just an echo of her own sense of the challenge of this mission? Something had seemed to say — enter if you dare. And Zanne's own magic had risen up in answer. It was odd too that she'd been given a nickname so like her own name ... as if the unfocused mind-magic of a highly promising talent was hovering around.

Perhaps it wasn't very likely. Still, she liked the idea of discovering a mountain prodigy. She dismissed the young flores she had seen as easily as Lecte herself had done: she'd never known a man or a boy with more than a tiny gift for conjuring illusions. Maybe that little girl was the one? To find unrecognised magic and send a new student to Hillen would be a privilege, and a pleasant change from her usual work ...

She realised with a guilty start that she was keeping her new employer waiting and hurried into the house, putting the mountain prodigy out of her mind for a while.

It was almost dark before the haymakers stopped work. Zanne had found the people Lecte had told her to find: she now knew the name of the farm where she was staying, had met its workers and learned something about the family. She walked home to Slack Road with Mab and Truc and the child Sirato, whom everyone called "Rat". She was very tired. She had been sent to work without being offered a bite to eat or a chance to wash off the dust of the mountain: and she couldn't help thinking of other places in Inland, where a covener who appeared on the doorstep would be treated far differently. But she laughed at herself for this weakness. Zanne had been brought up in a strict little village where "living within What Is", meant bean porridge for dinner and no shoes except in winter. She'd often been shocked since those days by the luxury some Inlanders felt they could afford to take from the world — and said so, loudly and clearly! Perhaps she'd begun to forget, in her adventures, what the life of a real covenanter was like.

She was impressed by the Minithers' quiet ways. There had been no fooling in the hayfield, no horseplay by the cold silver and black stream where they went to bathe when the long day was done. And now she was sure it wasn't only tiredness that made the others move so slowly. Even young Sirato kept her head down and her arms by her sides, as if afraid to disturb the air by breaking through it. This is going to be a lesson for me, thought Zanne. A little time with these sober people will do me all the good in the world.

The evening was warm and still, the deep blue-green sky pricked over with stars above the crags. Zanne felt at peace with the world, weary but easy and pleasantly ready for her supper. She let herself imagine that she was what Lecte Slack Road had first thought her: a roadwalker, a dayworker, living from farm to farm. What a good life that would be. She wished it were true, and the whole other business just a dream.

In the big bare kitchen everybody sat down. Besides the three haymakers and Zanne there was a tall mournful-looking dark man, a boy younger than Sirato and the handsome flores whom she had glimpsed earlier. Lecte coldly introduced the new dayworker to her brother and his apprentice, and to her nephew. Gwil Slack Road took Zanne's hand. "I hope you will be happy here," he said, dolefully.

Zanne noticed how much metal there was. Minith was short of trees, she had seen metal in the haymakers' tools as well. Anywhere else in Inland it would have looked like shocking luxury: but not here. Everything was as plain as earth. She sniffed appreciatively at the steaming bowl of bean porridge.

"Oh, that smells good. I'm famished!"

The dour farmer frowned at her. "Take your place at table, Sunny. And do not use such extravagant expressions, that's not our way here."

Zanne raised her eyebrows, but meekly sat down.

"Would you like me to say the Covenant promise for us?" she asked cheerfully. It was a custom some Inlanders liked, as a blessing before meals. "Though I'm sure no one needs any magic to help them enjoy the good food."

She laughed. No one else did. Old Truc looked as if something had bitten him, the little girl stared with round eyes and then quickly ducked her head.

"In Minith, Sunny, we don't joke about the Covenant."

The meal began then, in complete silence. Perhaps it was that silence or the failure of her very innocent little joke; or perhaps it was something in the clasp of Gwil's cold hand, but Zanne didn't relish her supper. The plainness and the quietness that she wanted to admire began to oppress her. Also she felt watched by mocking eyes, by someone who seemed to enjoy her discomfiture. It wasn't little Rat, or Lecte. The culprit, she was sure, was that handsome flores, Rat's brother Holne. She had noticed already the embroidery on his sleeves and collar, where everyone else wore the plainest undecorated homespun: and the tender glances that fell his way from his hard-faced aunt. Holne seemed to be the pet of this household.

She caught him at last: staring. For a moment, he didn't look away. His bright brown eyes were cold and wary. Now why is that? wondered Zanne. She couldn't think what she'd done to offend. It seemed that the young man, like his aunt, mistrusted strangers on principle.

When at last the meal was over and Aunt Lecte began to speak, Zanne didn't understand. She got up from her place.

"Well, I'm very tired. Goodnight everybody, sweet dreams."

She knew where she was to sleep. Mab and Truc had already shown her the clean, bare bunkshed she would share with them.

Everybody seemed stunned by this simple announcement. Aunt Lecte raised an imperious hand.

"Sunny, it is the custom of Minith to tell over each day as it is ended, to measure how far we have fallen short of keeping the Covenant in thought and word and deed. Take your seat."

Zanne's mouth dropped open.

"Fallen short? But why should you — "

She noticed that the little girl was pulling desperate faces at her, and sat down.

"And first," Lecte went on, in the same grim tone, "We'd like to know a little more about our new worker. Tell us, Sunny. What brought you to Minith?"

There came a strange buzzing from around the table: "*Under the Covenant* . . .", mumbled all the Minithers, with lowered eyes.

Zanne opened her mouth, and shut it. No doubt this "daytelling" idea only *seemed* like a miserable empty ritual, nothing to do with the love and freedom of the Covenant. And besides, she had resolved to stay out of fights.

She sighed, and began again. It was about time she explained her real business. But although she couldn't refuse to answer the question, she felt somehow certain that she was heading for trouble.

"I'm looking for one of the great Makers," she explained. "There is an old powerhouse in these hills somewhere, and

Hillen Coven sent me to find it. I — ah, I'm hoping your meeting will be able to help me."

The faces of all the adults had turned to stone. Little Sirato looked from one to another, bewildered. The apprentice boy, better schooled, kept his eyes lowered.

Holne smiled, and pursed his lips, as if he was going to whistle.

Zanne had plenty of time to take in these reactions, because the silence this time was so long that she thought it was never going to end.

At last Lecte Slack Road spoke.

"Sunny, there is no great Maker in Minith. I don't know how ever Hillen Coven came by such an idea. If your story is true, that is. I expect you just made it up to make yourself sound important."

Zanne gasped. Perhaps fortunately her indignant response was forestalled by Mab, who leaned over and patted her hand.

"Why, you mustn't tell tales like that, Sunny. Next thing, you'll be having that uncovenanted Zanne of Garth down on us ... the one that ferrets out all the old things, the wicked woman!"

Mab suddenly recollected herself, and ducked her head.

"Reprove me, Lecte. I spoke out of turn, and without necessity — "

Lecte nodded. "The Covenant reproves you," she corrected. "Not I, Mab."

Now it was Zanne's turn to feel stunned. She couldn't think what to say or do, but only knew she couldn't stay in this kitchen a moment longer.

She got up from the table again. "I'm sorry, but I'm afraid I must leave you. I'm sure your — your daily household meeting is a good custom, but I'm not fit to join it at the moment ... I have some clothes to wash, I suppose I can do that in the scullery? Well — goodnight."

When Sunny was gone, the rest of them sat in dumb astonishment, wondering when the storm would break. But Aunt Lecte made no comment at all. Calmly she began to speak again, and the daytelling went on. There was a look in her eyes, however, which promised hard times ahead for that unrestrained, uncovenanted vagrant.

Zanne pumped water into the stone trough and found a big pitcher full of lardy soap. In here, as everywhere at Slack Road, everything necessary was plentiful, plain and neat. There was no sound from the kitchen. She had waited in the bunkshed until Mab and Truc came to bed, not wanting to meet any member of the household again tonight. She set herself firmly to wash clothes, until the quiet work had soothed her temper and calmed her confusion.

It would be strange to sleep indoors again. It had been a long, lonely walk from Hillen to these mountains.

She sat back on her heels frowning. "What am I to do now?" she asked out loud.

It wasn't the first time she had met with opposition from indignant local people. Some Inlanders took it as a personal insult when you told them that their countryside was harbouring relics of the past. However, once they were convinced they were very glad to have someone deal with the things.

But she had never met "Zanne of Garth's" shocking reputation before. She had declined to give Lecte her name at first out of embarrassment, because she detested the fame that had come to her through her strange talent. She'd known that even here in the mountains they were bound to have heard of the death of the great Daymaker — and sometimes people made such a stupid fuss, gaping and admiring. Now that childish impulse had landed her in trouble. It was bound to look like deliberate deception, however she explained herself.

There were drying racks against one wall. Frowning, she began to spread her clothes on them. She laid her hand on the bare bricks behind, knowing that on the other side of this wall must lie Slack Road's sunstove. Every dwelling in Inland had its sunstove: the heart of the house, magically kindled by the covener and kept burning all the year. She needed the comfort and reassurance of that hidden warmth.

The wall was cold as the touch of Gwil's hand. Zanne shivered, almost in fear. Then to her relief she felt the warmth of life, very faintly. Of course, she was being stupid: naturally the stove would be low now, at midsummer.

And yet — it was not only the household's reaction to her mission that was disturbing her tonight.

There is something wrong with this place, she whispered.

Mab, the red-haired kindly farmworker, had told her a little about the Slack Road family as they walked down from the hayfield: how the children's mother had died young after a long illness. Maybe that sad loss was enough to explain some of the atmosphere of gloom. For the rest, it could be just that Minith customs were unfamiliar.

She remembered the curious little battle she had had with Lecte at the yard gate. It had seemed as if the woman had detested "Sunny" on sight, and yet she'd been determined to take her in. It was Lecte who said "I suppose you want work": Zanne had only been meaning to ask the way to town. It was a puzzle . . . another problem to go with the rest, all running together to form this oppressed, uneasy feeling that she could not shake off.

I'll sleep on it, she decided. After all, if What Is didn't want me here, I wouldn't be here.

She couldn't help wishing though, that she had walked on and found a bed at another farm.

The girl slipped into the scullery as quietly as a mouse. She looked at Zanne sidelong, but she was drawn to the open pack. Crouching down on the floor she shyly touched Zanne's moonlamp, which was filling the room with a gentle night-time light. Beside the lamp lay a small silver brooch set with freshwater pearls.

"You'd better hide these," she warned. "You'll get into trouble if Aunt Lecte sees them."

The lamp's light came from Zanne's magic, but like the brooch it was an uncovenanted, luxurious looking object: a fancy market trinket from a big tradestown, the kind of thing no decent country person would own.

"I know what you mean," agreed Zanne. "But a friend of mind who is dead gave me the brooch, and the lamp used to belong to her as well. So you see I'm stuck with them."

"My mother's dead."

"Yes, I know. Mab told me."

Zanne went on hanging up her clothes. The girl watched her as if fascinated by a strange unknown animal, and kept an eye on the door at the same time. That sly shifting of the child's eyes made Zanne feel uncomfortable, but she pretended not to notice it.

"Rat is a nickname, isn't it," she said. "What's your real name?"

"Sirato. Siri — but no one calls me that."

"Well I will, if you like."

Suddenly Siri giggled. "You mustn't leave in the middle of the daytelling. That's wicked."

"It would have been wicked to stay — I mean, wrong. Wicked is far too big a word. I was not in the right state of mind to join in any sort of meeting."

"But it's only the *Covenant*. You only had to sit there. No one would have known if you weren't paying attention."

Zanne draped her last wrung singlet and came to kneel opposite Sirato, looking into her face. She leaned forward, and gently made the circle sign of the Covenant, on the child's brow.

"Siri, the Covenant is in the mind and heart of every individual who lives *by free will*, in What Is and by What Is ... Free will isn't something you can pretend about. It's either there, or it isn't. You would have thought I was crazy, wouldn't you, if I'd gone on pretending to eat when my plate was empty. There's no difference. The Covenant is as real as food."

The stranger girl had grey eyes. They were kind and bright but also, just now, rather solemn. Sirato realised with a sinking heart that she had been wrong about Sunny. However it happened that she was a covener without a meeting, she couldn't be one of those magic-traders. Aunt Lecte and the others were wrong too. Though she behaved oddly and laughed far too much there was nothing "un-covenanted" about this person. Siri was bitterly disappointed. She'd been imagining she had an ally.

She felt almost like crying, but instead pulled a face and jeered resentfully: "Oh, you don't need to tell me that stuff. We learn it in school. It doesn't mean anything really, does it."

Zanne stared in amazement.

Before she could begin to answer, the girl started forward. With a quick covert movement, she slipped the brooch inside Zanne's pack, and pushed the moonlamp so it couldn't be seen if anyone opened the door unexpectedly. Zanne watched this little performance uneasily.

"Siri?"

"Hush. *He's* there."

Zanne got up and peered curiously into the dark kitchen. She was in time to glimpse the shadow of a lithe young figure, slipping out of sight through the farther door.

"Spying on us — " whispered Siri.

"Was that your brother? But why?"

"To get us into trouble, of course. I'm supposed to be in bed. You be careful of him, Sunny. He'll tell tales on you."

With a scamper of small feet the little Rat whisked by her, and was gone.

Zanne was left staring at the last rinse water as it trickled down the clean and glistening scullery drain. She frowned worriedly, and then laughed at herself.

"Just a naughty little girl. She can't have *meant* any of those silly things."

Oh well, thought Siri as she crept up the loft stairs. She rubbed at her forehead, where Zanne's finger had made the Covenant sign: it tickled. At least Aunt Lecte would have someone else to pick on now. She didn't notice the magic until she was climbing into bed. A little of the moonlamp's glow had followed her from the scullery. The silver glimmer hovered around her pillow, like the ghost of a kind smile. She decided she would have to warn poor Sunny: Aunt Lecte mustn't catch her doing frivolous magic. An unaccustomed thought crept into Sirato's mind. She would do her best, she resolved, to take care of the roadwalker. As long as it didn't mean getting into more trouble herself.

Pitying her new friend, who trusted the Covenant instead of being afraid of it, she suddenly remembered the things she had said, in bravado, down there in the scullery. She started up, her heart drumming. If the Covenant had heard her!

But the faint haze of silvery light was strangely comforting. She lay down again, and fell asleep peacefully for the first time in many long nights.

CHAPTER THREE

MINITH WAYS

THE SUN WAS rising and the stars were fading. The new dayworker slipped out of the bunkshed as she had done every dawn since she arrived a few days ago, and left the yards. She crossed the open hillside to the place where the Burnhouse stream came leaping from the crags behind and to the west of Slack Road farm. This young river would gain a lot of water from various tributaries before it ran through the smelthouses and metalworks in Minith town a few vales further down, but it was already strong and vigorous. It roared and sang in the early twilight. The roadwalker made her way to a green grotto right by the water's edge. She stood on the level turf for a few moments as if in thought, and then she began to move — stretching and curling herself in an odd, slow dance.

It was part of a covener's training to develop the Link between body and mind. Years of practice could give the magically talented extraordinary physical abilities, but there was more to it than that. Zanne had been taught long ago when she first went to magic school that all kinds of effort are one. Magic works by sympathy, by the likeness between forms. As she taught herself to shift and hold her own body, she would be increasing her sympathy with that other physical body, the world: and therefore her ability to shift and hold the patterns in its fabric.

As she worked, Zanne was thinking with amusement of her first morning at Slack Road. The daily Link exercise was part of any covener's life. It had not occurred to her that she ought to explain this behaviour to anyone. So she had set out in the dark of dawn after her first night in the bunkshed, and found this place. She was just in the middle of a low lift, when there came a grunting and a scrabbling, and two rough sleepy heads popped up over the rocks. Open mouthed they gaped at the human body suspended half its own height in the air, balanced on nothing. Zanne laughed so much that she almost came down in the water.

Two solemn faces peered down as she fell, still laughing, to collapse on the turf. Mab and Truc had followed her. They clambered into the grotto, waited with dignity until she had regained control of herself, and then started to interrogate her. Was she sick? Why was she out here when she should be asleep? Was this a kind of game? If it was she'd better give it up. Under the Covenant there was work and sleep, meal-times and daytelling. There was no place for anything else in decent peoples' lives, except on a proper Covenanted holiday ... It took a while to convince them that she was doing something which was her duty. Even then, they agreed they would have to report the strange business to Lecte.

She had heard no more, so presumably Lecte Slack Road had decreed that the Link exercise was permitted. But the incident left Zanne with another uncomfortable impression to add to her lingering unease about Slack Road farm. After her problems at that first daytelling she had seen only more of a relentlessly stern and sober way of life: and heard more, in the hayfields as well as at Slack Road, of the superiority of Minith's version of the Covenant. The self-righteous tone was annoying, but still she'd almost come to believe that there was nothing wrong with Minith or Slack Road. She had herself been brought up in an isolated, opinionated village, where customs were strict enough to horrify many soft-living town dwellers.

But she couldn't imagine anyone in Garth following somebody around like that, or reporting on them to "authority". Surely it was a strange contradiction. If these people believed in their superior extra-strong Covenant they ought to trust their magic more and rely less on human surveillance. It seemed that everybody at Slack Road watched everybody else: reproving, restricting. What kind of virtue is it, wondered Zanne, that has to be enforced every moment?

The young river sang on. Zanne sat still as a rock, slowly rising out of the inner silence that ended her Link practice. Creamy small stars drifted down from the rowans and landed on her hair and hands.

She had not yet told anyone that she was Zanne of Garth. She had not tried to explain her mission again. She had decided that the best plan was to talk to Minith's covener, and enlist her help. But for that, it seemed, she'd have to wait until meeting-time. Aunt Lecte had calmly told her, when she said she would like to go down to town, that farmworkers had no time for jaunting about, except on Covenanted holidays. Zanne had chosen to eat at Slack Road's table: Zanne must accept the same terms as everybody else.

She would wait. She knew that was what Hillen Coven would advise. To find the undead past and put it to rest she needed the help of Minith meeting; and that meant every member, including obnoxious persons like Lecte Slack Road. There had to be a way. Under the Covenant, you could never make terms with a *part* of anything, it had to be the whole. Yet it was strange. She'd been expecting, half unconsciously, that the covener would come to find *her*. And not just because she was here on important business from Hillen. The covener must know that a stranger had entered her holding. If this had been Garth, Zanne's mother would have been up to this farm the day after Zanne arrived: full of curiosity and welcome.

Strange, strange...

Zanne drifted. She was under the rowan tree, but she was also in the great hall, under the mound of Hillen. Pillars like gnarled living roots of trees reached up to the coffered ceiling, fretted all over with tiny lights like stars. On the raised platform at the end of the hall stood thirteen chairs lacquered in midnight blue. Thirteen faces looked down at Zanne. Somehow she could not see them very clearly, though the pillar at her side felt rough and real under her hand.

Zanne? they said. *What are you doing back so soon?*

I forgot to ask you. I forgot to ask: What am I supposed to say to Minith's covener?

We don't know, they answered. *That is all we could have told you if you had asked ... You must speak for yourself. We trust you, Zanne. Do whatever you think is right, under the Covenant...*

The thirteen figures wavered and faded.

Trust me! cried Zanne. *I will find a way!*

But I am afraid.

She spoke the last words to herself, not to the Thirteen. She was back in the grotto, entirely. As soon as she had named it the fear leapt up and almost overwhelmed her. It was in this pretty grotto, in the song of the river — no, it was looming down from above — no, it was everywhere...

"Who's there?" shouted Zanne. She jumped to her feet. "Who's there? Come out!"

No one came. There was nobody there, she knew it. What she had felt had been a sense of real danger, not the pressure of spying eyes. It was gone. There was only the river, only the rowans and the grey-blue bulk of the crags above.

Zanne set off for the farmhouse in a bad temper, annoyed with herself for that odd fit of panic. She hurried: she knew that her extremely plain breakfast wouldn't wait. If she wasn't there with the rest she'd go hungry until midday, that was the rule. Gwil and Danno were already in their yard, noisily setting up for the day's work. Just as she reached the sled track that ran down from the mines, the clamour stopped. They had gone indoors to their breakfast. And at once another sound rose, sweet as a singing bird. Zanne stood still. The early summer sun touched her face, the lilac sky flowered with light ... Slack Road and all its surroundings suddenly became beautiful. Zanne didn't have a very good ear for music, she couldn't sing a note. Still her heart went out to this clear wordless song. It seemed to be a tune she knew, but someone had added to it all the wildness, all the space and emptiness of a mountain sky.

As she stood there, transfixed, a figure appeared on the path in front of her.

It was Holne, the farmer's nephew. Where had he sprung from? He might have jumped from the crags like a great cat, he had materialised so suddenly. And where had he been, so early in the morning?

Zanne did not begrudge Holne his petted status, or the way he never seemed to have much work to do while everybody else was busy from morning to night. It wasn't his fault if his aunt — and his father and the other workers — favoured him above the little girl. She'd have tolerated all that if he'd been as pleasant and sweet-tempered as he ought to be, having such an easy life. But Holne was not pleasant. He hardly spoke to his aunt and ignored his father. His favourite occupation was teasing his little sister, his favourite expression was a sneer. He was always hanging around whenever Zanne and Sirato were together, as if he grudged the poor bullied child any scrap of pleasure of her own.

The ugliness of his nature, Zanne thought, took all the virtue out of his good looks. Every time she saw him she found herself thinking she would not like to touch him.

She had resolved that she was not going to join in the chorus of approval. Holne was going to know that somebody at least was not fooled, and somebody was ready to take little Siri's part.

Holne stretched his arms and grinned, glowing with sleek sunburned vitality and making it impossible for her to continue down the path. He had the look on his face that she had noticed before: a hidden wariness behind the wide, white smile.

"Seems like another nice day," he remarked blandly.

"Yes, lovely. Excuse me." She wanted to find the source of that music. Holne didn't stir.

"Who is that playing the violin?"

"Playing the violin? Oh, I don't think so, Sunny. We don't make unnatural music in Minith. If my aunt Lecte found a violin on the farm, she'd burn it. Besides — " he made an elaborate show of listening. "I can't hear anything."

The bird had stopped singing. Holne grinned and stepped aside to let her pass. He followed after. She could feel his eyes on her shoulders and hear the soft pad of his feet all the way to the kitchen door.

At the table everyone waited, with varying expressions of righteous grief or sympathy: except for Sirato's father who scarcely seemed aware of his daughter's existence most of the time. At the last possible instant the bad girl darted in, her face red and her hair unbrushed.

"I was watching for the sheep!" she cried. "I went up the track — "

Poor child, thought Zanne, she lies as easily as she breathes.

Lecte compressed her lips coldly. "And are they coming down? Or not?"

Little Rat blushed even redder: she hadn't thought of that.

"N – no. I mean — yes."

Her brother laughed unkindly. "Silly little Rat, why tell stories if you can't back 'em up? Everybody knows you slept in."

Lecte opened her hands over the morning platter of beanbread and damson curd, offering the food a benediction that would have soured new milk.

"Under the Covenant — " she intoned.

"Within What Is," they all mumbled.

"Rat, you will give back the sweet paste from your portion to the Covenant. You have taken extra sleep instead."

Almost before the haymaking was done, it was time for the fleece harvest. Before Zanne arrived in Minith she'd imagined that this would be a great festival, and had been glad that she'd be in the mountains to see it. The rich and silky-soft dark Minith wool was famous all over Inland: the flocks that bore it must be a source of pride and joy, and their "coming down" a high spot of the farming year. But now she knew Minith better, she was not surprised to discover that Minith ways were different. There was no fleecing ground dedicated from time immemorial down in Minith town. There would be no feasting, no drinking, no games, no flowers. In Minith the flocks separated out and the animals came to their own farmyards. The fleece was stripped, the flock kept penned while the shepherd checked them over for any trouble present or threatening: and then they were driven out to return to the hillside, while the serious business of cleaning and baling and tallying the wool was soberly shared by everyone.

The only consolation was that when the dull process was over at last it would be meeting-time. She'd be able to sort out all the misunderstanding, and get on with her real mission.

"Isn't fleece harvest like this where you come from?"

Sirato and her new friend were waiting by the gate, for this time the flock was really coming down. To the Minither child, "the Fleece" was simply another chore.

"Oh no, not at all, Siri."

Sirato beamed. It was lovely not to be called Rat. In her own mind she was Siri now — it was almost like starting a new life.

"If this was Garth, when the sheep came into the yard we'd all pounce on them and dress them up in flowers. Then we'd race them to the fleecing ground and there'd be ribbon-pole dancing, singing, all sorts of things to eat. And the sheep, well, once they're stripped they just go crazy: running in and out of the houses, eating hats. They get so wicked, because no one's allowed to scold them and of course they know that."

Siri laughed, a rare sound, "Eating hats — ! Oh, Sunny, you're making it up."

"No, no. It's true, I swear. A straw hat is a mad sheep's favourite dish.'

Aunt Lecte had come out from the brickyard behind them.

"Get down from the gate, child."

Siri got down: eyes lowered, shrinking into herself.

Lecte gave the roadwalker a look of cold scorn. "In Minith," she remarked, "we don't make pets of domestic animals. They are for us to use as we are used by What Is, and that is how it should be. We do not kill them for meat and we do not play with them like toys either. We leave those ways to outsiders."

"But, Lecte, animals have feelings too. You can't just use a beast as if it were a hoe or a pitchfork. Maybe your sheep have a different temperament here. But your draft animals, your ponies: surely you have to have affection for them — "

In Zanne's version of the Covenant the hoe and the

pitchfork deserved affection too, and would give better service if they had it. But she didn't want to provoke the woman.

"Ponies?" murmured Siri.

"I must ask you, Sunny, not to put such ideas into the child's head. You should know, Rat, in other parts of the world certain profligate and greedy persons use animals to carry them on luxurious journeys, and in many other uncovenanted ways. You may thank What Is that such practices are no business of yours."

A dark dusty blot had appeared on the track. The Slack Road sheep trotted together, docile and silent. Without another word "Sunny" opened the gate, and helped Lecte to guide the flock into their pen. But her eyes were smouldering. She didn't mind being insulted herself: but Zanne's mother, the covener of Garth, made her calls round the Mid-Inland farms on the back of a little brown pony. It was too much. This arrogant intolerance was unbearable.

The day after the flock came down, the household of Slack Road woke to find their farmyard transformed. There were knots and garlands of wild roses and frothy chervil tied up along the walls and fences. Every ewe and lamb had a blue or yellow ribbon tied round its neck or wound in its horns and New Summer flowers threaded into the rich dark fleece along its spine. The tup was resplendent in a crown of green rowan berries. The sheep pranced and winked and ate each other's decorations. Sirato gasped and clapped her hands.

"Oh, how lovely!"

Aunt Lecte didn't even glance at her, much less at Sunny who was standing by grinning rather shamefacedly. Gwil Slack Road almost smiled, then sighed and retreated to his brick kilns.

"Very pretty," said Lecte, her words dropping like chips of gravel. "A little too pretty for honest Covenanters. Of course, that's only my opinion."

Mab and Truc began to take the decorations down, quietly and without any sign of either amusement or annoyance. Sunny's joke had fallen rather flat. But the worst of it was that the sheep, corrupted overnight, decided they liked being dressed up. It took the best part of the day to part them from their finery.

The hot weather set in in earnest about this time, and there were long, sweating days of back breaking work before the wool was baled. All things considered, by the time the fleece meeting day came Zanne was very happy to walk out of Slack Road farm gate and down the track to the town she had not yet seen. Minithers were too sober to make friends easily, but she had a few acquaintances from the hayfields whom she'd be pleased to meet again. Surely when the whole meeting was joined together, she'd find a better atmosphere.

She walked with Mab and Truc behind the family, feeling more cheerful than for several days. She tucked her arm in Mab's, impulsively, as the grey settlement came into sight.

"I'm so glad it's meeting-time at last. You must be glad too, Mab. You'll have a chance to go and see your niece."

She liked Mab: whose natural kindliness and spirit kept peeping out from under the Slack Road gloom. She had heard her two companions whispering in the bunkshed sometimes, about Mab's young relative who was ill. Mab had news of her when she went down to the dairy at the next farm to get milk — Slack Road had no milch cows of its own, it was thought the brick dust was bad for them. The dairy was a centre for what in Minith passed for news and gossip, but Mab rarely related any of what she heard. No doubt Aunt Lecte would have flattened any such talk as "unrestrained" — even this concern for a sick girl.

Mab started.

"Our Karin? What do you know about that?"

"Why — I heard you telling Truc. I'm sorry if I — "

The study farmworker seemed to control herself with an effort. "Sunny, my dear," she said, reprovingly. "We aren't *glad* to go to meeting. We do it because it's right."

She recovered her arm and hurried to catch up with Gwil and Lecte, leaving Zanne puzzled. She supposed that was a Minith way of saying "mind your own business".

Minith town was an important place, being the centre of the whole of this part of Inland. But there was no market here, no streets of houses as in an ordinary tradestown: only the complex of furnaces and metalworks along the Burnhouse, the meeting house with its bell-tower and a few pensioner cottages.

The meeting house was a silver flecked beehive, roofed in Minith green slate in a complex spiral pattern. It looked huge, ridiculously large, alongside the little cottages. But the crowd outside it today showed the real size of Minith meeting. People were still gathering as the Slack Road household arrived. Sirato slipped away from her aunt and stayed protectively close to Sunny, who was bound to do something shocking if she wasn't watched: and pointed out the different families. There were the Darklakes, the Breakwaters, the Crags, and others; who had come in, on foot of course, from farms in the lonely valleys. With them mingled the craftspeople, the usual crafts of a farming community and also the numerous metalworking clans: Miners, Burners, Smiths. Everyone was talking seriously and sensibly about the weight of the fleece bales and the yield of the mines. Zanne looked hopefully for some sign of holiday spirit, and saw a girl with red hair and a freckled turned up nose executing what looked like a dance step or two, to the amusement of a group of flores.

"Who's that, Siri? The nice-looking flores with the red hair"

"Oh, that's Karin Silvermines."

"I suppose Karin is a common name?"

"Well, I don't know any other. Our Mab is her auntie."

"Time to go into meeting now, Sunny. Off you go now, little Rat"

It was Mab, who had come to find them. Sirato scurried off to where the other children had formed a line and were marching off led by a pair of white-haired pensioners.

The red-headed girl was still dancing. Zanne turned to the woman beside her; and she could see the likeness.

"There's good news for you, Mab. If that's your niece Karin — she looks about as sickly as young Holne!"

Mab too was watching the lively girl. As Zanne spoke, her face suddenly twisted: with pain or grief or some other strong emotion — it could even have been anger, though that hardly seemed appropriate.

"Ah, the poor child — " she sighed, half to herself. "Why is it always so? Always the dearest. Maybe it only seems so because they are all dear to us . . . "

She looked at Zanne sharply. "Now that's twice, Sunny Roadwalker. You mind your business. Don't let me have to reprove you again."

"What's wrong with her, Mab?"

The red-haired farmworker sighed in exasperation.

"Why nothing, Sunny. Nothing at all. Can't you see that?"

Together they entered the dark hive of the meeting house, and took their places.

The cone of the meeting house roof was supported by a cobweb of ingenious metal in which voices floated and were lost: strange echoes rose from the hollow flags. Zanne was at the back, she could not see the covener or hear any of the speakers well. Although the crowd outside had seemed large the house felt empty as a barn, as if the people were not real; or else their minds were elsewhere. It's because of the daytelling, she reminded herself. The meetings they have every night in each household mean more to them than speeches made by the outsider sent from Hillen.

Still the sense of emptiness disturbed her. She looked at the Minithers and saw the sheep penned at Slack Road, huddled sadly together. Not willing members of their world, keeping its laws happily and lovingly: but cowed, obedient servants. I will speak, she thought. I am a part of this meeting, because we are all one in the web of Inland. I'll get up and sing them a song, dance for them. I'll tell them they've forgotten how to play, which is forgetting how to live...

What she really ought to do was stand up and tell the meeting and covener her name, and why she was here; and put an end to this delay.

But at Slack Road Zanne had been sure she was in the right. Now she was surrounded by faces like Lecte's: dignified, calm and sombre; and she couldn't be so secure. She stayed quietly in her place, afraid that she wouldn't be able to announce herself without giving offence to Minith ways. She could imagine the expressions on all these hard sober faces, when the roadwalker declared that she was Hillen's emissary. They would challenge her, and she would make some hasty retort — Zanne had been warned, she knew her own faults. She waited for the right moment to speak, searched for the right form of words... The moment and the words never came.

When the meeting was over she came blinking out into the sunlight. She felt confused. This was the event that was supposed to solve all her problems. What had gone wrong? She wished she had more idea of what had been going on. Of course it had been the same as any such gathering: discussion of weather needs, complaints and haggling about the uses of magic. Lecte Slack Road had been among the speakers. She had made some remarks about the "roadwalker" to whom she was giving shelter and even seemed to praise Zanne (as far as she could catch the words) as a good worker. But the tone had been decidedly unenthusiastic. Had there been something about "the sick of this meeting" — someone, a child, now thought to be beyond help? It must be very hard to lose someone through untimely death, mortal illness was so rare in Inland. In the crowd coming out behind her Zanne saw two people, a man and a woman, leaning on each other's arms, the ones who had stood to acknowledge their neighbours' sympathy: and would have gone to offer her own, but didn't like to intrude on such grief.

Apparently it was the Minith custom that only adults came into the meeting. The children were still tucked away in the pensioners' cottage schoolroom: Minith's flores had spent the hours just waiting outside on the grass. Zanne noticed that though most of the young people were sober and quiet, there was one little group that had become quite lively. She expected to see these rebels quickly *reproved* — but curiously enough the adults ignored them. Holne Slack Road was there. So was Karin Silvermines.

Minith seemed to have quite a collection of "pets", exempted from all the strict rules. What a strange idea, she thought.

As Zanne watched, the grieving couple came up to the group of laughing flores, and led red-haired Karin away.

That was odd. If there was a child mortally sick in Karin's family, surely she would not be in such high spirits?

She stood frowning, and a heavy hand fell on her shoulder. She looked up and there was Carad Breakwater, the supervisor from the hayfields. Lecte Slacke Road was with her. Zanne had seen them sitting side by side on the elders' benches. From the look in Carad's eyes, Zanne felt sure that the older woman knew about the stupid prank played on the sheep in Slack Road fleecing pens. She could only be grateful that Lecte hadn't told the whole meeting.

"Sunny," said Lecte, with deceptive gentleness, "I think you said you wanted to talk to our covener?"

Suddenly, Zanne knew she had been outmanoeuvred. There was an expression of quiet triumph in Carad's eyes, and Lecte looked almost sorry for her. She had missed her chance to speak out in meeting; and now she wasn't going to be given a chance to speak to the covener in private.

Why that should make a difference she couldn't tell. Surely there were no secrets between a covener and her people?

But there was no time for wondering and it was too late to retreat. She was lead to a small group of people: all of them elders of the meeting. The dark wall of backs covered in sober Minith cloth parted. The figure in the middle of the group was revealed as a tall woman, broad shouldered, with light brown hair cut square around a plump pink face.

"Covener Anlys," announced Lecte, "this is Slack Road's roadwalker, Sunny."

Zanne felt her face reddening. She did not particularly like being introduced as a vagrant.

"She's a good worker," said Carad condescendingly. "A little unrestrained, but we will change that if she stays with us."

Zanne was a small woman. The tall, well-made Minithers seemed to tower round her. Their covener was tall too, but she gave an impression of softness, not strength. She had the kind of body that comes when muscle runs to fat: slack and loose, not round and comfortable. Zanne remembered her vision of the Thirteen in the rowan grotto. She had thought that morning only that Hillen Coven wanted her to make her own decisions; and then her strange fit of panic had put the vision out of her mind. Now she knew for sure. There was something wrong, wrong, with Anlys Covener...

"Tell Anlys what you told me, Sunny."

Lecte's calm voice prodded her. There was no way out. Knowing it was useless, Zanne held out her hand.

"I should have come to you before this — " she began. "Perhaps you know why I'm here already, I mean, magically ... I've come about the lost powerhouse."

"Powerhouse?" said Carad, sounding disgusted at that term, which came from the lost past. "You mean a great Maker? What story is that? There's no such thing in our country."

It wouldn't dare to be here, said her tone.

"Yes, it's just a silly story," said Anlys — to Carad. She looked over Zanne's head, and didn't seem to see her offered hand. She nodded vaguely as she turned away. "Work hard, young roadwalker. And do as you are told. That's the best way, in Minith."

The weather almost broke that meeting day. There was no lessening of the heat but before sunset the whole sky had vanished behind a blanket of thick dim haze. Sirato wandered about the yards, her stomach heavy with twice as much supper as usual. There was nothing special to eat on meeting days but at least there was plenty, for a change. She had no chores because it was a holiday. Unfortunately anything else she might like to do was too unconvenanted to contemplate. She had started going back to her secret place whenever she could, Sunny's presence somehow gave her courage. But she wouldn't have dared to play unnatural music on a day like this even if there was noise in the yards to cover it. The Covenant would be bound to punish that. It would be more fun to live in one of the further valleys, so you could spend all the day before walking down, and all the holiday time after walking back.

She settled at last leaning on the hurdles of the sheep pen. Sunny was in there: moving about among the animals, stroking them and whispering to them. There was no need. Truc and she had already examined every one of them for foot rot and bad teeth and ticks and whatever else goes wrong with sheep. Siri had never seen anyone behave like Sunny now. It was funny to see how the sheep responded, stretching up their newly naked necks and bleating as if they were talking.

She took out of her smock pocket a withered posy of flowers and a strip of blue cloth. She had rescued them from the midden and kept them ever since that exciting morning. She would hide them in her treasure box soon. Sunny must have torn up some of her clothes to make the "ribbons". The very idea made Sirato shiver with horror. But it might be a good thing. The roadwalker would be less conspicuous if she wore only Minith clothes — in Minith shades of brown and rust and grey.

Her friend saw her and came over. They walked up to the bunkshed and sat outside it. This had become their private meeting place, whenever they had time to be together. The roadwalker drew up her knees and rested her chin on her folded arms. She sighed heavily.

"Siri, why didn't your brother help us with the fleece? Why did Truc and Mab and Lecte and I have to do all the stripping ourselves?"

Sirato shook her head sadly, but she was grinning a little. The roadwalker was a slow learner. "Don't you know? My brother doesn't have to do anything he doesn't want. Besides, no one messes with animals more than they need. That isn't the Minith way, it would be unconvenanted. The beasts don't like it, either. Sunny — is it true? In other parts, do coveners kill sheep? Do people really eat them as well as take their wool?"

"It's true, Siri. I eat meat myself, and I have killed for meat sometimes."

"Ugh. That's horrible. I don't know how you can stroke them and pet them, when you kill as well."

Zanne looked down at her own hands, her covener's hands. She remembered the feel of a living body between them, and her own voice saying the killing words: *sister, don't blame me, I will die too, and be eaten* ... She had been disturbed from the start by the Minithers' attitude to their animals. She felt sure it wasn't kindness that stopped them from killing. It seemed more like a refusal to accept that web of love and death and dependence that binds all things together — including humankind. But she didn't know how to tell the child what she felt. Or even if she should try.

"Tell me about the moonlamp girl," suggested Siri. In Minith nobody told stories: it was reckoned the same as telling lies. But Sirato was developing a taste for this un-covenanted entertainment.

So Zanne fetched out the silver trinket from her pack. Sirato was allowed to hold it and play with it (this was what she'd been hoping for) while Zanne told the story of her brave friend, who had owned this strange treasure: very strange to Siri because it was clearly Covenant magic and yet so fancy and pretty it was also obviously, attractively, *wicked*.

"When I was young," began Zanne.

"But you're not old — "

The older girl chuckled. "Younger, then. I was very wilful and naughty. I ran away from home. I decided to go treasure hunting, because I wanted something more exciting than life on an Inland farm. My friend, she was called Dimen, came with me, just to try and keep me out of trouble ... "

Zanne looked into the past, smiling at bittersweet memories.

"So we set off to find the great Daymaker of Mid-Inland. I was going to wake it up and bring back the dead past. That was my choice journey, Siri, although I didn't know it when I started. We travelled through the forest that goes right up to the boundary of Inland there: and we met the forest people. You think you live a strict life here, but the foresters would beat you. They think chairs and tables and houses are needless luxuries, they scarcely wear clothes. They live as wild things, within What Is. You couldn't get further from the people of the past. Their covener knew what I was up to, but she let me go on. Old coveners are like that, especially the Thirteen. They wouldn't lift a hand to stop a bad thing by force, not if it was to save the whole of Inland ..."

She sighed, and began staring over her knees again.

"The story ..." prompted Siri gently.

"Oh yes. Well, on the other side of the forest we were in the badlands, the Outlands where the raiders come from. They never reached your mountains I don't suppose, but those outlaw bands used to terrorise my part of the country. They caught us, me and my friend. They knew we were half-trained coveners and they wanted our magic: mine especially, because my magic still worked in the badlands, where no one keeps the Covenant."

"It must be a funny sort of magic."

Zanne smiled wryly. "That's what everybody says. Anyway, we ended up in the den of the chief of all the outlaws. She was a covener herself, in a twisted sort of way. She — ah, she used her mind-magic on me, Siri, and I nearly gave her all the power of the Daymaker to play with. I would have done it, but for my friend Dimen. She saved me, and Inland. In the end she fought a magic battle with the chief of the outlaws and she won. The outlaw bands were dispersed, and Mid-

Inlanders now sleep easier on winter nights at the dark of the moon. Oh yes, and after Dimen's victory I decided the Covenant was good enough for me after all, and I came home again."

She did not mention the destruction of the Maker, and Siri knew so little of the world outside Minith that she did not recognise the story of Zanne of Garth. If Zanne couldn't announce herself openly to the meeting it seemed bad manners to whisper her secret to a child.

Siri sighed happily. "Is that the end? It's a wonderful story. I wish I could have adventures ..."

"Do you? You shouldn't wish that. My friend died to destroy that outlaw chief, Siri. Adventures are not good things, they only make good stories."

Sirato let the silver light well through her fingers so her skin glowed like rose petals. She was sorry about Zanne's friend, but she didn't know how to say it. She'd very rarely, in her short life, been sorry for anyone but herself. She was wondering secretly if there was any way of sneaking this beautiful thing out of Zanne's pack and into the hiding place in the toolshed.

Zanne smiled. "That's not quite the end of the moonlamp story. All Dimen's things were lost, somewhere out there in the badlands. But two years afterwards I was staying at a waggon inn — that's a place where you can sleep for the night if you're travelling a long way by road. It was quite another part of Inland, but rather wild and on the edge of things. A woman I had never seen before came up and talked to me. She knew my name but she wouldn't tell me hers. She gave me Dimen's moonlamp. In the morning she was gone, and I've never seen her again."

"Was she a forester? One of those wild wood people who helped you before?"

The roadwalker shook her head. "No. She was a raider:

an outlaw."

"Oh! Then why — ?"

"That's the way things are, Siri. People are rarely good all the way through; or bad. That's why you should never make up your mind quickly, about anyone or anything."

The long warm twilight had passed, the muffled sky showed not a glimmer of light. Siri noticed that the moon-lamp was fading. Obviously her friend's little store of funny magic wasn't strong enough to keep it bright for long. She huddled closer and thought with dread of the journey back across the yards and up to her bed.

"I think I'll go for a walk," said Sunny. 'It's such a beautiful night. Will you come with me? We could go up to the Burnhouse stream and sit and listen to the water. I love the stars, but I think I almost love this better: it's as if there's only the earth, wrapping you in its arms."

Siri bit her lip. She wondered if it was a joke. She had a horrible feeling that it was not. To go out of the yards, to walk on the mountainside in this blackness...

She shuddered, and after a long silence at last whispered: "I am afraid of the dark."

"*Afraid* of the dark?"

Her friend sounded astonished.

"It belongs to the Covenant," explained Siri. Aunt Lecte would have been angry with her. But though Sunny was as bad as any of them about the Covenant at least you could talk to her. She would listen, if she never seemed to understand. "People always say, night-time is It's time. That's why I'm afraid. Especially here, you know, because the mountain is looking down on us: and sometimes I think the mountain *is* the Covenant. I can feel It watching me. And I've always been bad, so I know It's going to do something awful to me..."

The child didn't know what she was saying, didn't know

how much she was revealing about her people.

"Siri, child, there's nothing to be afraid of — "

"Yes there is," affirmed Sirato, with absolute conviction. But she couldn't tell about the "Rat" dreams: not here, not in the dark.

"Siri, supposing you were blind? Supposing you'd been born that way: you wouldn't be *able* to be frightened of the dark then. It would just be natural to you, it would be What Is. And so — "

"There are no blind people in Minith. Or if there are, they are shut up like mother was when she was ill. If something like that happens to someone, it means they've been wicked. It means the Covenant is angry."

By this time the thick watching blackness was pressing so close that it had pushed Sirato right up against the roadwalker's side, and her small hand had fastened itself tenaciously on a fold of the older girl's smock.

Zanne looked down. She had an extraordinary impulse, for a moment, to pull away from that little clinging hand as if it was something unclean. Feeling disgusted with herself, she put her arm firmly around the child's shoulders, and drew her close. She stopped defending the Covenant then and talked about comforting things: the village where she was born and the woods around it, the lovely days you could spend tree climbing and nutting there. When Siri had stopped trembling she found to her joy that the moonlamp had recovered. It shone brighter than a candle lantern in her hand.

"You can borrow it," said Sunny. "Take it with you now."

Sirato didn't wait to see if the roadwalker really meant it. She scampered away clutching her treasure, silver wrapped round her like a cloak: away from all this horrible talk of night and darkness and the Covenant.

Zanne stood up and walked to the yard gate, and leaned over it gazing into the scented darkness. Her moonflow had begun tonight, she could feel it pulling through her body. The flow had started late for Zanne, she'd still been a child when she destroyed the Daymaker. It was still a significant time to her, not just a commonplace part of life. She imagined always that on these days she was closer to the earth, and to magic ... As if all days weren't part of the same cycle.

But now when she tried to give herself up to the peaceful mood she needed, and which the flow usually brought to her, she could only think of Anlys Covener — a covener who would not touch a sister's hand. And the Covenant of Minith: the plain and simple agreement to do no harm to the world, which had somehow become for little Siri a monster. Yes, that was the only word. A monster, with teeth and claws.

Unseen, in the black night, the bulk of Minith mountain loomed over her.

Something cried, outside the gate but close by.

Zanne started. She had heard that sound before, the same long sobbing cry. That was the beast she had heard by her camp on the bare mountainside.

"A wolf," she muttered. The Minithers didn't keep dogs. The wolves in this country must be a strange breed, to come so near human habitation at midsummer.

Zanne went back to the bunkshed and sat outside it for a long while. She was alone tonight. Truc and Mab had gone visiting their relatives; and Danno too was with his family for this rare holiday of the Minith year. She sat there scowling and biting her knuckles, as if hoping that would help her make up her mind.

"Oh dear," she whispered to the night. "Oh dear ... "

CHAPTER FOUR

A FIGHT IN THE DARK

OLD TRUC AND the dayworker climbed up a stony track to the shoulder of Minith mountain. The sun was bright and hot, though not as hot as it must feel down in the valley. The sky was blue as a robin's egg, with a few trails of high fair weather cloud. As the shepherd strode along he stooped occasionally and picked up a handful of thin soil, rubbed it through his fingers and showed it to his companion. His quiet placid voice kept up a gentle lecture: the fleece was gathered, the hay was safely in, thanks to the Covenant. Now the land had to be tended through the long hot summer. The state of these high pastures must be watched with care: bad feeding now would mean light fleece next summer; and there was the risk of fire, and the magic of the meeting working hard already to keep the small grain harvest safe through a drought; and of course the mines drawing on it too . . .

The piles of black and brown wool, that the local people called "blue" and "red", had been sorted, washed and baled: the bales were waiting in each farmyard to be carted to the waggon road. Very little of the first-class wool would be kept for Minithers' use. It was a matter of pride with them to put the rest of Inland first, and supply their own needs from the fleeces that "fell away". Notoriously, the kind of beast that refused to come down to the yards would have poor wool and less of it. It was because they resisted the gifts of Covenant magic that those sheep didn't come to be harvested as they should.

Truc was pleased with the vagrant dayworker, in spite of that trick with the ribbons and flowers. She stripped the fleece well, she was neat and fast and handled the animals better than Mab or Lecte. There were never enough natural beast-tenders in Minith, it was a problem at every fleece harvest . . . Truc quelled that thought. He knew it couldn't be otherwise, under the mining country's Covenant.

"Now remember," he grunted, as the path grew steep. "We're not here to play with the beasts. No more of those tricks, my girl."

"No, Truc."

Ever since she had started her covener training Zanne had found rest and renewal in returning to the work of an Inland farm. Most, if not all, of Truc's sage monologue was as familiar to her as bread. She didn't know much about mountains but she did know about sheep: and the trials of balancing one crop's needs against another's. All her life she'd heard farming people worrying and complaining in just this tone. The old shepherd made her feel that her anxiety about Minith ways was nothing but prejudice and misunderstanding.

They came to the place that Truc called "the shoulder". It was obviously a gathering place for the flocks, because of a single old twisted thorn which they used as a scratching post. The tree stood in the centre of an area where the earth had been beaten bare by cloven hooves. Scraps and tangles of wool lay about, caught in snags on the branches and in the rocks at its foot.

Truc showed his dayworker a bunch of pierced metal tokens hanging from a thong that was looped through a hasp driven into the tree's trunk. All over the mountain she would find "token trees" like this one. Sometimes the "tree" was a boulder with a hole in it, or a cairn. "But we call them all trees," he explained. "To keep it simple." Every sheep-keeping farm had its own token. As Zanne and Truc walked the hills today they must slip a Slack Road token to the head of the line at each marking point, so other beast-tenders would know where they had been. "And if you strip a fleece that's not ours, you bale it up and leave it by the nearest token tree."

Down below them Slack Road was neatly laid out: the back of the farmhouse and the mountain facing yards. A bundle of newly naked sheep came up and peered at the humans, dancing skittishly nearer and nearer. Zanne could see someone leaning on a yard gate, idle as always. She had not yet worked out exactly what Sirato's brother did for a living. Perhaps he helped his father: but it didn't seem to take up much of his time.

"Truc, you know there's something that puzzles me. Minithers have such respect for the Covenant. You all work so hard — except for a few that don't — "

She didn't want to mention Holne by name, feeling she had no right to make personal criticisms.

"What's the reason then for all this 'restraint'? Don't you think it sometimes does more harm than good?"

One of the sheep came up boldly in a sudden rush on the basket that held Truc's midday bite. He shouted and she bounced away, quite unrepentant.

"There's a bad element in every flock," remarked the old shepherd patiently. He might have been talking about the sheep. "Sometimes it's the Covenant's will it should be so, no fault of their own. We just do our best to make them few, according to what we know. It's not a thing an outsider can understand."

She could tell from his tone that it would do no good to

press him further.

Truc divided up the bite, pointed out landmarks again and made Zanne repeat once more the directions he had given her. They would part now to cover separate ground and he was obviously concerned for her: it was the new worker's first day alone on the mountain. Zanne was touched, and ashamed of her own thoughts. As the old man stood to leave her she grasped his hand warmly.

"Truc, I know I've been a trouble to you. Thank you for reproving me — I mean about the ribbons. I won't fool around like that any more."

The Minither shook his head sadly and drew his hand away. "Ah, there you go: extravagant again. You'll have to learn restraint, Sunny. As far as an outsider can."

But she thought he was smiling as he strode away.

The task of hunting down stray fleeces had come very conveniently for Zanne. For the first time she could make a start on the search that had brought her to Minith. She didn't like the fact that she was setting about this in secret; but it seemed the best way to deal with her problems. She would locate the lost Maker on her own. Once she had proved it was there, the Minithers would come round. She realised she was going to get no help from Minith's covener. She thought she understood why Hillen Coven had been so mysterious on that subject. Clearly there was something badly wrong with that woman, Anlys. But it wasn't Zanne's business so she'd been told nothing about it: and she had better leave well alone.

It wasn't going to be easy to steal time from her farmhand duties. To be fair, Lecte Slack Road expected no more of her workers than she expected of herself, it was just that she seemed determined that every moment of every day should be occupied — if not by necessary tasks then by invented ones. Luckily the kindly old shepherd had set the pace today and as far as she could judge he had generously under-estimated the new worker's capacity. He probably assumed she would spend half the day getting lost, or chasing "bad elements" around the rocks.

The mountain's peak was a mass of blue-grey boulders piled like a giant cairn. Zanne's path skirted the Minith side of the pile, where down below but high above the valley the famous mines were busy, back in full action after the lull of the double harvest. She found a place where she could lie and look over onto the flat shelf outside the most important workings, with Minith town hidden below. Miners scuttled like ants, bringing out the baskets of raw rock and piling it into the stone crusher. Others took the separated ore away, and others shovelled tailings onto the sleds that would be hauled off and flung down that glassy slide above Slack Road. Truc had cracked a rare chuckle when Zanne told him how much she admired the silver-flecked building blocks, and how she'd always thought it must be hard magic that produced that effect. "That's not silver," he told her, flattered by her ignorance. "That's mica, and we don't put it there. We wouldn't spend our time in such a wanton way."

He was no miner, but every Minither knew the rock. As he tested the soil for the effects of drought he hadn't been able to resist picking up pebbles too to show her: the dingy white with black speckles that feels so strangely heavy — that's lead, and poison to work without the Covenant. The quartz with the glittering trace of copper or gold — and a trace is all the past left us, he said. But with our magic, we can glean it and gather enough. He spoke of the metal always as if it were a live stuff like wheat or wool. Smelting, Zanne discovered, was a word for outsiders. In Minith they burned the rock like wood, boiled it like milk, worked it like dough; wove the different metals together like threads on a loom.

Truc was careful to explain that he was not a metalworker

himself. He could fool around with a little prospecting but he would never be allowed to work underground, or down in the town. It wouldn't be right.

Before she'd been watching the working for long, Zanne had devised an ingenious system of pulleys to carry the rope baskets of rock to the crusher. She was also thinking of the sled run. The sleds went down so fast, it seemed a pity all that force just went to polish rock: couldn't it be transferred some way to the punishing work of turning that crushing wheel?

She laughed at herself. Minithers — or any other decent Inlanders, would be appalled at such ideas. The time of the tools that work without hands was gone forever.

There were no draft animals on the flat shelf. Even the great stone crusher was moved by human power and magic alone. Zanne remembered Lecte Slack Road's distaste. The Minithers kept dairy cattle and poultry she knew, and they had a few pairs of oxen shared for ploughing and drawing heavy loads. But they had no pets: not even barn cats or sheep dogs; and here at the centre of the mining peoples' lives nothing that threatened their special Covenant was allowed.

Zanne thought she was beginning to understand the Minithers. There was old Truc, the beast-tender. You could see in his eyes and in the gentle way he handled his sheep, his natural affection for the animals. But though he accepted cheerfully his lowly calling he still felt that it was "wrong", or at least demeaning, to be a shepherd. Zanne remembered the Foresters in the wild wood, who mistrusted all the usual crafts and would scarcely touch metal. These rock-people were like Foresters in reverse. It must seem to them that metal out of the rock and animal nature were so much opposite they must never mingle: a miner's hands should never touch an animal. And the "restraint" they practised was as near as they could come to being one with the rock they served; as those other strange people — dressed in skins and leaves — became one with the creatures of the wild wood.

She had decided, on reflection, that she'd been right in her first assumption outside the meeting house. It was Karin Silvermines the lively red-head, not a brother or sister of hers, whose parents had earned such pity and sympathy from the rest of the meeting. Minithers counted harmless youthful rebellion as a sickness — for in the country of rock, it was outright rebellion to dance and sing outside the meeting house. She had a glimpse now of how Holne had achieved his special status. At least they seemed to treat their "bad element" kindly. There had been real tears in Mab's eyes, and the parents had led their lost sheep away very gently.

It was a strange way to live, and hard on all the young people — especially those like Siri who were not naturally restrained but were too timid for open rebellion. But Zanne had no right to accuse anyone of intolerance. She'd had shocking proof of that last night, when poor little Sirato had nestled up to her. Afterwards, it was the memory of that shudder of disgust which had convinced her as nothing else that her fears about the mountain community were not to be trusted. Whatever distorted ideas Siri had, she was just a child: it was totally wrong to condemn her. If Zanne could respond so unfairly, what right had she to judge Lecte, or any of these people?

After all Sirato was a naughty girl, and she probably twisted or misheard things said in her presence, as any child might . . .

Zanne stretched out a hand and ran it through the air, above the lip of her viewpoint. A faint bright prickling on her skin marked the presence of a magic warding, to prevent silly lambs from tumbling down into the stone crusher. She must have crossed such a warding — they couldn't always be felt — as she crossed the unseen boundary of Minith. Keep out! it said. Do not disturb! She had broken through, and now — as Lecte had said — she must accept Minith's ways.

No — it was impossible for a whole Inland meeting to be as far in the wrong as she had begun to imagine. The fault must be in Zanne herself. It had to be. She would get on with her own work, and leave the local customs alone.

It was a great relief to have come to a decision. Zanne left the ledge above the mines, and went looking for stray sheep.

About an hour after noon by the sun she crossed a giant's pavement of dull grey splashed with white quartz, with uncountable bright flowers growing up between the cracks. There were two fleeces baled behind her: one for the Crags and one from a beast she thought belonged to Breakwater; nothing for Slack Road yet. Now her scanning eyes lit on a place where the pavement ran into a rock wall. There was a polished horn of protruding stone, just at a comfortable height for scratching woolly shoulders, and around it some skeins and tufts of fluffy litter. Zanne chuckled, and sat down to wait.

Before long two ewes, weighted down with their unseasonable burden, came trotting up to take advantage of their private alternative to that thorn tree on Minith shoulder. A large fat lamb was with them. They spotted Zanne and their ears flicked indignantly. Shouting threats and glaring at her they paced to and fro. But they were feeling the heat, and the scratching post was alluring. The first ewe, an especially black one with a white spatch across her brow, sidled closer. She almost surrendered without a fight, but at the last moment remembered her proud reputation for wickedness and tried to bolt. But Zanne had her by the horns. The sheep kicked. Zanne laughed and danced out of reach, wondering if Truc would count this as "playing".

But she held on and at last, with a throaty sigh, the animal stood still.

"Now then, was it worth all the fuss? See — it doesn't hurt at all."

She rubbed the ewe's knobbly intelligent brow, and laughed at her outraged expression. "I shall call you White Spatch."

In a few expert strokes the overripe fleece was free. Zanne tweaked out ticks and checked the ewe's feet and teeth. As White Spatch trotted away, looking bitterly affronted, the other recalcitrant came up of her own accord. Zanne stripped and deticked her as well, somewhat encumbered by her lamb who wanted to play this new game too. She named the second ewe "Curly", because of her especially springy coat. Soon the fleeces were bound and two curious-looking goatlike creatures were skipping away. The nubbly undercoat was slate blue, quite different from their heavy fleece.

"Get along, you beauties," laughed Zanne. "Go and find a pool and admire yourselves."

Maybe Truc wouldn't like the ewes to have names, but Zanne knew her own limitations. She simply *could* not tend anything without befriending it.

When the sheep had gone she sat down to eat her midday bite of beanbread and barley water. The sound of her own laughter had made her feel lonely. At home this would have been such a different day. After the fleece harvest in Mid-Inland bands of friends and pairs of sweethearts would take to the hills, making a picnic and a pleasure jaunt out of the search for strays.

High overhead the mountain larks were singing: *lonely, lonely, lonely*... Zanne closed her eyes and laid her hands on the stone: searching its nature, finding its possibilities. The earth is one, in all its transformations. It is only necessary to reach the deep level of identity and you can be anywhere, everywhere ... Soon she could feel the yielding turf of the sheep downs, she breathed the softer lowland air; she could hear laughter and slow Mid-Inland voices. And the same larks were singing, in the same blue sky.

"I am still in Inland," she told herself. "I am still safe at home."

Deep, deep inside ... She felt herself mingling with the rock, her body of flesh coming apart in tiny starbursts of dissolution ...

Zanne sat up, blinking. She had better be careful. These heady mountain breezes seemed to affect her magic. A little more of that, and she'd have been sitting here made of stone. And generations of Minithers could have brought unruly children up to see what happened to the roadwalker who tied ribbons on sheep.

The work that Truc had given her was done. She had covered all the ground without glimpsing a single living creature except the sheep: not even Truc himself. The mountain that Minith called *the* mountain was far more massive, far more complex than it appeared from below. But now she turned her back on the populated valleys hidden by its bulk and began to explore the hinterland of Minith, beyond the unmarked boundaries of the high pasture. She didn't expect to find the lost Maker anywhere near human habitation.

The rocks and thorn trees gave way to bare rounded upland, the upland to more crags, with long banks of scree and little vegetation. Once a small stream led her into a narrow pebbled gorge with walls that rose and towered higher and closer, until she passed through a cleft like a door onto the shore of a long lake. The water was the colour of beaten steel, reflecting nothing of the narrow blue strip of sky overhead. On its surface was a constant flickering motion, though there was no wind.

She couldn't get by that way, the screes that plunged into the quivering mirror were too steep and treacherous, so she turned back. Just half a vale away she found herself in a valley that might have been next door to Garth, with a golden-green young oakwood surrounding sunny meadows. There were wild ponies grazing there: one red, one dun and one dapple. They weren't shy at all, but came up eagerly to make her acquaintance. She gave them the fragments of her bread and cheese, and they followed her for a while hopefully.

As yet, Zanne had no special plan. She only meant to explore and get the feel of the land. As she scrambled and wandered half her mind was attentive, laying sights and signs away for later study. The other half was beginning to feel distinctly bewildered.

There were still hours of daylight left when she decided she ought to turn back. It was a pity, but in a way it pleased her to be constrained like this, fitting in her special work around the farm tasks. It made her feel like a real covener — looking after the meeting alongside her own work or craft.

There was no chance of getting lost, the mountain's blue bulk was a clear landmark. In a green ferny gully well within the pasture boundaries she halted and sat down, to reflect for a moment.

Zanne had found small buried remnants of the past close to Inland villages. The only other time she had seen a great Maker it had been in the Outland, a dead place where nothing would live or grow. Child of the little hills and woods of Mid-Inland, she had never seen a mountain before the start of this mission. The word suggested desolation and emptiness; and that was what she had expected to find, with the mining people living and keeping their flocks on the edge of a sort of desert. It was not what she saw here. Zanne knew as much about the old powers, and their effects where they had survived into Inland's time, as anybody living. She knew that if there was a great Maker anywhere about its presence must be felt. These mountains should be dead — not blooming as they were, glowing with wild vigour and life. She had wondered a little when she first arrived and crossed the high country alone, and saw none of the distortion or ugliness she had expected. But then everything had been strange. Now that the country was more familiar, the contradiction was even more striking.

Perhaps Hillen Coven had simply made a mistake?

No, said her magic sense. There is no mistake. The old power is here. But where? Formless, but insistent, she felt the trace. *Here* ... To the east, away from Minith, lonely crags and peaks seemed to stretch out forever. Somewhere over there this blurred impression must have its strong focus. Her search had only just begun.

She was about to set off again when she saw the cave entrance. Truc had warned her about the danger of old forgotten shafts. He had also made it quite clear that Minith Covenant did not approve of outsiders visiting the working mines. He had said nothing about natural caves, which was what this happened to be. Ferns and blue bellflowers overhung the slip of darkness. Zanne felt drawn to it as if to a spring of cool water, after the long heat and glare of the day. She glanced at the sky. The sun was already out of sight, bathing the Minith valleys in the summer gold of its decline; and she still had to pick up the fleeces she had baled.

She was getting hungry, that was another consideration. However it wasn't as if there would be honeycake for supper, or a big Mosden custard pastry, flaky and melting and oozing creamy sweetness. She had done her day's work. If she chose to forfeit her boiled greens and bean porridge in exchange for a little free time, how could anyone complain? She made sure of her hank of baling twine, her empty pouch and bottle, and the shepherd's culter: a blunt hooked blade set in a wooden handle. She could imagine how Truc would feel about farm tools left forgotten out of doors. With everything safe on her belt and her staff's cord looped around one wrist she scrambled up and into the cave. There were signs that others had been before her — perhaps prospectors — but not for some time.

The cave became a passage into which the light followed her. Its walls were emerald green with moss, and tiny ferns and flowers grew underfoot. Then the passage took a steep turn downwards. Light vanished. Zanne felt her open eyes bathed by the underearth darkness, black and cool. She stood for a moment drinking it in: the darkness that always returns; and then walked on, picturing hidden wonders which she would in a moment reveal. There might be coloured minerals, sheeted rock drippings like frozen waterfalls, stalagmites and stalactites. Maybe a Minither would laugh at her and say this was the wrong kind of mountain for such displays, but in the dark she was free to let her imagination play. She had taken several steps before she remembered that Siri had her moonlamp and she could not see where she was going even if she wanted to. But she could still touch the walls and roof of this passage and her staff would warn her of breaks in the floor, so she was in no danger. The dark in itself was beautiful.

Pad, pad.

The underground world was not entirely silent. Water dripped somewhere, and occasionally a stone that shifted underfoot rolled away, rattling against others. Zanne decided that the following tread she heard was the echo of her own footsteps.

Strangers should keep to the roads ...

If Minithers really felt about the rock the way Foresters felt about the wild wood, then it was wrong of her to explore in here. It's so easy for humans to break and change things without meaning any harm. Maybe even a hole in the ground has a right to be left alone, to be itself with no help from prying eyes or even blind ones ...

Zanne decided she would venture just a little further, and then turn back. She was thinking about Sirato now. The little girl had been at the back of her mind all day. Maybe Lecte was not deliberately cruel, maybe she was doing her best for her niece in her own way. At first glance you might say Holne was the one being spoiled, but there are other and more dangerous ways of ruining a child's nature besides over-indulgence. All that Siri was learning from her aunt's hard training was how to skip her chores, how to lie; and how to hate the Covenant while pretending to respect it. Supposing she really had a buried talent for magic, which Zanne still suspected, that made the case ten times worse. Zanne knew what magic can become in a ruined, evil mind.

Just as she formed this thought, a small voice seemed to whisper very distinctly in her ear: *I am afraid of the dark.*

Where did that come from? Zanne started and glanced around, uselessly, in the darkness.

Was someone trying to speak to Zanne's mind, using her own thoughts? Either someone who didn't care that to penetrate the mind of another is forbidden in Covenant magic, or someone so ignorant they didn't know what they were doing ...?

"Siri?" she cried out loud. "Is that you, Sirato?"

No answer.

It struck Zanne then that whatever was trying to reach her — a premonition of her own, or some other mind — she was being given a warning. Of what? She took the knife from her belt and lifted it. Bright as a blade — by the rule of likeness she conjured the polished metal. But the small light she had made glimmered on nothing but damp rock.

Nothing to be afraid of: her passage seemed to be coming to an end, that was all. Its charm was gone now that it was visible. Zanne felt chilly and her feet were cold, she thought of her dull supper with vivid regret. Then, lifting the knife higher, she saw something that made her forget all her discomforts and the eerie warning too. There was a cleft, up in the wall on her right. Beyond it she had a glimpse of open space, of level walls and a flat floor.

Zanne did not imagine that she had found the lost Maker. She was far too close to the populated valleys. But any sign of the people of the past was exciting to her. Telling herself it was her duty to investigate, she tucked the knife back into her belt and began to climb. She could make a light again when she was up there.

Something moved behind her, swift and powerful. There was a sound, a deep harsh noise between a cough and a snarl. Zanne's foremost hand had just closed on the lip of the cleft. Before she had the slightest chance to react the thing had landed on her back. It was big, it was heavy, its breath was hot. She was slammed against stone with incredible violence. Gasping, she clutched the rock. In a moment she realised that was no good. She let go and fell, into blackness, the thing under her.

"Under the Covenant!" she shouted. "Under the Covenant! Peace! Peace! I am not prey!"

It wasn't that she thought a beast could understand human language. But words were Zanne's way of communication. She must use them, and let the magic bond between all creatures of earth translate: if it could.

She had rolled out of the animal's reach, but now she couldn't touch it she felt really blind.

With a scrabbling rush it came again, smashed her down, her teeth against gravel. The ferocity of the attack was terrifying. And now with all the strength her practice of the

Link exercises had given her she was clinging desperately to a mass of powerful writhing muscle. As long as she held close it had no space for the killing bite to her throat. The thing seemed to know what she was doing, and flung her free. Her head cracked against stone. But Mid-Inland farmgirls have hard skulls: Zanne's hand at the same time reached out. Her staff, which she had dropped at the foot of the wall when she began to climb, flew through the empty air. She couldn't see it but she caught it; and wailed aloud at the pain of that extra small magic. On her knees, with her back against the rock, she faced the invisible assailant. It rushed her twice, in terrifying silence, and slammed against the barrier of good ash wood. It came again. Zanne had reversed the pole, shortened it and dealt the most ferocious blow she could muster . . .

Something retreated then, pad, pad, into the dark.

Zanne lowered her staff, slowly, and groped for the forgotten knife in her belt. Not that it would have done her much good: it was meant for cutting string. The blade light showed no sign of her attacker.

What *was* it?

Not a wolf, not a bear. It must have been a wild cat, a big, big, wild cat. Big cats were known in all Inland's wildernesses. But they were rare, seldom seen. And they didn't attack humans. Under the Covenant no animal would do that unless sorely provoked. Was this place a wild cat's lair? The air was sweet. She had seen no sign, felt no trace of animal presence.

Zanne put her head in her hands and shook it muzzily. She couldn't be sure what kind of animal it was. The fight had been like falling into a whirlpool. She tried to remember details — its pelt, its size; but there was nothing she could grasp. She was astonished at the sheer malevolence that she had felt. There must be something wrong with that beast. She would have to warn the people at Slack Road. All the shepherds must be warned. A big cat that would attack like that was a danger to the flocks: a danger to anyone.

She was very frightened that it was going to come back, but still it was a long time before she could make herself move. When she stumbled out of the cave entrance it was already twilight. The fern gully looked strange and haunted. Zanne's legs gave way under her. She was shaking, trembling all over with reaction. And the beast was still watching somewhere, she was sure: waiting for its chance.

When a soft and heavy muzzle touched her, she woke up again almost screaming. It was one of the wild ponies. "What are you doing here?" gasped Zanne. "Aren't you afraid?" But it only nudged her belt pouch and whickered gently.

The yard at Slack Road seemed to be full of people and lanterns. Lecte must have been getting worried. Why should anyone worry? This was Inland, not the Outlands where bad things happen. No, it was Minith: where strangers should keep to the roads. Keep to the roads and pass on by ...

As Zanne swayed with weariness, her confused impression of bustle and blurred lights resolved into a girl's face with bright eyes and pointed chin, peering up at her out of the gloom. "Oh, how did you catch the pony?" cried Sirato.

Zanne slid to the ground. The dappled pony stood blinking, as bemused as his rider. Truc lifted a candle lantern to the roadwalker's face, so the light dazzled her eyes.

"You've missed your supper," he declared solemnly. "Did you cover all your token trees?"

"Yes I did." Pride held her upright. Couldn't he see that she had been mauled and beaten? Didn't he wonder what had happened? Minithers don't wonder — it's unrestrained to wonder. "I stripped two Slack Road fleeces, they're up by the rock pavement where there's a scratching stone. But don't you see, I've been attacked . . . I must tell the covener, warn the meeting. There's danger up there."

Truc lowered his lantern.

"You can fetch them down tomorrow."

He stumped heavily away, towards the dark bunkshed.

Someone took Zanne's arm, making her cry out in pain. Someone must have led her indoors. When her head cleared she found herself sitting by the sunstove in the kitchen. She was still confused by Truc's reception, and a little dazed. It hadn't been easy to guide the unbroken pony and keep herself on its back. But here was Lecte Slack Road suddenly turned kind and gentle. She had roused the buried sunheat, she had a bowl of warm water that smelled astringently good and was bathing Zanne's shoulder. The torn sleeve of her smock lay on the hearth.

"I was attacked," mumbled Zanne. "A rogue mountain cat, I didn't know they came so big . . . At least I think that's what it was."

"Where were you when this happened?" asked the farmer calmly.

"In a cave. I was exploring. Lecte, this might be quite serious. Your flocks might be in danger, even other shepherds. Will you call the meeting, or tell the covener? I don't know how you deal with emergencies here . . . but whatever's usual — "

"Oh, I don't think I will trouble the meeting," said Lecte.

The strong herbal scent was making Zanne dizzy. She blinked at the older woman.

"You will not — ?"

Lecte's handsome face was closed and sure as the mountain.

"You did wrong to go into any cave, Sunny. The creature you met was doing no more than its duty. You deserved to be reproved. In Minith we do not meddle and pry and wander away from our proper business."

For a moment Zanne was almost convinced by the force of the woman's certainty. It was so much like what people might say in Garth. It was so much like what she had thought herself, before she succumbed to temptation. And Lecte didn't believe in Zanne's mission, so as far as she was concerned there was no excuse at all. It was true. If Zanne had come straight home with her fleeces like a good covenanted worker, she wouldn't have been hurt.

"No!" exclaimed Zanne, throwing off her bewilderment. "I never heard such superstitious nonsense in my life! As if What Is would misuse a free creature to 'punish' anyone. There's a rogue and dangerous animal on your doorstep, where *under the Covenant* it has no right to be. If you won't tell your meeting, I will."

Lecte smiled, without humour. "Tell as you please. But you would be better advised to accept the warning."

"What warning? What do you mean?"

But the other was carrying the bowl and torn sleeve away. "Good night, Sunny. Don't be late for breakfast. I imagine you'll be hungry enough."

Zanne lay in the bunkshed. The others were deeply asleep: she could hear Mab snoring gently. She was snoring because she was sleeping flat on the earth floor. Zanne had limped into the shed to find that the others had piled their mattresses together to make one soft wide bed. They insisted that she take it, to ease her bruises.

Minithers! She would never understand them.

The bunkshed door creaked. Something scuttled across the floor. Zanne gasped and clutched for her staff — she was still on edge. It was only Sirato. She crouched by the pile of mattresses.

"Ssh. It's me — "

Something was pressed into Zanne's hand: she recognised the shape of her own moonlamp.

"I thought you might want it."

Zanne made a tiny hollow of silver around them, and the girl's face appeared, looking pinched and anxious. She produced something else from the pocket of her smock: a piece of cheese between two oatcakes.

"I gave your pony an apple," she whispered. "I knew you'd want it to have something. Oh, Sunny are you badly hurt?"

Zanne thought of Siri's long walk back to bed in the dark she hated, and was immensely touched.

"No, I'm not hurt. Only bruised and scratched. Your aunt was very kind, bathed the worst bits and bound them up — "

"She's *not* kind," hissed Siri. "She knew. Holne's been out on the mountain all afternoon, he only just got back. I think she sent him to look for you. She knew something had happened. I bet she planned it — "

Zanne sighed. She was in no mood to deal with such a preposterous idea. "Siri, no one could plan what happened to me. It was just a poor old sick cat in a bad temper. Probably it had toothache, it had awful bad breath."

Siri giggled faintly.

"Now go back to bed."

The small shadowy figure stayed for a moment. "I didn't steal the food either. It came from my own supper."

Zanne arranged herself around her bruises, somewhat comforted. If nothing else was going right, she was at least doing a little good here to one damaged child.

But sleep was hard to come by, and not only because she was sore. So Holne had been out on the mountain, had he? Zanne stared into the dark: wondering, wondering — for so long that Siri's wild accusation began to seem not so wild after all. Now that she was safe and her fear had subsided, she still felt that the rogue beast had been a very odd one. Even with her Link strength, was she really capable of fighting off a full grown mountain lion that had forgotten the Covenant? She had had a lucky escape.

Or had she?

CHAPTER FIVE

SIRI

SIRI POURED APPLE juice and water from the pitcher. They were getting near to the bottom of the barrel, she knew. Slack Road had no orchard. The juice was traded, which meant (under the Covenant) that you had to be even more careful than usual not to waste a drop. She screwed up her face and wished fervently that the worst wouldn't happen. But it did. A great brown blob of slimy apple pulp slithered into her beaker. Siri shuddered in disgust. She glanced sneakily to the head of the table. Aunt Lecte wasn't paying attention. If she was quick she could hoick it out with the end of her porridge spoon and smear it under the table top out of sight.

Sunny wouldn't do that. She would swallow the vile slime cheerfully. She hated wicked waste as much as Aunt Lecte. Siri pondered on this. Watching the roadwalker and listening to her talk, she was beginning to get a faint idea of what it might be like: to keep on doing all these unpleasant little things not because anyone forced you but because ... it was magic. Because, in some tiny way, swallowing the apple pulp or not would make a difference to Inland. She hesitated. But the habit of years was too strong. Little Rat was not capable of such an act of heroism. The metal spoon end darted into the fat brown earthenware mouth. With incredible swiftness the slime was caught, disposed of, and both Siri's hands were back above the table.

Aunt Lecte always liked to see them there. Any part of a Rat out of sight, she said, was bound to be in mischief.

At this part of the summer, the bean harvest as they called it, everybody separated for long hours of evening chores after an early supper. She could hear her father and Danno in the brickyards; and Holne had vanished somewhere. Siri was alone with her aunt, who was sitting doing nothing at all. It was most unlike her. She had even cut the daytelling quite short. But Aunt Lecte had been behaving strangely ever since Sunny had that fight with the mountain cat. She kept Siri close by her in the garden, slaving over the bean rows and soft fruit canes. But she was very quiet; didn't even make sarcastic comments about the pace of her niece's picking. A guilty conscience, thought Siri. That's what it is.

The attack was supposed to be forgotten, Siri was forbidden to talk about it. But only a day or two after it, Carad Breakwater and some of the other elders had come up to Slack Road. They had disappeared into the counting room, the study next to the kitchen where Aunt Lecte and father kept all their accounts, and Siri had heard them muttering in there for hours. The door was thick, she couldn't make out what anyone was saying.

Siri knew, in a childish way, what these gatherings of the elders usually meant. In a little while there would be another face missing from that group of bold, bad flores who played games and talked loudly even on a meeting day ... someone would vanish the way Rian Mountainside had vanished long ago. And Siri would be scolded if she ever spoke again about "the one that's gone". But this time she was certain that something different was going on. She had taken the risk of asking Mab.

"What are they talking about? Is it Sunny? What are they going to do to her?"

Of course Mab wouldn't tell but she was flustered. She

even forgot to reprove Rat's curiosity, just begged her not to go asking her aunt such questions.

"May I leave the table, Aunt Lecte?"

"You may."

A trestle by the sunstove was piled with long beans, jars and a vat of preserving liquor. Siri eyed the horrors resentfully. Her hand was already sore from that nasty stringing knife. Aunt Lecte looked at the trestle too: but as if she didn't see it.

"There are no more chores for you today. You had better go straight to bed. Mind I don't hear you running around up there."

"No, Aunt Lecte ... Under the Covenant," rattled Siri, "I thank What Is for my good food."

She slipped off her stool and darted away with her beaker, bowl and spoon. When she'd rinsed them at the scullery pump she peeped out of the door to make sure no one was in sight: scurried across the yard and out onto the hill beyond. Naturally she had no intention of going to bed.

No farmwork ever took Siri up to the Burnhouse stream. She would have been afraid to venture even this far from the beaten track, but it was broad daylight and she knew that she would find Sunny there doing her exercises. She usually did them before dawn but while recovering from her bruises she preferred to wait until evening when a day's work had loosened her muscles. When Siri had first heard of these exercises she'd thought Sunny wasn't such a fool after all. It seemed like a good excuse to get away from your tasks: and apparently Aunt Lecte couldn't call it idling. But when she saw "the Link" she was disillusioned. It looked very much like more hard work.

Sirato climbed down into the grotto and sat quietly waiting for her friend to finish. As she watched the older girl she thought of the day when she had seen the stranger appear — how excited she had been, how it seemed as if everything must change. In many ways Sunny had been a sad disappointment. It had always been a joke, the way Aunt Lecte called her "uncovenanted". She was worse than any Minith elder in her own peculiar way. But now she was even giving up those peculiar ways, and turning into a proper Minither.

The night Sunny had come home all bloody riding on a wild pony had been exciting. Sirato had heard the shouting in the kitchen and felt thrilled by her friend's rebellion. But by the next morning Sunny had changed her mind. She wasn't going to defy Aunt Lecte and go down and tell the meeting after all. She said: "I'm eating at your aunt's table, working on her farm. I'll respect her judgement — for now." It sounded as if the roadwalker was learning to swallow her anger, to say thank you for being reproved and forbidden to speak. If it was so, Siri didn't blame her. She understood that "for now" part, as well. Only too often she'd said the same sort of thing to herself, after some punishment or other had fallen especially hard — *just you wait. Just you wait until I'm big....* It didn't mean anything. It was a way to bear the misery of being small and helpless, something you could keep by you and gnaw sometimes in the dark.

But supposing it wasn't like that? Suppose Sunny really was biding her time, and planning still to complain to the meeting: to accuse Aunt Lecte of setting the wild cat on her? Siri chewed a grass stalk and wondered uneasily. Maybe she ought to tell her friend about the elders. She didn't understand herself exactly what was happening: however, she was sure Sunny understood much less. She simply wouldn't listen when you told her how things worked in Minith.

It was no use, she didn't dare ... Besides, what could she say? *I don't know what you're planning, Sunny, but it won't work. Minith isn't like your Inland. It's no use being brave here, it doesn't do any good . . .*

"Sunny, would you swallow apple pulp?"

The roadwalker was doing nothing now, just sitting quietly with her legs crossed. Her eyes seemed to come into focus from a long way off.

"Apple pulp?" repeated Zanne, mystified.

"You know. The slimy bits that float around in the bottom of the juice barrel."

"Yuck — no. Why would anyone want to do that?"

"For — for the good of Inland," explained Sirato, embarrassed. "Because waste's wicked."

"No need to waste it. Pour it on the compost heap." The dedicated covenanter suddenly went off into peals of laughter. "What else do you think I should eat, Siri? Cowpats?"

Sirato scowled. "It's not funny," she muttered. "I'm trying . . . trying . . ."

"Trying to do what, Siri?"

She couldn't answer, only bit her lip and glared.

Zanne was thinking of the warning that had reached her just before she was attacked. She had been waiting for a chance to approach the younger girl, to find out if the buried talent was really there. She would have to go carefully. She remembered how frightened she had been the first time she really felt the power within her, when she was a little girl herself.

"Never mind. It's my exercises, they make me light-headed. Siri, would you like to see some magic?"

"Oh — *yes!*"

Zanne went to the edge of the stream. She lay down and fished in the water and brought out a smooth pebble, bright and wet.

"Do you only dig for metal in Minith? Don't you ever find gemstones?"

The brown glistening stone had gone. A ruby the size of a pullet's egg lay on the roadwalker's palm, shimmering like a great clear drop of blood.

"Ah — " Siri sighed delightedly. "May I touch?"

"Of course."

"But this is illusion," said the child of Minith sternly, holding the counterfeit between finger and thumb. It was very lovely.

"Quite right. I can't fool you. You know more about these rocks than I do."

"Could you make it real?"

"It could be done," responded the covener thoughtfully. "There is no end to transformation: everything becomes everything else if you follow far enough. But it wouldn't be very practical. To make a ruby out of your granite or limestone would take — oh, enough expense of magic to turn Minith into a hole in the world. Still, there is something I can do instead . . . Siri, don't you have a grass in this country that you call 'cut-finger'?"

"Why, yes."

"Give me the thing that cuts."

Siri darted into the long grass and pulled a ribbed blue-green blade. She was careful: cut-finger had an edge like a scythe for unwary hands. The egg-shaped pebble lay on Sunny's hand again, turning dull and dry in the evening sunlight.

"I don't like to make shifting magic without real need. I might disturb your covener's balance of things. But this is such a little, it won't hurt."

She took a single gentle breath, and as she released it drew the grassblade across the pebble. It fell neatly in two. Only the outer shell was brown. The centre was a crystal of deep violet, pure and bright.

"Oh! Amethyst! Real magic!"

"Yes, Siri. But not mine. I cut the mineral, I didn't make it. You can thank your mountain for that."

"Is it mine? May I keep it?"

"Yes, if you like."

Sirato's eyes glistened. She reached out for the river jewel, almost managing not to snatch. Her fingernails scratched Zanne's palm like eager little claws.

"I'll keep it in my treasure box, in my secret place — "

She hadn't meant to say that. She broke off, stricken. Her eyes went to the mountain in sudden fear: and then she realised Sunny was watching her with a strange, grave expression.

"Sirato," said the covener. "I want to ask you something. I want to ask you — have you thought about what you will be when you grow up? When I was your age, I remember I used to worry, because it seemed as if I had no talent for any ordinary trade. Is that the way it is for you?"

"Oh!"

The greed with which Sirato had snatched the jewel vanished from her face. She looked horrified. "No one knows — " she cried. "You can't know, you can't know ... it's my secret — "

Zanne had half expected this sort of reaction. She waited for the panic to pass: but instead of calming down Sirato suddenly went rigid. She was staring upwards. After a moment, Zanne saw what she was looking at.

"Holne, come down."

Siri's brother dropped neatly from his perch among the rowans and stood grinning. Zanne noticed how surefooted he was. And how clever at hiding himself, even from a covener.

"Spying again!" cried Sirato. "You've got no right! This is not for you! Boys who meddle in magic ought to be whipped!"

"Siri! Don't be so rude!"

In other parts of Inland people said, more kindly, "men who make magic only make fools of themselves". Zanne might have known Minith ways would be more harsh on that point as on everything else to do with the Covenant. She was surprised to see in Holne's face that the taunt really stung him. She would not have thought he would care for magic at all ... according to her latest guess about his interests.

But the wounded look vanished and the big white annoying grin reappeared almost immediately.

"Where's the harm?" he asked, mockingly. "A *cat* can look at a covener — isn't that what they say?"

He winked broadly.

Zanne almost laughed out loud. Really, this young man was quite astonishing. But she managed to keep her face blank, though his impudence reduced her to silence.

"What's the matter, Sunny? Cat got your tongue?"

"You always spoil everything for me!" wailed Sirato shrilly. "Go away, you beast!"

She clutched the amethyst pebble, baring her sharp white teeth as if about to fly at her brother and bite him.

Holne smiled more widely than ever. "Oh, I'm a beast, am I?"

Lightly, he crossed the turf and caught his sister's shoulder before she could duck away. Zanne noticed how alike their vivid features were: though Siri's eyes were burning with rage and Holne was laughing, or pretending to laugh. He shook the child a little and turned her to face Zanne.

"Be careful, covener," he said. "You don't know everything. Not even everything about this little Rat. She may surprise you yet."

Siri twisted around and bit his hand. Holne gasped; for a moment the teasing mask slipped and Zanne saw another face — fear, anger: she couldn't tell which. Then he let Siri go.

"You're supposed to be in bed, Rat. You'd better be there soon — you know someone's bound to tell."

He jumped up, grasped the rowan branches and swung himself out of sight.

The Burnhouse went on purling and singing in its bed, the grass was still as green and the flowers bright. But the grotto had changed. There was no peace in it anymore.

"I hate him," muttered Siri between clenched teeth. "I'd like to *kill* him."

"Siri, don't say that. He's your brother. Under the Covenant, Holne is part of you and me, and we are part of him. If he hurts us we ought to try and understand why."

She was talking to herself as much as to Sirato. She might feel tempted to dismiss Holne as a spoiled, spiteful brat and laugh at his antics; but that wasn't good enough. She had to reach him somehow. She had recently come to the startling conclusion that the success of her whole mission might depend on her understanding of Lecte Slack Road's nephew.

But Siri did not know what was on Zanne's mind. She felt betrayed.

" 'Under the Covenant'," she jeered furiously. "Under the foul, beastly Covenant — "

Glaring at Zanne, she threw the two halves of the amethyst pebble into the river.

"You're just the same as all the others. I don't want your magic. You can keep it."

The treasure was lost. Tears sprang into Siri's eyes. She ran away, hugging herself in her thin little arms: hating Zanne, hating Holne. The only comfort was that she had not told her last secret. She had been saved from that.

In the beginning Zanne's suspicion about that "mountain

cat" attack had been merely a wild idea, that came to her out of nowhere in the course of a sleepless night. But the more she tried to remember about the animal in the cave, the more unfocused her memory seemed. The thing that had attacked her had no fixed shape, no defined presence. Soon she was almost certain. Her confusion came from the fact that it had not been a beast at all — but a tall and strong young man, with a catskin tied round him. Zanne's pride was injured. She had fallen for Holne's prank completely. It had been a very rough joke and the bruises were real, but that didn't improve matters. She, a covener and a strong one, had been frightened half to death by a boy's trick.

Then she started to wonder why he would fake such an attack. There must be a reason, he surely wouldn't risk something so outrageous just for fun. She thought of a young man with time on his hands, a young man who had had years in which to explore the Minith mountains. It came to her in a flash of inspiration — *Holne must have found the Maker!* And he didn't want anyone else to find it. He had been suspicious and resentful of the new dayworker ever since the night she arrived: Zanne had always wondered why. Now it made sense. He had heard her say she was here to seek the thing out, so he had plotted to scare her off. He must have been waiting for a chance to get her alone, just as she'd been waiting for a chance to begin her search.

Zanne was not as shocked as she might have been. She remembered well, from her own youth, how fascinating the marvels of the dead past could be. She couldn't quite get over her almost physical distaste for the handsome youngster, but she felt more sympathy for him, not less, if this guess was right — in spite of her bruises. After all, if Holne was wild, Lecte and the other Minith elders were finally to blame. It was a stupid combination: to bring young people up so strictly and then, if they rebelled, just to abandon them to their own devices.

After that strange little scene in the rowan grotto, there was no doubt left. Holne had definitely been her attacker. He had obviously been testing her, to see if she had any suspicion. She hoped she'd managed to soothe his anxiety on that score.

To prove or disprove the other part should be easy. Holne might be very good at concealing his tricks, but Zanne was a covener after all. She would be watching him from now on, and following him whenever he went up into the mountains. He wouldn't stay away from his treasure for long. Sooner or later, he would lead her to the Maker.

Sirato did not know about Zanne's new occupation. She only knew that she seemed to have lost her friend. Sunny was nowhere about: whenever she wasn't working she just vanished. So there was no one for Siri to tell, about the things that were happening at Slack Road. It wouldn't have sounded like much, anyway: her father and her aunt whispering together with grim faces, Mab and Truc getting so silent, and making up so many chores that kept them inside the yards. They sent Danno away "for a holiday with his family". Sunny probably didn't even notice that, apprentices probably had holidays all the time in her unimaginable, different Inland. But Siri knew. Something terrible was going to happen. Not only to Sunny but to all of them. It had started with that wild cat . . . it was getting closer.

It was in her dreams that she discovered what the terrible thing was. She had finally been so wicked that the mountain was to be allowed to have her. One night she woke up whimpering and scrabbling to escape and found Aunt Lecte leaning over her with a rushlight. She cried out in fear and hid her face, her aunt looked so horrible. When she dared to peer between her fingers the figure was gone. It might have been a dream. But if Aunt Lecte was getting into the dreams that was even more frightening.

Sunny wouldn't save her. Sunny had abandoned her after what happened by the river. She wouldn't protect anyone from the anger of the Covenant. She was on Its side.

She decided to run away. It was quite simple, there was nothing to be prepared. The idea came to her one afternoon when she was cleaning out the henhouse. (She had scoured it once already, but her aunt wasn't satisfied.) She wondered at once why she had waited so long. But Slack Road was the only home she had ever known. When she kissed her father goodnight after supper he stroked her hair and looked at her so sadly she almost burst into tears and blurted out that it wasn't goodnight, it was goodbye. Then he said, "Try to be good, Sirato. Try to obey your aunt Lecte. She knows how you must live." So Siri swallowed her tears and made no sign.

She lay in bed waiting and waiting until the summer night was nearly over. The space above the loft partition had turned from black to dark grey. She got up — she hadn't undressed. She had two oatcakes she had saved from supper tied in a handkerchief. She looped the little package to her belt and added an old water bottle she'd found among the discarded odds and ends in the loft. She made a bundle of her winter cloak, which she had sneaked from its place in the clothes closet in her aunt's room: and was ready to go. She had no hope of escaping from the Covenant, or even from Minith. Most likely when she reached the edge of the mountains there would be an invisible fence there, like the one that kept the sheep out of the hay. But she must try. It was too horrible to stay here waiting for the formless terror to take shape.

False dawn lightened the sky but there was no warmth in it. Siri was shivering down to her bones, as you do when you have been awake all night, watching the dark until you think you have really gone blind. She crept out of the scullery and across the yards, slipping from wall to wall bent double and almost running on all fours. In the slack yard the air was still hanging with grey dust: several sleds of tailings had come down the mountain yesterday. Sirato didn't bother to pray for protection. She didn't want anything the Covenant could give her. Up above, the mountain loomed black against a deep blue sky that was scattered with fading stars. Siri cowered, and scurried for the old toolshed. She slipped quickly through the maze of dim shapes that she she knew so well: and stopped dead.

There was a light.

Someone had moved the loose brick from above her secret place.

She saw a dark shadowy movement, big but low down, near the wall. There was an animal in the shed — a beast, she could see its green eyes glinting as it pawed over her precious treasure. Sirato screamed. She dived into the space between the lumber pile and the wall, a tiny desperate bundle of teeth and claws.

"Leave that alone! That's my mother's!"

The animal lifted its head. It sat back on its heels and became her brother Holne. He was holding mother's violin in one hand, and the bow in the other. She could see his face, his hateful smile, by the grey light. She knew then what he was going to do but could not, could not believe it.

"You're up early, little sister."

She lunged for the violin, but he easily held it out of reach.

"Or have you taken to staying out all night, like me?"

"I don't care if you stay out all night. I won't tell, I won't tell. Only give me that — it's mine!"

Holne laughed, it sounded like rattling pebbles.

"There's nothing you can tell, little one. There's nothing

anyone can do to me. What are you up to, Rat? Are you running away from home?"

She didn't bother to deny it. The cloak bundle lay between them on the floor.

"What if I am. What do you care. You'd like me out of the way, you hate me."

For a moment, if she hadn't been fooled by Holne so often, she would have been confused by his expression. Suddenly he wasn't laughing, and he looked so sad —

"You're mistaken, Rat. I only wish that there was somewhere you could run to. But there isn't. You can't leave Minith. None of us can, least of all my sister."

"Give me that violin!"

Holne shook his head. "Close your eyes," he said. "Close your eyes or go away, poor little Rat."

He put down the bow, but kept his foot on it. He took the fragile shell of wood by its slender throat and swung it against the wall. There was a terrible sound, a sobbing wail of murdered music. Holne dropped the pieces, picked up his mother's bow and broke it across his knee.

As soon as Holne had left the toolshed another figure, shrouded in a dark cloak, slipped out of the dawn shadows and went in.

Not a sound came from the corner behind the lumber pile, where Sirato was lying with her face buried in her arms.

Zanne stood over the crushed and huddled body. If Siri had looked up then she would have wondered what had happened to "Sunny", the young vagrant her aunt had condescended to employ. Zanne's hood had fallen back. Her gaudy hair was cooled to silver by the colourless light, her dun cloak indigo in the shadow: the moon in a night sky. Her face was very grim as she knelt beside the pitiful victim of Minith's Covenant.

"Siri? What is it? What happened?"

At the touch of Zanne's hands Sirato suddenly came to life. She jerked away.

"Leave me alone," she cried hoarsely. "Leave me alone — " She burst into loud, racking sobs. "My music, my music, it's broken. I hate you all — oh my music, it's gone forever ... "

Then Zanne saw just what Holne had done. All around Sirato on the floor were scattered fragments of polished wood. She picked up one, fragile as a sea shell: and she remembered the wordless song that she had heard once, coming from these yards. So Sirato was the musician. The sobs had quieted. Sirato lay rigid, one hand clinging to the instrument's broken neck.

"Siri — " asked Zanne after a moment. "Is this your secret? The one you thought I had guessed?"

The girl sat up. Her face was smeared all over with dust and tears, she rubbed at it drearily.

"Yes."

It didn't matter anymore. There was no reason to lie. "It was my mother's violin. I found it here, after she died. Aunt Lecte would never let me be a music-maker, I know. But I could come here sometimes and try to play. It was all I had — Oh mother, mother ... "

She hid her face.

"But why did Holne do this?"

Siri shrugged her shoulders. Wasn't it obvious? "Because he hates me. Because — because he knew no one would blame him. Unnatural music is wicked waste ... under the Covenant."

Zanne reached out. She took the small hard hands in both of hers, repressing firmly an odd little shudder — a memory no doubt of all those times this child's words had shocked her. And now her covener's sense told her unmistakably that music, not magic was the craft Sirato was born for. The "untrained talent" at Slack Road existed then only in her imagination; and she must have warned herself, unconsciously, in that cave. Fleetingly she was disappointed. But there were more important concerns at the moment. She saw she desolation in Siri's eyes and finally all her resolution to withhold judgement and be tolerant, was shattered like the violin.

"Sirato, don't say that. Siri, you've got to forgive me: I've been very cruel. I have been lying to you. You have been quite right all along. The Covenant that you know, *is* horrible, it *is* cruel ... and you've done nothing wrong at all in hating it and defying it."

Siri stared dully.

"All I can say is, though I don't expect you to believe me, — it's not meant to be like this. The real Covenant is gentle and kind. And no one, no one in any other part of Inland I know, would stop you from making music ..."

She hesitated. But she couldn't bear to lie to this child anymore.

"There's something else. I'm not who you think I am, Siri. Do you remember when I first arrived I told you all I had been sent by Hillen Coven, to find an old powerhouse, a Maker that's hidden in these mountains?"

Siri nodded listlessly. "Oh yes. It was a made-up story."

"No, Siri. It was the truth. My name isn't Sunny, it is Zanne, Zanne of Garth. I'm the wicked woman Mab told you about. But I only 'dig up the past' where it has been buried alive. That's my work. I hunt down old poisoned relics, and give them good, covenanted death."

Sirato went on staring. She was still stunned by what Holne had done. Another Covenant, not like the one she knew? She had begun to imagine that, before, but how could she trust it now? She didn't want to take such a risk. And yet against her will: even now, when everything, everything had been taken from her, she was roused by Sunny's story. It was an adventure, a real adventure.

"Oh, Sunny," she gasped hoarsely. "I mean — Zanne. Is it true? If it is, you can trust me. I won't tell! I'll help you! I can keep secrets!"

Zanne was caught. She hadn't planned this. Here she was, trying to rescue the child and straight away involving her in more deceit. But she could see no other course for the present. "No, you'd better not tell. Let the grown ups go on believing it was a silly story, for now."

Siri drew a long breath.

She glanced at the winter cloak, that lay among the glittering fragments of a broken mirror.

"I was going to run away — " she said blankly.

Zanne knew that it would take more than a few consoling words to undo the harm of years. But at least some of the bitter, desolate look had gone from Siri's face. She squeezed the girl's hands.

"No — don't do that. Don't misunderstand me. You have a right to leave here, and I'll help you as soon as I can. But running away isn't a good way to start a new life. Wait a little longer, Siri: and when I've done my work we'll leave Minith together."

"Aunt Lecte — "

"Don't you worry about her. You're eleven years old aren't you? I was younger than that when I left home to learn my trade. I'll deal with Aunt Lecte."

Looking into her friend's new face, so strong and stern, Sirato could believe it. She felt a shiver of unwilling hope: then her eyes fell on the broken mirror.

"But it's broken. Oh, it was all I had of my mother. Now she's really dead, really dead — "

"Child, your mother doesn't live in a box of polished wood. She lives in What Is, the same as you and me. And if your music comes from her she isn't lost. You will find her again the next time you pick up a fiddle, which will be quite soon. We'll buy one at the first tradestown down the waggon road, after we leave."

The light that came through the hole in the wall had brightened from grey to gold. Soon the household would be stirring. Siri scrubbed at her face again, but guessed she wouldn't be making any improvement. The first tradestown down the waggon road! That sounded so wonderful. In spite of herself, she was dazzled. She would have to get indoors quickly, and wash the tearstains away. No one must suspect ... All at once she felt brave and purposeful. Zanne had given her more than a promise of freedom. For the first time in her life little Rat had work to do that meant something. She was going to help Hillen Coven.

"Your cloak's wet," she noticed suddenly. "You'd better hide it, or they'll know you've been out in the dew."

"Yes, I was out all night on the mountain. I was trying to follow your brother," added Zanne, frowning.

She had had to give up that attempt. The young man was too crafty. And something, maybe the presence nearby of the lost Maker, seemed to hinder Zanne's magic up there.

Siri's eyes brightened, vindictively. "Is he your enemy? I told you he was. I bet he knows all about the evil Maker."

"Siri, don't talk about 'enemies'. That's not the way to help me. And I didn't say 'evil', either. The relics of the past don't mean us any harm. They can't help being what they are — "

Siri ignored these rather feeble protests.

"Don't you worry, Sunny. I mean Zanne. I'll help you get him. You just tell me how."

Zanne knew she should tell Siri it was wrong of her to hate her brother. Holne too was the victim of Minith's Covenant, he'd simply been hurt in a different way ... But she couldn't put much conviction into her defence of that young man at the moment.

"You'd better go and get ready for breakfast," she said instead, "before anyone catches us idling together. I'll hide the broken violin so your aunt won't find it." Looking at the piteous wreckage, she had a sudden impulse and took her moonlamp from the pocket of her leggings.

"Here — " she told Siri, in the urgent low tone of one conspirator to another. "You'd better keep this. You never know, we might be separated and you might need to reach me quickly. The moonlamp will always know where I am."

When Sirato was safely out of the way, Zanne left the old toolshed with her waggon cloak over her arm. She stood for a moment, frowning. She had seen Holne leave the shed. She had not heard him walk away. She walked around the back of the building. There he was, sitting cross-legged and careless by the hole in the wall. His black curly hair shone in the sunlight: he was smiling as always. Zanne glared.

"I don't understand you, Holne," she said at last. "Once, I heard someone playing a violin, do you remember? You must have known that it was Sirato. You protected her then. You kept her secret ... You must have been keeping it from your aunt for a long time. So why this? Oh Holne, that was so wicked!"

Holne's bright eyes watched her. She could not read them: they might have been doll's eyes, made of brown glass.

"I changed my mind."

Her hand was itching to slap, her magic itching to do worse. But as she struggled to find words to express her contempt, words failed her altogether. There was something strangely horrible about the way Holne sat there so coolly. Why had he stayed? He'd had plenty of time to get away. She had a sudden unpleasant idea that Holne had often been near to her without her knowledge: hiding as he had hidden in the rowan grotto; invisible to her magic. Why had she not sensed his presence? What kind of creature was Holne? Was he so lost that nothing of the Covenant could reach him? The hairs on the back of Zanne's neck prickled. She had been badly mistaken. There was nothing remotely amusing about this young man.

"Zanne of Garth," said Holne. "The maker-lover, that's what they call you around here. I heard you say it: '*the relics of the past don't mean us any harm* — '. Minith meeting wouldn't like that kind of talk."

"Are you threatening me, Holne Slack Road?"

The young man's smile had become a grimace.

"You don't understand. You don't understand half as much as you think you do, covener." Suddenly something came to life behind the cold eyes. He lifted his clenched fists as if he was going to hit out at Zanne.

"I had to do it!" he cried. "I had to do it! It was for her own good! Oh, you'd better get away from here, Zanne of Garth. You've been warned once. Get away, before it's too late. And leave Sirato behind. She's ours, you can't have her."

That was enough. That he should imagine he could scare her off — and this morning he wasn't even wearing his catskin. Zanne was furious.

She laughed. "Holne, I don't have to argue with you. Nor am I going to accuse you of anything I can't prove, so don't expect that satisfaction. But understand this: I know your secret. And what I don't know, I'll find out. I'll do what I came to Minith to do, and when I leave Siri will leave with me. There's nothing more to say."

She turned on her heel and marched away, afraid that if she stayed a moment longer she would really lose her temper . . .

Holne sat by the wall. If Zanne had looked back then she would have seen something strange. The insolent young man wrapped his arms around his knees, shivering hard in the warmth of the early sun. "You don't know my secret," he whispered. "You *don't* know, and I hope you never will . . . "

Holne shivered and shook and hugged himself, breathing hard as if he was trying not to sob out loud. The next moment, he jumped up and loped off across the yards to the farmhouse. The white grin was in place again, hard and bright as ever.

In the warm odorous henhouse Siri slipped her hands in and out of the nesting straw, searching for eggs. Outside, Slack Road's poultry clucked and crowed in their run, gobbling up her running-away oatcakes along with their usual grain. She squatted back on her heels and took the moonlamp from her pocket, smoothing her fingers over the dull silver lovingly. The pain of losing mother's violin would come back, but for now it was almost overwhelmed by the wonderful dream. To live among people who didn't call her wicked. To make music every day without having to hide ... *Oh, I'll do anything you say, I'll help you all I can*, whispered Siri. She had learned about the evil "makers" at Anarad Pensioner's school. Anarad had probably told them about Zanne of Garth too, but Siri didn't remember: she never paid much attention to lessons. Aunt Lecte had said there was no Maker in Minith, and she never lied . . . but if Siri had to choose she would believe Sunny. Together they would beat Holne and find the old Maker and kill it, and then walk away and never come back. The chief coveners at Hillen would be so grateful they would hold a great feast — with musicians, and magic flowers, and honeycakes . . .

It was a lovely vision. Pretending to believe it, Siri could forget about the whispering and the shadows that had always surrounded her, that were growing so close and terrible now. But inside she knew. The good dreams are never real, the nightmares always are. Sunny — Zanne — didn't understand fear, she didn't believe in evil. Maybe in her own world she was right. But not here ... not here. Siri glanced around her, shivering, and hid the moonlamp away again, furtively; like a guilty secret.

CHAPTER SIX

THE GUARDIANS OF THE MOUNTAIN

THE GREAT MOUNTAIN slumbered under a pall of heat. Zanne paced the parched and crumbling sheep tracks, her toes wincing at hot pebbles. After the fleece harvest she had walked up here and been consumed by homesickness for Garth. Today she felt no desire to reach through this landscape to another. She had to study these particular rocks, these bare uplands, and find out their secret.

The strange thing was that she was looking for a lost Maker in a country that had never known the people of the past. Generations ago when the first covenanters came looking for metal they had traced the bright veins, the blood and nerves of the mountains, far away from the exhausted workings of the old time. The people of the past had stripped everything: where they had harvested nothing would grow again. In Mid-Inland, in the patchwork fields and little woods where Zanne had been brought up, farms and villages and little bustling towns lived and thrived on the green grave of a vast ancient city. You couldn't walk a vale without seeing a cluster of old misshapen stones in the corner of some field, or a swathe of different colour in the grass that marked the route of a vanished road. Minith was not like that. Its mountains had always been empty. Towers of light never grew out of these crags: there was not even the ghost of one of the old great roads within many days' journey of Minith town.

Most of the inhabitants of Mid-Inland thought of the "ruin stones" and other relics as a nuisance; if nothing worse. If asked, they'd probably say Minith's foundation was better. The Minithers had started afresh, planting the new growth in uncontaminated soil. But they'd be wrong, thought Zanne. New things don't come from nowhere. They spring from the old, someway. The Minithers have been able to forget that, and it has done them no good. They've grown proud and self satisfied: so sure of themselves they've twisted the Covenant all out of shape and they don't even know it.

Up here on the heights, with the mines and the settlement out of sight, the blue mass that Minithers called *the* mountain lost some of its powerful identity. It was just one of the waves on a vast lake of stone, that seemed to have been frozen in an instant at the height of a tossing storm. Zanne wished she could bring Siri here. If she could walk on the mountain's back and see it in proportion: splendid, but only one of many, she might begin to lose her superstitious terror. But though the barriers had really begun to break down now that Zanne had told the child the truth about herself and her mission, there was still a long way to go. Minith children were taught to be afraid, it seemed, as soon as they could toddle, so that they would grow up sober and restrained — living in the middle of this glorious wilderness and never knowing it, never daring to venture off the beaten track. "Only bad children wander," explained Siri. "And then the mountain punishes them. When they grow up they get sick and die like my mother. Holne's like that — " she added bitterly. "Aunt Lecte tries to pretend he's not. But he is, he is. And I hope he dies of it soon."

Zanne tried to persuade Sirato that a tendency to idleness and a taste for embroidered collars wasn't necessarily an illness: but the child wouldn't have it. She was still deeply under the influence of Minith's Covenant.

If it wasn't for Siri, Zanne would have left Slack Road by now. Since the morning when she had caught him smashing Sirato's violin she hadn't spoken to Holne, nor he to her. She was fairly sure that he would keep her secret so long as she didn't accuse him: he would not want to raise the subject of the lost Maker. But it was becoming quite an ordeal — this secret duel with the farmer's nephew, carried on right under Lecte's eyes.

And maybe it was her own unease, or maybe it was the unrelenting heat, but the whole household seemed to be suffering with her. Gwil's apprentice had disappeared. The brickmaker himself had become totally silent and withdrawn: workers from Minith who came to help him in the kilnyard arrived and left again without saying a word to anyone, as if visiting a house under a curse. Meals in that big kitchen were agonising. Holne teased his sister with an edge of cruelty: and the nastier he became, the more the rest of the household seemed to defer to his whims. Siri cowered and looked sly, hugging her secrets: the farmhands ate glumly and seemed to have fallen out with "Sunny". Over all the tall black woman presided with a face like carven basalt . . . never smiling, speaking always in the same cold measured tone. If a rock could talk, it would sound just like Lecte.

But if she could leave the child, where would she go? Minith meeting held together. She could be sure without trying that there wasn't a house in the valleys that would willingly take in a dayworker who had walked out on Lecte Slack Road. She'd be even less likely to find any household that would welcome Zanne of Garth. The fix that she'd got herself into seemed more hopeless every day. Worst of all was the knowledge, inescapable now, that a whole Inland community had lost its way. The Minithers had been left alone too long. Something must be done. Hillen Coven must be told . . .

There was no relief from the oppression out of doors either. Truc had told her, with gloomy pride, that she must not look for a break in the weather now. These rare burning summers, once they set in, never varied until Leafall. She was up here today firewatching and checking the state of the pasture. The flocks became so depressed in conditions like these they had not the sense to move on themselves. They would have to be driven from one scorched moor to another: and in the end fed with baled hay carried up from the barns.

"It's like the hour before a thunderstorm," muttered Zanne. "But the storm never breaks."

At least the heather had so far survived. It was just coming into bloom, colouring the great stone lake purple with blue crags for tossed spray. Zanne collapsed onto a thick springy bed, and gratefully unstoppered her stone bottle of barley water.

The only solution, she told herself — as if it would cure the drought as well — is for me to find that Maker.

She stared into the wilderness, her back to Minith, and gradually her eyes became fixed. She put down the cool bottle slowly, unconsciously.

It did not trouble her too much that there were no other relics around. It had been fairly common, she knew, for powerhouses to be built far from the towns and cities of the old time. What troubled her, almost frightened her, was a growing certainty that the focus of power was *here* — close to Minith town. There was no need to scour those distant peaks. Indeed, she now felt that the state of Minith's Covenant was the best evidence she had that the Maker existed at all. But she could not find it. She was looking for something massive: a block of masonry as big, almost, as an Inland village. How could such a thing still be hidden from her? And where was the pool of obvious physical distortion, the blight on all living things, that had to surround the centre where a power of the old world met and struggled with the new? She didn't know. She felt ignorant and chastened. It seemed her understanding of the lost past was not so complete as she liked to imagine.

Kee-ah.

The buzzards circled lazily overhead, their great primaries spread like black fingers on the blue. In her belt pouch she had a strike-a-light and a candle end from her own pack: a provident travelling covener doesn't rely entirely on magic. She was going to go back to that cave she had found, and investigate the tantalising cleft in its wall. She did not think the "mountain cat" would attack her again. If it dared, she'd be ready this time. It would find out that Zanne of Garth was quite a different adversary, when not hindered by her sympathy with what she thought was an innocent wild animal.

Go back! Go back! Go back!

A fat brown grouse shot away, its wings brushing the heather.

Zanne started and looked up, following the bird's flight, to where one of the Minith sheep lay like a small dark cloud drifting on the purple sky. Slowly, replugging the barley water, she stood: peering with narrowed eyes. The blot was too far away to be anything more than a featureless blur. But to Zanne, who had followed the ways of Inland sheep for many years, it looked wrong. She headed up the slope. When she was closer she stopped, stared again and began to run, not bothering to find a path but scrambling straight uphill, stumbling over heather roots and jumping jutting rocks.

She need not have troubled. The ewe was dead. It had been dead for some hours. The calling of the buzzards took on a new meaning: they had already had both its eyes.

Even though the flocks of Minith were large by Inland standards every animal was counted. Only a few lambs were raised each year, just enough to maintain the balance between the need for wool and the available pasture. This was loss, real loss. But far worse — it was a breach of the Covenant between the people of Minith and their flocks. The sheep gave their fleece. In return they must be safe from all danger. No natural predator should touch them unless in a time of real famine. A few weeks short of rain didn't make that kind of emergency.

Zanne looked at the rust-red wound in the ewe's throat. What kind of killer tears out a beast's throat and then leaves the carcass lying untouched? She remembered Siri's eyes, round and shocked at the thought of killing animals for food. She did not know why that memory should make her shudder now. She did not know either, why she was standing ten paces away, gawking. What was there to be afraid of in a dead sheep?

But she was afraid. Her mouth was dry, her knees were shaking. She had felt like this before, in the cave where the wild cat attacked her. She had forgotten until now — fear, this fear ...

She forced herself to go up and examine the body. It was one of her own. Zanne knew all the Minith flocks by sight as individuals: that was a matter of course. No Inland shepherd had to mark her animals to tell them from her neighbours. But some of Slack Road's animals had become real personalities to her; and this was one.

"Oh Curly. Poor Curly ..."

She remembered the day she had come up here to collect stray fleeces, and caught Curly and White Spatch by their private scratching post. Poor old Truc. She had never dared to tell him his sheep now had names: and yet she knew he too would be heartbroken by this loss.

Zanne wept. She wasn't ashamed of crying, only of the strange fear that persisted, making her hands tremble. She drew the circle sign of the Covenant on Curly's knobbly brow, and wished her a good death.

"I don't know why you frighten me like this, Curly. We all die, we are all eaten. I eat meat myself. I might have killed you as a covener kills if Minith was different, in somebody's barnyard before a feastday — "

But not like this.

At last, belatedly, she remembered the rogue mountain cat. She knelt by the carcass, feeling bewildered. This death seemed to prove that the beast in the cave had been real all the time, and Holne had been teasing her with his brazen hints. Did that mean her conviction was mistaken, and he knew nothing about the hidden Maker? She couldn't believe that. Holne was not innocent. He had some guilty secret, some reason to fear and resent the presence of Zanne of Garth: and what else could it be?

The puzzle would have to wait. She was Zanne the shepherd now, not Zanne the Maker-killer. A dangerous predator had broken through Minith's warding: a rogue that killed not to eat, but wantonly. Whatever Lecte Slack Road thought, this would have to be taken to the meeting. Zanne heaved a sigh. She laid her staff within reach, got down and pulled Curly onto her shoulders. After the reception she'd had last time she wasn't going to leave her proof on the mountain. The buzzards and other scavengers would have Curly in pieces soon if she stayed here.

The dead animal was very heavy . . . Zanne reached for her Link strength, and found it shaky and slow to answer: the fear was still there. It would be wrong to take anything from Minith, after this evidence that the warding was already weak. She looked up to the world-holding sky, where spiralling wings still drifted. Kee! cried the buzzards reproachfully. But that enormous power was too diffuse and too far away for Zanne to reach just now, with her troubled mind. She sighed again, and started on the long walk.

At last she trudged into the yard. She didn't mean to make a dramatic entrance. But Mab was just passing with a pile of sacks on her way to the roadshed, talking over her shoulder to Gwil and another Minither who were standing at the gate of the brickyard. A waggon convoy would be passing on the distant road soon, and Minith building materials seemed to be in great demand this season. Siri and old Truc were by the henrun. Siri was pretending there was something wrong with one of her pullets, so she could consult with the beast-tender and keep clear of the brick packing. Into this populated scene came Zanne, with her burden. Mab heaved her sacks under one arm and called: "Truc — Sunny's brought a poorly ewe down."

Zanne ducked her head and let Curly drop onto the silver-grey cobbles. She sat down herself, sweating and exhausted.

Mab exclaimed indignantly at the treatment of a sick animal. "Hey — that's no way to use her!"

Gwil Slack Road put his hand on the other brickworker's arm, and stopped the young woman from running forward. For a moment Zanne looked into the silent man's eyes. She saw there grief and horror that seemed out of all proportion —

Truc came running.

And now everybody saw the rent in Curly's throat.

"I told you," declared Zanne, when she could get her breath. "I told you. We have a killer up there, up on your precious mountain."

The household of Slack Road stood as if paralysed. Truc knelt by the body. When he looked up his face was haggard. "Where did you find her?"

Gwil whispered to the other Minither. She ran to the roadshed; and then Lecte appeared, drawing off her packing gloves. She didn't look at the sheep but went to her brother and gripped his arms, her handsome face more bleak and bitter than Zanne had ever seen it.

"Be strong — " she murmured.

She looked around. "Where is he? Where is Holne?"

Zanne didn't understand. She thought Lecte must have got to know about her nephew's irresponsible teasing.

"Oh yes. I believed him when he tried to make me think he was the one who jumped on me in that cave. It was stupid of me, and means we've wasted time — "

Lecte turned away from her. "Truc, is it one of ours?"

"It is, Lecte."

"Put her out for the foxes then."

Brother and sister disappeared into the farmhouse. Siri too had vanished. Mab and the woman Zanne didn't know stood gaping not at the dead ewe, but at Zanne. Old Truc got up, came over and made the Covenant circle in the air in front of her face, the first time she had known any Minither use that sign.

"Oh, it was a bad day for us when you came out of the mountain, Sunny Roadwalker. It was a bad day, and this is a worse one."

Zanne was exasperated. "What's the matter with you all?" she cried. "Your pasture warding has failed, that's all. . . ."

The three Minithers went on staring with stricken eyes across the hot grey yard. "It's the guardians," whispered Mab. "It's the guardians. They've broken out again."

In Minith valley the heat had settled breathlessly. The pensioners' cottages squatted patiently under it, like animals unkindly penned in the sun and unable to creep off and find shelter. Behind the cottages, vegetable fields that hadn't yet been harvested looked tired and sad, in spite of the Minithers' ingenious and carefully tended watering channels.

Zanne came down the grey stony track, alone. She stopped at the fork by the metalworks and glanced, with regret, at the track that went on through the flat narrow valley to find at last the waggon road. She would dearly love to shake Minith's silver dust from her shoes and go. The town was very quiet. It was usual in Inland's country settlements for daily life to be lived out on the farms: a village would only fill with people on meeting day or at a festival or when the carrier came. Silence in Minith was different, and a little eerie. Inside the long grey complex of yards and sheds by the river the burners and the weavers of metal should be loudly at work: but not a sound emerged from there. The town seemed dead.

It was half a moon since Zanne had found Curly the ewe with her throat torn out. The day after that a shepherd from a neighbouring farm had come to call at Slack Road, with a very grave face. No one told Zanne what news he brought, but she guessed anyway. That was the last day that anyone came up from town to work in the brickyards: and Lecte announced that the firewatching was cancelled. From now on no one, not even Truc, was to go alone to the mountain pastures. Slack Road began to feel like a place under siege.

The trouble wasn't only affecting Slack Road. On the fifth day after Curly died, a little girl came running into the yards with a message. Lecte left her kitchen and set out on foot into the hills. She reappeared after several hours — Zanne had not known her to leave the farm before, except to go to the fleece meeting. At the daytelling that night she told the household that she had been to a meeting of the elders, at Breakwater farm. The guardians are fully aroused, she said. Several animals have been taken. We must, of course, thank the Covenant for this reproof: but we will be keeping doors and shutters closed and staying near the house from now on, to avoid accidents.

She did not list the dead. It was from Mab and Truc that Zanne got that information, conveyed in whispers at night in the bunkshed. Mab had heard all the news when she went down to fetch the milk. She wasn't supposed to indulge in any unnecessary chattering on that errand, but this time the horror of the events was too much for her. Ten full grown and valuable ewes were gone; and three of this year's lambs. The lower farms where dairy cows were kept had lost two good milkers and Minith's only bull calf; and one of the little brown cattle called "cheesemakers" had been killed on the higher pasture. Every killing had been the same as the first: no trace, no spoor to identify the killers and the animal left lying bloodied but untouched; unless foxes or other scavengers had found it. There had been no attacks on human beings. But shadows of fear followed the miners to work, rattled at shed doors; waited by the poultry house for the child who came out with a scoop of corn.

It was the guardians all right. Zanne's foolish notion about a single rogue mountain cat was nonsense. This was a whole plague of killers, striking twice in the same day many vales apart: climbing walls and breaking into barred sheds. Nothing defeated the guardians, and nothing would stop them until the punishment was over ...

Zanne paused at the end of the pensioners' row. The Minithers had no inn. They used one of the pensioners' houses as a social meeting place and gathered there to drink tea. Zanne suspected that though the metal yards were empty, Anarad Pensioner's front room was not. She had seen the curtains twitch as she went by.

All over the valleys it would be the same. Eyes looking out from shuttered windows, doors locked: as if a ferocious band of raiders had descended on the mountains and was besieging every homestead. Children weren't allowed to go to school, no one walked alone, night or day.

The eyes behind Anarad's curtains were drilling holes in Zanne's spine. Against her will, her shoulders shifted uneasily. She knew she shouldn't be here. Truc and Mab had explained her position to her as they huddled around the single taper Lecte allowed them, since they had to keep the door barred and windows shuttered. Sunny had stirred up trouble with the guardians, by her uncovenanted ways and by her prying into secret places. She had better not leave the shelter of Slack Road for the present. She was responsible for the plague, and some Minithers might be unrestrained enough to forget themselves and resort to violence.

"I'd advise you to leave Minith," sighed Truc. "But I'm afraid the guardians would be permitted to have an accident with you if you tried to cross the mountain now." He shook his head sadly, obviously picturing the poor roadwalker with her throat righteously torn out.

"But what *are* these guardians?" cried Zanne.

Mab leaned forward, her red hair catching the light: kind, sensible Mab with her honest, homely eyes.

"It's happened before," she told Zanne. "Not in the time of anyone living, but people still remember. The guardians are always among us. Sometimes they have to break out, to remind us of our duty. We haven't been keeping the Covenant strict enough, that's what it is."

"Don't fear, Sunny," said Truc. "Lecte's a wise woman. She won't let anyone harm you, for she knows you're just the instrument. You wouldn't have been allowed to come here and stir up trouble if we didn't some way deserve it. Nothing happens without purpose, within What Is."

The old man spoke with a kind of mournful satisfaction.

There would be no meeting, no attempt to restore the pasture warding. The gathering of the elders at Breakwater had settled everything. Everyone was to stay indoors as much as possible, to avoid what Lecte called "accidents", but otherwise no one was to take any unusual measures to escape the punishment. On some farms this would mean the animals were not even brought in to the doubtful shelter of sheds and barns. It wouldn't be right, said Lecte, to put up any resistance. The Covenant had roused the guardians. It would be wicked and unrestrained to hinder them in their task.

Lecte was not the only fanatic. On her defiant lonely walk into town Zanne had seen many sheep and cattle wandering the open moorland still. Zanne of Garth had never known she could feel so helpless. She could teach young Siri. But what could she do with adult Inlanders who sincerely believed this kind of pernicious nonsense?

Her back must be as full of holes as a colander by now. But Zanne hadn't come down to town to talk to the tea drinkers. Firmly, grinning sourly to think of the excitement she would be causing, she took the path that lead to the meeting house on its green, and Anlys Covener's cottage.

Zanne had her own idea about these mysterious killings. It was more sensible than the Minither version, but almost as unpleasant. She would agree with the Minithers this far: they were dealing with no natural predators. Further, she would agree that she was herself indirectly to blame for the plague.

The killers were not wolves or wild cats or bears. They were human. If Holne Slack Road could dress up in a catskin to try to scare off a meddling stranger, then he and others could continue and extend that vicious game. She'd been wrong in assuming Holne was the only one who had found the Maker. He must have allies — maybe that whole group of rebel flores. The children of Minith either learned to be docile and to embrace willingly their parents' hard and miserable customs: or else, like Siri, they learned to hate the

Covenant secretly and to long for any kind of escape from its laws. If some young people in that state of mind had found a Maker, she could see how it would become their treasure and their consolation. They wouldn't be able to use its power, but they would know the power existed and that it was "evil", "wicked" — in other words utterly opposed to the magic of the Covenant, which they had learned to hate.

If their treasure was threatened, they would be bound to put up a fight: and the old superstitious story of "the guardians" served their purpose. The slaughter would continue, no doubt, until Lecte Slack Road withdrew her protection and the meddler was driven away. The plan was horrible. But then Minithers were not brought up to love their beasts. To use and be used, that was how Minith saw life. In the end, these ruthless killers weren't so far astray from their elders' teaching.

She had tried, without success, to get the household at Slack Road to listen to her suspicions, speaking in general terms. She had more sense than to accuse Holne without proof. Mab and Truc looked at her as if she was crazy, and Lecte — who had always seemed an intelligent woman — absolutely refused to listen.

Since the first and only meeting she'd attended, Zanne had been leaving Minith's covener out of her calculations. She had felt she had no right to get involved in Anlys's problems. If she had lost the respect of her meeting, that was something between the older woman and Hillen. But at least Anlys too was a stranger, and a covener. She could not possibly believe in the idea of wild animals being assigned to "punish" Minith for obscure and imaginary crimes. She must know her own people, she could probably name the members of the killer band fairly accurately. However much she allowed Minith elders to bully her in normal times, surely she could be persuaded to try and put a stop to this horrible nonsense.

Anlys Covener had no trade or land. Her little cottage sat all alone by the meeting house: a clear indication, Zanne now saw, of her isolation; of the way she was allowed no part in the life of the valleys. The covener was in her garden, watering a row of beans. She pretended not to have noticed that someone was coming, and made a kind of furtive lumbering dash for her front door. Zanne forestalled her, crying, "Covener, stop a moment — " But her heart sank.

Anlys Covener came to the wicket gate, the big rather shambling figure Zanne remembered. She did not open it.

"We have to talk, Anlys. I don't want to interfere with your meeting but there is something very nasty going on here, and I think I know who's responsible — "

She spoke in a rush, trying to make her point before Anlys could escape: but then found herself looking into the other woman's eyes.

It was a shock. She saw there that she had been right in her first assumption, long ago before the fleece harvest meeting. The recognition Anlys had been afraid to show before was miserably clear now. The big woman knew Zanne, had known her errand all along . . .

"There's no need to tell me — " said Anlys bleakly. "I know. I am responsible."

It was the truth. It silenced Zanne. She stood perplexed. She had been sent here to find a Maker and give it death. She did not know what to do with all these other problems. They were too big, too far reaching. Why don't you leave me alone? she wanted to cry. I don't know how to help you, I just want to get on with my work!

"Why don't you go back to Hillen?" she burst out. "I mean, if your meeting won't listen to you — "

To her distress, she saw that the older woman had begun to weep. Zanne didn't know what to do. She was ashamed, because she hadn't even given a thought in all this time, to how Anlys must feel: a covener who had failed, who had lost her people.

"Anlys, I'm sorry. Let me in. Let us talk . . ."

Tears ran down Anlys's face, her broad soft shoulders were shaking.

"I wish you had never come here — "

"Oh please. I'm to blame. I should have come to you before. Maybe I can help — "

"No one can help me, no one. I can't go back. I can't leave Minith ever — "

As she spoke the big woman began to back away, wincing and flinching as if it was actually painful for her to face those bright, shadowless grey eyes. She ran into her cottage and slammed the door behind her.

She had left the water sluice open, her beans were drowning. After a moment or two Zanne climbed over the wall, picked up the little sluice barrier from where Anlys had dropped it and settled it back into place. It was a flake of Minith slate, smoothly worked. The irrigation channel that came out to the covener's cottage was a trough of stone, in sections well mortared together. It climbed over the garden wall in a series of neat steps. Zanne admired it. Trust the Minithers — they could even make water run uphill.

When she stood up, Holne Slack Road was at the wicket gate, watching her.

"Have you been there long? I might have known you were somewhere around."

Holne shook his head. "Oh, Anlys isn't afraid of me."

"Then what is she afraid of?"

"You wouldn't believe me."

"Try."

She climbed over the wall again. In fact, she thought Holne had given up spying on her. Since the guardians began their work he had spent a good deal of time shut up in his bedroom. At least, that was where he was supposed to be. Lecte made appetising little meals for him, which usually came down again untouched. He was "overtired", she would say. Zanne found Lecte Slack Road's doting blindness pitiable. But her own feelings towards Holne had cooled somewhat. He was not evil incarnate. He was a naughty boy, whose naughtiness had been allowed to get wildly out of hand. His trouble was nothing compared to Anlys's shame. She almost felt glad to see him.

They were all alone in the hot sunlight. Holne glanced around as if looking for eavesdroppers.

"Holne, please trust me. I, well, I've been in trouble myself, in my time."

He almost looked as if he might.

"Come on now, admit it. You don't believe in these guardians. Oh, I can see how the story started. There must have been a long bad winter once, with wolves coming down and taking off sheep and maybe even seen in the yards. That kind of thing can be very frightening. It would be just like Minithers to decide it was a 'punishment'. That's how the superstition began, don't you agree?"

Holne shook his head.

"No, Zanne. Zanne, you're wrong—" He leaned towards her and whispered, though there was no one in sight. "You're so wrong about what is happening in Minith. You see everything, but you don't see the truth. Have you really looked at the bodies? You'd know then. The wounds are made by teeth, teeth and claws. Not knives, nothing human. You have a good look, next time."

So much for common sense. By the time she'd thought of checking the evidence the first time, Curly's body had vanished—"dragged off by foxes". Holne must know she wouldn't get a chance to look closely at any other body, unless she found it before anyone else did: which was unlikely since she was supposed to stay shut up indoors. The marks of teeth — Holne and his gang must be faking that appearance, and now he was disappointed that their cunning was being wasted on the gullible.

She scowled at him. "Holne Slack Road, that's the last time, the very *last* time I give you a chance to be sensible. The marks of teeth indeed! You young ghoul. You and your friends are having great fun, aren't you? Well, I think it's disgusting. Now go away and leave me alone."

That seemed to sort him out, for the moment anyway. She turned her back and when she looked round he was halfway up the path to town, slouching along head down and shoulders hunched. It looked as if she'd made some impression on him this time. She certainly hoped so.

Left alone, Zanne walked around the Minith meeting house. Worried and restless, she was trying to make a plan that would cure it all, from Anlys's shame to Sirato's broken violin. She wanted to go back to Hillen and ask the Thirteen. But no vision came to her, and the hot quiet made her head ache. It wasn't fair of Hillen Coven to send her here all alone. They must have known that Minith's problems were too much for one young girl. The mountains leaned down over Minith out of the blue like huge animals: half-human animals because they seemed to be enjoying her failure. She read the names that were carved on slabs of slate nailed up on the bricks. In Garth, the names on the meeting house walls were whitewashed over in time and the entries began again. She supposed here there must be a pile of filled slabs somewhere. She found Siri and Holne's mother. Rian Mountainside had died young, she had been told. There were no dates on the roll of names, but there were several Mountainsides unnaturally close together, she thought. And the same with several other family names. She remembered what Siri had said: *the bad children, when they grow up, they die ...*

She walked round the cone again. But this distraction soon palled. She couldn't see how Minith's dead could help Minith's present trouble. And the headache was getting worse every minute.

It was not in Zanne's nature to tolerate such a state of mind for long. Blocked in the task she had been sent out to do, she couldn't sit and do nothing. Things came to a head that evening in Slack Road kitchen. Ironically, it was Holne who had given Zanne an idea. The atmosphere in the grey-walled room was stifling. Four slender tapers in metal holders leaned towards each other in the centre of the table. Tiny threads of blue oozed from the flames and crept along the tabletop. There wasn't a breath of air to raise them: and no light from the summer evening managed to force a way in around the window shutters.

The silent meal was over. Gwil Slack Road sat looking at his hands, Siri picked at a crack in the scrubbed wood. Lecte's voice went on remorselessly, detailing a day spent besieged by horrors as if there was nothing remarkable about the way they were living. "Under the Covenant — " they all muttered, at the proper intervals. Mab had made a tiny mistake in filling out the tallies for the brick cart: it was discussed in depth and Mab nodded and murmured righteously — "Thank you for reproving me, Lecte."

"And now, does anyone have any other news?"

Zanne gritted her teeth. She particularly disliked that last question of the daytelling, because it sounded so casual. Yet if Lecte were to deviate from the formula by a syllable: if she were to say "But now — " one night instead of "And now — ", Zanne was convinced the whole room would be thunderstruck, gasping in shock. Minith ways! When she thought of all the time she had wasted trying to find them commendable, she didn't know whether to laugh or to cry.

"I do."

"What do you have to tell, Sunny?"

Zanne looked deliberately across the table at Holne. "I have to tell that I am going to spend all my time out of doors from now on, keeping watch around our yards and our neighbours' yards and up on the mountain with the sheep. I plan to start tonight."

Slack Road was one of those farms where the flocks had to take their chance of being "punished" out in the open.

"Would anyone like to come with me?"

There was a stunned silence. Siri stopped picking at the table and gaped at her friend. Truc forgot himself so far as to speak before Lecte.

"Ah, no my girl. That's brave but it's wrong and foolish. We mustn't watch, we mustn't see them go by — "

Lecte looked at him, and he broke off.

"Truc is right," stated the farmer. "We Minithers believe in accepting What Is, without reserve and without complaint. If you cannot manage that, young woman, at least you must realise that you can do very little on your own. I advise you to stay in your bed."

For a moment Zanne was too angry to speak. Holne sat there, straightfaced. She was almost ready to denounce him, shout out that one of the killers was sitting right here — but that would do no good. Not yet. There was a better way.

"I don't see the connection," she answered tartly, "between 'accepting What Is' and a sheep with its throat torn out. All right, you won't believe me when I tell you these killers are human. But whatever they are, I am a covener, of sorts. Are you saying that I have no power to protect? Maybe you're right and I can do very little alone. But think, if the five of us went out there, willing our flocks' safety with our minds and hearts. . . . We owe them that, don't we? Isn't that what the Covenant means?"

She had left someone out of the count of adults and flores. No one else seemed to notice but she thought she saw him smile.

"That's enough, Sunny — "

Mab turned to her and spoke as if to a child.

"Sunny, my dear, I'd come with you. But don't you see, if the punishment must fall it's wrong to try to protect your own. Why should Slack Road be safe and some other farm suffer?"

"That's enough, Mab!" Lecte slapped the table with her open hand. "Sunny, I can't stop you from pursuing this foolish plan — "

"You're right. You can't."

The household winced together. Nobody ever spoke in that tone to Lecte ... The dark severe farmer and the small stranger with her tousled yellow head and clear eyes, faced each other as if a fist fight was about to break out between them — and then a childish voice rose, tremulously.

"I will."

Everybody looked at Siri. She swallowed hard, but faced them. It had taken her so long to get up the courage to speak no one remembered the question she was answering.

"I'll come with you," she quavered. "I'll come and watch on the mountain. It's cruel to leave the poor sheep out there alone. They must be so frightened."

Holne laughed, as if with genuine admiration. "My, you've changed, little sister."

Siri flushed, and darted him a savage glance.

"You will do no such thing!" snapped Lecte.

"I will! I will! Z-Sunny, tell them I will — "

Zanne was taken aback. She hadn't stopped to think when she asked for help. She didn't want Sirato with her tonight.

"Siri, I'm afraid it's not for me to say."

"Father, tell her I may. Lecte's not my mother! She can't say what I ought to do. Not when it's C-covenant business!"

The confrontation between Lecte Slack Road and her dayworker was lost in Siri's pleas and tears. She got no support from her father, or from Zanne either, and was sent to bed crying bitterly. Zanne hated to let her young friend down, but for the moment Lecte was justified. Siri must stay at home, where she was safe.

Siri dreamed. She dreamed that the full moon of Old Summer came floating into Slack Road loft. Its big fat shape peered over the partition and started to roll down the wall, which was a horrible thing to see because it had a face that kept being squashed into mush against the planks. It leaned over her pillow, just a head all round and white; and its blue features writhed in frightening disorder. "Get up Siri," it said. "Get up and come with me."

"No," she cried — and now she remembered she had been called like this before. It was harder every time not to obey. "No, no. I won't do it."

Then the moon turned into Aunt Lecte, standing at her bedside with a candle lantern. Siri realised that she was awake.

"Get up," said her aunt again.

She got up and stood shivering in her nightsmock, though the loft was very warm. She was afraid Aunt Lecte was going to beat her for her back answers after supper. Her aunt had never beaten her before, she had other ways of punishing. But Siri had never been so defiant before either.

Aunt Lecte put the lantern down on the floor. "Turn around."

Siri felt her arms taken by the shoulders from behind. She felt a tug, and another tug. She was being shaken about as if her aunt was combing painful tangles out of her hair. But that wasn't what was happening. A cord went round her elbows, and another round her wrists.

"Aunt Lecte, don't — "

"Be quiet. Come with me."

Siri stumbled down the stairs with her arms tied behind her and her aunt's hand gripping one shoulder. She was too frightened and confused to resist. Aunt Lecte was often hateful, but she didn't do things like this. It must be a dream. Down the stairs, along the stone passage, into the room beside the kitchen. The counting room was a thick walled private place that Siri rarely entered. There was nothing in it but the big desk and a few hard chairs, the air was cool even now. Aunt Lecte opened a door in the wall revealing a small empty closet. There was a straw mattress on the floor inside, and a chamber pot in a corner.

"Lie down."

"Aunt Lecte — "

"You're to sleep here, from now on."

"Aunt Lecte, please — "

Aunt Lecte lifted the lantern so Sirato could see her beautiful dark eyes. "You will not go out on that mountain. Not tonight or any night. I know how cunning little rats are but I will keep you safe. Even from the Covenant itself."

"Please, please, Aunt Lecte. I won't go out. I promise, I promise — "

The closet door closed. No glimmer of light remained. Sirato stood rock still for a moment. Then she screamed.

"Father!"

No one came. Up above in the stifling silent house, Gwil Slack Road stood by an unshuttered window, looking out. He put up his hands, ingrained forever with the silvery dust of the brickyard, and covered his face.

Zanne had waited until full dark to leave the bunkshed. She had then walked, unconcernedly, down to the farm called Cowmeadow, which was the next homestead along from Slack Road on the track to Minith. She had spent two or three hours sitting on a gate keeping company with the cows who were penned up there. Minither dairy cows were a broad-backed and rangy moorland variety, with red or white and roan hides and evil-looking horns. They were surprisingly friendly considering how little they were accustomed to human affection: and tonight they seemed so grateful for Zanne's presence that it hurt her to leave them. But she had said that she was going to visit the mountain as well as the yards, and she didn't want to disappoint anyone.

The cows all hurried after Zanne to the far end of their pen as she slipped down from her perch, but no one in the dark house of Cowmeadow stirred or showed a light at the noise of this small stampede.

"Be safe," whispered Zanne making the circle sign, "In What Is and with What Is. Be safe for tonight, my dears."

The moon was nearly full but it was drifting in and out of sight between the sultry hot weather clouds that gathered every evening and never let down any rain. Zanne smiled to herself as she strolled back towards Slack Road. The killings nearly always happened at night. It was easier to slip out of a house unseen if you were supposed to be in bed. She did not think that anything would happen this time. It would be tomorrow night or the night after. The guardians wouldn't be able to resist her bait. They would try some trick to scare her again — and then she would have them.

She was perfectly confident. She had her magic: and one other advantage that the killers, brought up in Minith's distorted ways, would not suspect. She was not in the least afraid of the dark. Her only worry was the obstinacy of the Minith elders. What kind of evidence would they need? Would they believe Zanne if she dragged their young people to them literally red-handed? Probably they'd accept nothing less.

There were no lights showing at Slack Road. Zanne decided she would climb up to the first shoulder to that token tree where the flock often liked to gather, and stay with them there until dawn. She crossed the brickyard, moonlight lifting glints of silver from the cobbles under her feet, towards the gate that led out onto the mountainside. When she'd unfastened the latch she turned and looked back: wasn't that the sound of someone crying?

Uneasiness shivered in the air. Zanne was trying not to judge, trying to remain calm and even tempered in all this. In reality she was very, very angry. How dare these bullies take the lives of innocent beasts? How dare they pollute the serene magic of Inland's night with fear? Why, she would almost feel afraid herself now, if she let herself give way.

A shadow, a lithe moving shadow, slipped along the wall of the old toolshed. Zanne's breath hissed.

Something moved behind her.

She whirled around, in time to see the gate which she had opened slowly closing all by itself. It hit the latch, bounced off and tried again.

Chink, chink.

Zanne stared, fascinated.

Somebody doesn't want me to go out there.

Don't be a fool, Zanne. You're doing it yourself, you pitiful coward. You're more scared than you can bear to admit.

But she knew that wasn't true.

Siri?

She had thought that the hint of magic talent in her young friend had been disproved. But here it was again. I'll be sure, this time, thought Zanne. It won't take long. I can explain to her as well, why I didn't want her with me tonight.

She hurried silently up the stair to Siri's loft. Behind the partition the outline of the small bed was barely discernible in the gloom. Zanne bent down whispering Siri? Siri?: and found nothing but rumpled bedclothes and her own moonlamp tucked under the thin, hard pillow. Siri must have decided to join the night watch after all, thought Zanne guiltily. She took the lamp, surprised that it had stayed behind. She knew that Siri kept the precious talisman with her always.

Down in the dark hallway again she paused. Sirato must be looking for her outside somewhere. That was the end of playing bait for tonight. She'd have to find the child and bring her back before anyone discovered she was missing. Now where would Siri go first? There was no light in this windowless passage. The unseen walls of bare brick played tricks on her eyes, making silver sparkles more like little stars rising and spinning all around her. This is not my country, she thought. All of it is strange, all of it down to the bones.

Something whimpered, close beside her.

"Siri?"

The whimpering grew to sobs at the sound of a friendly voice, and mingled with the sobs was a frantic scrabbling.

Zanne burst into the little counting room. The moonlamp she still held in her hand suddenly burned white and bright. She saw the locked closet shaking, reached into the lock with her mind and shifted its wards. The door fell open outwards. Zanne saw the little figure crouched there, the pallet and the twisted cords lying on the floor behind her. Siri burst into renewed loud sobs and pitched herself out of the terrifying prison, into Zanne's arms.

"Oh I was so afraid — Oh, Zanne — "

Zanne held the hard bony little body tight and made soothing noises, too amazed and horrified to ask questions: and then a yellower light joined the whiteness of the moonlamp. Lecte stood in the counting room doorway with a lantern. She was fully dressed, as if she hadn't been to bed.

"Did you do this?" cried Zanne.

Siri's thin arms were marked with dark red weals. It was unbelievable.

"Is this what the Covenant means to you?" she shouted. "For once a child finds the strength to speak out for herself — so you tie her up and lock her in a cupboard. Lecte, you're grotesque. I can't believe I'm in Inland — "

Siri had been frightened into silence by her aunt's appearance. She stood trembling violently, hiding her face.

"This is not Inland, this is Minith," said Lecte in her voice of stone. "The world is different here, and beyond your understanding, Hillen girl." She held out her firm and shapely dark hand.

"Come to me, Sirato, child. If you can't sleep in the closet, you will share my bed, where I can watch you."

"She will do no such thing! She'll go back to her own bed, and you will leave her alone."

Zanne was about to add that she would keep watch in Siri's loft herself, to make sure of that — But Siri had her own ideas. She wriggled free from Zanne's arms.

"I won't!" she cried shrilly. "I won't go to bed. I'm going out on the mountain. I want to help to guard the flocks! I want to help the Covenant — the good Covenant, Aunt Lecte, not your hateful one! You're wicked! wicked! I'm never sleeping in your house again!"

Lantern light and moonlight gleamed on the snailtrack tears on Sirato's burning cheeks. She faced her aunt desperately, chin up, eyes flashing.

Aunt Lecte seemed to grow smaller, her hard face quivered. It was as if after all these years her bullying had collapsed at the first sign of real resistance.

"Sirato, child — please — "

"No! Don't touch me! I'm going with S-Sunny."

Zanne did not really believe that Lecte was wicked, only harsh and unimaginative: incapable of understanding how terrifying that punishment had been. Sirato would be quite safe now, safer in Lecte's care than out on the mountain. But to force the child to stay would have been a cruel betrayal.

"All right, Siri. You're a brave girl. Let's go."

Lecte let them pass: the yellow-headed outsider and the small girl in her nightsmock, bare legged and shivering; out into the haunted night. Her lamp was still burning, a bright blot on the dark shape of the house, as they left the yards and began to climb.

Zanne dimmed the moonlamp and gave it to Sirato. The true moon was hidden again but enough light seeped through the cloud to show rocks and bilberry bushes, sedge tussocks and heather.

"Night isn't very dark really, is it," whispered the girl. "It's not as frightening as I thought it would be."

Zanne had decided they would walk up to the shoulder and back again. That would be enough for Siri to feel she had done something worthwhile; then they'd go back to the bunkshed. Serious pursuit of the sheep killers would have to wait for another night. Siri's hand squirmed in her grasp.

"Zanne, do you really think it's a gang of bad flores? Not — not *the guardians?*"

"I'm sure of it."

"I bet Holne's the leader of the gang."

"I bet he is too."

Since the killing began, she'd been careful not to discuss Holne's part in it with his sister. She didn't quite trust Siri's power to keep secrets of that kind. But tonight everything seemed to be out in the open.

"Let me go, Zanne. We can't chase anyone like this. We have to split up — "

"On the contrary." Zanne was firm. "We have to stay together, so if one of us sees anything the other will be a witness."

The rough, skinny little fingers wriggled excitedly. The gloom had deepened and their owner was almost invisible: it was like trying to hold onto a small wild animal.

"Let me go — "

"No, Siri — "

Suddenly the small animal gave a convulsive start. Zanne had heard it too — over to their right, a rushing pattering sound of many feet running together.

"Oh!"

It can't be so easy, thought Zanne. Holne heard what I was planning. Tonight they'll lie low, in some meeting place of theirs, and plan a really good scare for when I'm off my guard ... The running feet were coming closer. Human or not human? She couldn't tell, and she couldn't see.

"Give me the lamp, Siri — "

She groped for Siri's other hand, not wanting to make a light until the sound was near enough for a clear view of whatever caused it.

"Oh Zanne, they're coming. Quick, quick, let's run — "

The child jerked herself free.

"Siri! Come back!"

Zanne leapt after Sirato and caught her smock, but it whipped out of her hands. It was exactly as she'd feared when she wouldn't let go of the girl's hand. The moment they were parted the moon vanished altogether. Sirato vanished with it. Zanne called to her, and called to Dimen's lamp with her magic. But if it woke, Siri was behind some rock or other and no light showed. Siri was a naughty girl and wouldn't come when she was called. Why should she be obedient? She had never known any kindness, never known respect or friendship from the adults who ruled her. But how strong she was suddenly. Only an hour ago she had been locked up, sobbing with terror: she was so afraid of the dark.

What had happened to Siri? What had made her so brave?

Zanne stopped calling, realising the girl wouldn't answer, and hunted silently. She had left whatever path there was and was jumping from boulder to boulder. When the ground levelled out it took her by surprise. She had reached the shoulder. A dim unearthly landscape stretched before her: she could see the twisted skeleton of the old thorn. "Siri?" she cried. Then she heard the pack again. They had changed places. She wasn't the hunter anymore, she was the hunted. Fear rushed over her like a strong wind. Terror, terror: she was not human. She was helpless and cowering, pressing her muzzle into the warm fleece of her neighbour, stamping with her hard small feet to keep her place and a wall of bodies round her: all of them pumping and pulsing with the same abject surrender. When the guardians come there is only one thought — *take someone else, not me*. Take the little girl in the nightsmock, out here defenceless somewhere — she's yours, you can have her.

The storm of terror passed. Zanne was lying face down in the dew wet heather, in the murky light of a half shrouded moon. She jumped up remembering: I'm not a sheep. I'm a shepherd, and the phantoms of fear cleared from her mind. Where were the Minith flocks? They must have taken flight, further into the wilderness. No, she could see something that must be them: a huddled moving mass under the token tree. With a shock of something like elation, she realised that huddle wasn't the sheep. It was her quarry. She began to run again: determined to see, to be sure ... What were those figures doing, shadows on darkness? She couldn't make it out. They must have heard something. There was a flicker of many twinned green lights turned towards her, reflecting moonbeams that now slipped again through the clouds.

Zanne stopped. Human eyes don't behave like that ... Human or animal, the pack was on the move again. Zanne put on speed, not caring if they could see her.

She could not run fast enough. They were gone. Zanne stood under the token tree alone. Feeling defeated and somehow guilty she collapsed there, sat back on her heels and looked around her. There was a pale patch of something dangling from the lowest branch of the thorn. Zanne reached and pulled it down. She was holding a piece of material torn from a Minith smock. The stuff was linen, of good quality. Her fingers traced a line of elaborate decorative stitching. But the linen was stained, darkly and wetly. It marked Zanne's hands in the moonlight.

She had her evidence.

"Siri?" she cried.

Surely they wouldn't hurt a little girl —

On this mountain, she thought, anything was possible.

She came down the track from the shoulder as fast as she could run on the rough track. The moon had reappeared, but it showed no trace of Sirato. What had happened to the child? Zanne's fears were cloudy and horrible. She could understand now why Lecte had been prepared to take such desperate measures to keep the little girl indoors ... She was hurrying so that she rushed slap into the lantern light, noticing nothing until it blinded her. Dazzled, she blinked at Lecte Slack Road and her brother. Both of them were *armed*: Lecte with a pickaxe handle and Gwil with a metal-headed hoe.

"You're too late with those," she told them angrily. "You've lost another ewe I think: I expect we'll find her in the morning."

"Where is the child?" demanded Lecte, in a desperate voice.

At that, for the first time, Zanne's fears settled in one

terrible shape. Her fingers closed on the bloody rag she had been so glad to find.

"You don't think much of your flores, do you," she jeered — because she couldn't bear to believe the worst. "Do you really think they'd attack a child as part of their nasty game?"

"You don't know what you are talking about, you young fool. *Where is she?*"

"I don't know," confessed Zanne. "She ran away, I couldn't hold her. I was coming to get help."

Gwil Slack Road dropped his makeshift weapon, with a sob of horror.

"Oh, my child. My poor Rian's daughter. Lost — lost!"

"Well — come on, let's *find* her!" cried Zanne, bewildered and frightened by this sudden despair.

Sirato came out of the dark. No one had heard her approaching. She looked very small. Her eyes were black and huge in her pointed little face. In her two hands she held Dimen's moonlamp: the faintest possible glow of silver slipped through her fingers.

"Sirato!"

The incomprehensible Minithers both took a step *backwards* — as if they thought they saw Siri's ghost. Lecte recovered first. "What have you been doing out here alone?" she demanded harshly.

Sirato looked from her father to her aunt. Her fierce bravery seemed to have faded. "I was lost," she quavered. "I was scared."

Lecte dropped her axe handle and pounced on the girl, gripping her shoulder and lifting the lantern to her face, then put her arm around Siri with unexpected tenderness.

"She is safe, still safe ... I thank What Is. Come child, we'll take you home."

Siri seemed dazed and did not protest.

"Lecte," said Zanne to the farmer. "I have evidence now, and I mean to take it to the meeting. It concerns your family. Do you understand?"

But it seemed as if the war that had been declared at the daytelling was already over.

"Do as you please," said Lecte Slack Road wearily, turning with her brother, the silent child between them. "What do I care. I will save what I can of what's mine ... under the Covenant."

Zanne did not go back to the bunkshed. She didn't intend to desert Siri. But she felt that her time as a dayworker was over, and she had no right to a bed at Slack Road anymore. She walked down to Minith and slept in a patch of unmown grass up against the wall of the meeting house. Nothing disturbed her, no strange shadows prowled. The night was stuffy and airless; but chill as well before dawn. She missed her waggon cloak.

When the sun had shrunk and changed from red to gilded white and her dew damp clothes were drying, she roused herself and went to the tower beside the cone which held Minith's great meeting bell. It was for use only in emergencies, but this being Minith naturally everything was in perfect order: the rope unfrayed, the tackle neat, the great mouth shining up in the roof as if it was polished daily. Ding DONG ding DONG ding DONG. Hanging on the bell rope Zanne remembered a day when she, as a little girl, had rung the Garth bell like this to call the people: Fire! Raiders! Flood! She wished that the threat today was something so straightforward. When the great brazen double note first sounded, Anlys Covener came out of her cottage door as if on springs. She saw Zanne and nodded dismally as if she had expected this summons, and accepted it: then she disappeared once more.

All through the morning the Minithers gathered. Zanne

had been afraid they might ignore the bell, as soon as word got round that it was no fire but only the meddling stranger causing trouble again. She didn't know what she would have done then. But they came: farmers and pensioners and miners and metalworkers. By noon she thought all the nearby population had arrived. She went and rang the bell again to make sure people coming in from farther afield understood that the meeting was still waiting for them. The Minithers settled on benches inside the house, or vanished into various cottages. No one spoke to Zanne and she spoke to no one. She had had a wash and a drink of water from the public basin on the edge of the meeting house green. Nervousness stopped her from feeling hungry. The silence of the crowd made her feel young and awkward. She knew it was going to be difficult to convince these people of what she knew. They were so proud. They'd rather any horrible story than the shameful truth.

At dusk they were all inside. Two of the older men, dressed in dark clothes and looking important, took lamps out of a cupboard and went around hanging them and lighting them. The elders settled together in front of the speakers' platform under the peak of the cone. Someone was despatched to fetch the covener. Zanne sat up on the edge of the platform, keeping out of the way. She was beginning to feel that she hadn't called this meeting at all: Minith had convened itself.

Unobtrusively she examined her evidence again. It was a piece of creamy unbleached linen. The quality was excellent. Quite a few of the younger people wore linen cloth: it was tradegoods and therefore a luxury item, but it was also very hardwearing and practical. However, only the unrestrained, the young rebels, ever wore embroidery: and Zanne could identify this particular stitching even more closely than that. She had seen it a hundred times. He did the work himself, she believed. She couldn't picture Lecte taking on such frivolous work, even for her beloved favourite. This strip of cloth came from the collar of a smock that belonged to Holne Slack Road. No one else.

Anlys came quietly in and sat on one of the speakers' chairs: as self-effacing as anyone of her bulk could possibly be.

"Well then," said one of the elders. "Are you going to tell us why you rang our bell, young woman?"

It was Carad Breakwater.

Zanne gathered her forces. She was going to tell them the whole story this time. However little they liked Zanne of Garth, they couldn't entirely disregard the fact that she was Hillen's emissary. There was certainly nothing to be gained any more by holding back.

"There's something I'd like to ask, first of all. Will you allow your flores to join us?"

The young people were outside. She had a feeling there were many gaps in their ranks — Holne definitely wasn't there. But she'd like to feel she'd given the culprits a chance to face her, if they chose to.

"Only adults attend the meeting. That's the Minith way, and we see no reason to change it."

She accepted that: she hadn't expected to gain the point.

"Very well. I rang the bell because we have sheep killers in the pasture. Well, you all know that. I know that most of you believe these killers are — are not natural, and that they somehow have a right to terrorise and kill our flocks. That's not so. These killers are not wolves or wild cats, but they are perfectly 'natural'. They are human, they are Minithers like yourselves: and now I can prove it."

This was not easy. She could see Lecte with the elders, Gwil and Truc and Mab together further back. Whatever happened she was going to cause pain to that unhappy household. She reminded herself of the innocent creatures, dying in uncovenanted terror — and took out the strip of fine heavy linen with the elaborate cross-stitch border: worked in a neat, strong hand that quite a few people here would have to recognise.

"This is my evidence. Take the cloth, touch it. You don't have to believe my words or even your own eyes. By the Covenant that binds us all, you will know what is true."

The Minith faces looked up at her — pale from the mines and metal works, deep red brown from the fields: a few "black Minithers", with features darkly clear as Lecte Slack Road's. No one said a word. Zanne tried to give the strip of cloth to Anlys. Anlys would not take it.

At last Carad Breakwater spoke again.

"Why do you say 'our' flocks, stranger?"

Zanne felt the hostility, suddenly released, hit her like a clenched fist.

"I am not a stranger," she said, showing no resentment, "in any part of Inland. We are all under the same Covenant. Your flocks are mine, as I am one of you — "

"Don't worry. We know who you are."

The air crackled with sour triumph. Zanne had rung the bell. But this meeting was being run by Minith.

"We know who you are," repeated Carad, "Sunny the roadwalker. Your real name is Zanne of Garth. It's not surprising that you prefer to conceal it. Why, everyone in Inland knows about the little girl who fell in love with the evil past, who almost destroyed Inland trying to get the great Maker working again. Even here in the wild mountains we're not such bumpkins as not to know your story. And now she's grown up, this wicked girl wanders the country-side digging up old secrets that should be left alone. That's what you came to Minith for, isn't it, little Zanne. You think we've got one of your beloved Makers here."

Zanne gasped. She glanced, she couldn't help it, at Anlys.

The Minith covener flushed crimson and would not meet her eyes.

"But I tried to tell you!" she cried. "Yes, I'm Zanne of Garth. I was just about to say so!"

Carad laughed: the other elders smirked. A ripple of humourless, scornful tittering went all through the meeting.

Zanne forced herself to stay calm. She forced herself to remember; *she must win them over*. Impossible as that seemed there was no other way: and her enemies in this hall knew it.

Carad stood up. She came to the platform, and plucked the piece of linen from between Zanne's fingers.

"What's this? A rag with blood on it. Sheep's blood, I suppose. Why not! What are you, little Zanne, but a wandering meat killer by trade? How do I know how you came by it? I do know that you won't and can't believe that in Minith at least the Covenant protects itself from your kind. You want to tell us who is responsible for what we are suffering now? We will tell you. It is Zanne of Garth."

The tittering had died. A murmur of grim assent went around the benches.

"That's not true!" cried Zanne. "The truth is — some of your flores have found the Maker. They are the one who have 'fallen in love with the evil past'. But what they've found isn't evil, whatever you may think. It is merely in the wrong place and time: that's why Hillen Coven sent me to give it covenanted death. It's your young people who don't want to see the Maker destroyed, not me . . . and so they are using this plague of terror to try to drive me away — "

Silence. The faces stared at her, every one of them cold and blank as stone.

Carad said: "Zanne, that is *not* the truth."

Another of the elders stood up, Trevi Burnhouse, the speaker for the mining families. He declared loudly. "If

Hillen sent you here, you can go back there. You may be able to fool the Thirteen but you can't fool us, maker-lover."

"Maker-lover!"

"Go back to Hillen!"

"Leave us in peace."

"You've done enough harm already, little Zanne — "

The voices grew bolder, louder: they came from every side. Lecte Slack Road sat among the elders, without a word. It was her silence, among all the voices, that most enraged Zanne. For she was absolutely convinced that the reason Lecte did not join the chorus was that she knew all about Holne and his friends, and hated this charade as much as Zanne. But she would not speak.

Zanne looked around the meeting house. She saw all the smug, closed, self-satisfied Minithers: not one single dissenter — and her control snapped.

"So that's your answer is it? Blind stupidity, prejudice, superstition. Oh, the Covenant knows I have tried to understand you Minithers, but you've broken the back of my tolerance. I'd rather have one of your sheep-killing flores than any hypocritical adult here. At Hillen we are taught to use magic. Not hypocrisy and cruelty and self-satisfaction. You want me to go back to the Thirteen? Well, I'll be glad to, and leave you to your poisoned minds and your poisoned mountains! You disgust me, all of you!"

She heard herself then, and stopped. It was too late. She could not call back the angry, ugly words. The spoiled covener, hunched in her chair, seemed to be weeping softly as if her last hope was gone. Zanne couldn't bear to look at Lecte Slack Road. She had a feeling that at this moment Lecte pitied her.

Zanne had been shouting. Carad Breakwater spoke again, very quietly.

"We've heard enough, I think. The meeting is over."

She sat back in her place. The elders nodded and murmured to each other. Then someone at the back of the room stood up and soon all the Minithers had started to move. Dignified and grave, with an air of triumphant virtue, they filed slowly out of the house. Anlys Covener shuffled down from the platform and went with them, and the old men in dark clothes began to collect the lamps.

Zanne was left all alone in the gathering dark, with her defeat and her shame.

CHAPTER SEVEN

THE OTHER SIDE

IT WAS SUNFALL, the deep centre of the Inland year. In Garth and in many other places the grain was being brought in, with long days of hard work and a great deal of noise and cheerfulness. In Minith the small mountain harvest of oats and barley wouldn't be ready for another month or more. This year, especially, there was nothing to disturb a silence almost deeper than winter, the silence of the earth as it turned in its neverending cycle from waking towards sleeping: for this year, again, from life to death. Up on the mountain the sheep still left out to pasture had fled far into the east, and no shepherds followed them. Sunfall was as quiet and empty as the snow of Year's End.

Zanne came down to the token tree cautiously, though she knew there weren't likely to be any Minithers about. She checked the metal rings and confirmed that no one had been here for many days. The beaten earth was shrivelled and cracked. Zanne got down on her hands and knees and crawled over it, peering closely. After a while she sat up, examining something she held between her fingers: a few threads of dark yarn, no more. The night when she had lost Siri on the mountain haunted her. Shadows moving here, in this natural gathering place. What had they been doing? Frowning, she tucked the threads away in her pocket.

It was hard work climbing in the heat of the day. She

reached her camping place and dropped onto a pile of heather that she had cut for a bed. Stripping off her smock she wiped the sweat that was running on her face and arms. Overhead the sky was the same as it had been day after day: blue steel without a cloud. She could wring water out of her singlet. She drew up her knees and leaned her chin on her folded arms, staring gloomily at nothing.

Zanne knew that she ought to be on her way back to Hillen. It didn't matter now whether or not she found the lost Maker. She couldn't destroy it. This was not the Outland, and the opposition she had to deal with did not come from uncovenanted raiders. If she tried to enforce her own magic here, against the will of Minith's people, she would rip holes in the very fabric of this part of Inland. Long ago Zanne had learned the strange truth about her world, the mystery hidden within its commonplace appearances. Down in the depths of things, Inland was not made of rock and earth and water. It was made of meaning and magic — and every rock stood, every blade of grass grew only through the countless thoughts, wishes and desires of all Inlanders, balancing and checking one another. Her teachers at Hillen had told her so often: *don't believe that as a covener you act by the will of the people because that is right or virtuous. That may be — it is also the only way possible, in magic; in our world.* How many times had she tried to learn that lesson and be guided by it — but still it seemed it hadn't sunk in.

Zanne cudgelled her hot forehead with her fists. Over and over again she saw herself on the platform in Minith meeting house, forgetting everything but her own injured pride: shouting insults, destroying all hope of reconciliation between her mission and these proud, stubborn people.

The Minithers were absolutely right. It was because of Zanne that their flocks were suffering the depredations of the guardians. It might be that the hidden presence of a

Maker was doing insidious damage to the minds and hearts of Minith meeting, but she had missed her chance to cure that harm. Since it seemed she could not help she ought to go away. She was doing nothing. She had even given up her search for the Maker, since there was nothing to be gained by finding it now. If Holne and his bullies discovered that she was hiding up here and killed more poor beasts in protest, she would be guiltier than they.

And yet, and yet, Zanne could not leave. Too many people had said, or implied: *you have started something by coming here, some process that we can't control* ... She felt like a stone that has been dropped into a still pool. At first nothing happens, only the bubbles rise and the ripples spread. Then slowly, slowly, the hidden presence begins to stir. Gradually, as it rises towards the air, the monster takes shape...

It was the Thirteen who had thrown her into this pool. Maybe they didn't know any more than Zanne what would be disturbed: and she must wait now, wait and see.

She had fetched her belongings from the bunkshed under the eyes of Mab and Truc, who watched sorrowfully, making her feel like a child in disgrace. Truc had a generous pack of journey food for her, provided by Lecte Slack Road. Zanne had accepted it with thanks: which wasn't easy. The family kept away, even Siri. Poor little Siri, she was on her own again now, and that was one of the worst things.

There was water on the mountain still in hidden mossy clefts along the spring line, and she had a small supply of dry food of her own to supplement Lecte's provisions. When it was all gone, she supposed she would have to give in. Zanne groaned and wondered if she had any good reason for lurking up here at all. Perhaps it was just that Zanne of Garth, arrogant and obstinate as any Minither, could not endure to admit she had been defeated by a gang of young village bullies.

Siri was very unhappy. She had never been quite so miserable before in her life, except maybe when mother died and that was a time she didn't remember. At the beginning of this summer she had had her music and her secret place; and her dreams of escape, one day. Now she had lost everything. There was a bolt fitted on the outside of her bedroom door and every moment that she wasn't locked up in there she was watched. She wasn't allowed to leave the yards for anything. What made it all worse was that father approved of everything that Aunt Lecte did. Always before she had been able to console herself: poor father, he wasn't strong but he would defend her if he ever dared. Not anymore.

Siri knew that she was being punished because she had made friends with Zanne. She had to pretend that she believed it when Aunt Lecte told her that Zanne was wicked, and had been sent away by the Covenant. Inside she tried to stay loyal, but it was hard. Day by day her idea of the good Covenant, the real Covenant, was slipping away from her. Zanne was gone forever. What good did it do to try to be the sort of girl she would admire?

The only comfort Siri had was in her dreams. She would never have thought she could enjoy them. But since she had no hopes or secrets left she didn't mind turning into the creeping, scratching thing. It felt better to be that than to be Sirato. They came now even when she wasn't asleep. She might be working in the sheds under Lecte's eyes, with Mab right beside her, and she would suddenly get that dream feeling. The women didn't seem to notice anything. Siri would giggle and smother the sound in a cough: she pretended she was holding herself back so the change didn't get too obvious. It wouldn't do to turn into a rat right in front of Aunt Lecte. As soon as she was alone in her bolted room she would sneak out of bed and scurry around the floor. She would hide under the bed and pretend she was waiting to bite at Aunt Lecte when she came in to check the prisoner. So far, she hadn't really done it. But she had such sharp teeth, bright teeth in the dreams: Siri wanted more and more to use them.

She was so horribly hot too. Why didn't it rain? And why did they make her wear clothes when she already had a coat of fur?

It was noontime in the slack yard, another day of Sunfall with the heat falling like a dead hand on the farm under the mountain. This yard was always the hottest place of all short of the inside of a brick kiln. The mountain loomed over it like the half-closed lid of a box and there wasn't a scrap of green or a breath of air to give any touch of coolness. It was a day for doing nothing, a day for lying by the Burnhouse with your feet in the water or for hiding in a darkened room. But Aunt Lecte had been full of dour energy since the roadwalker went away. She had decided today that they would clear out the old toolshed. Siri didn't care. She had almost forgotten about her secret place. Aunt Lecte hauled everything out into the burning sun, stripping off oilcloths and sorting out the tools that needed repair or cleaning. Siri was set to burnishing various small metal parts with a sanding block dipped in water. She was quite sure that most of these old broken bits and pieces were rubbish, good for nothing but to be melted down. She decided that her aunt had gone mad. How Zanne would have laughed at the two of them. Minithers make work as if they're afraid of stopping, that was what she used to say. But for Siri it wasn't funny. Her salt sweat dripped on the sanding block. It was so hot: and worse than hot. There was something in the air that was making Siri's head buzz and sing. Slyly, she slipped her hands down and began to scratch. Her nails were sharp: she soon managed to make a big tear in the sleeve of her smock. Underneath she felt the fur, hot and damp from being covered up...

Siri gasped out loud. She was awake, she was not dreaming. She pushed back the torn sleeve and looked: and whimpered in fear.

No, oh no.

Just then, Holne came into the yard. She had not seen him for days. He had been shut in his room, Aunt Lecte said he was not well. Siri guessed his badness had caught up with him at last and he was going to die, like mother. She didn't care. She was glad. But here he was, and he didn't look ill at all. He wore only a singlet and leggings, his bare shoulders glistened tawny brown. He strolled up to Aunt Lecte: she didn't seem to see him but kept working away. "Go to sleep, Aunt Lecte," he said. "You'll get sunstroke if you keep this up."

Aunt Lecte fell. Holne pulled her by the arms until she was lying in the shade. He looked at Siri then, a long sad look.

"I don't want to do this," he told her. "But I can't stop myself. You understand, don't you, sister?"

She understood that there was now no one to stop *her*, from doing what the mountain wanted.

Then he jumped up over the high yard wall. She saw his tawny brown body shooting away, up the shiny channel of the sled run.

And now Sirato felt as if she was splitting in two, as if every separate part of her was splitting. As hard as Sirato cried No! another creature cried Yes, Yes. The mountain broke up into tiny sparkling pieces that fell on her like a dry grey rain, dancing through her body: changing it, changing it bit by bit.

She began to cry. She scurried into the toolshed (it was so much easier to run on all fours). Her hands scratched and scrabbled in the packed dirt. She sobbed no, no, but they were no longer a little girl's hands, they were the scaled, clawed paws of an animal. They reached into the secret cavity and pulled out Sirato's last treasure. If Siri had been a good girl she would have found some way to give the moonlamp back to her friend. It was almost stealing to keep something when you knew someone only meant to lend it. Probably the magic wouldn't work any more, because of that. She hugged the trinket. Oh please, oh please ... *under the Covenant.* She was trying to cry, but her eyes were no longer the kind that can shed tears.

Zanne's camp was on the far side of the mountain, facing away from Minith town. There was a stand of boulders behind it where she could hide if necessary, and the open heath stretched all around so that nobody could take her by surprise. After her visit to the token tree she sat for a long time thinking over her reasons for staying in Minith, trying to make them seem good and trying to put the scraps of evidence together. The purple masses of heather burned and burned. The air was so heavy with heat that it had a taste, like metal.

What a day, muttered Zanne to herself.

The blue sky seemed to roll and roll as if with tumultuous clouds. It was as if the storm Minith had been waiting for had broken at last: but the rain was dry rain and the thunder silent.

Far away across the heather she saw something moving. At first she thought it was an animal, some little secretive kind of animal. It moved in starts, hopping and scurrying and stopping to peer about. The heat haze was deceiving: all at once she saw that this little mouse or rat was actually human-sized — somebody creeping towards her camp. With an exclamation of annoyance she grabbed her waggon cloak and pack. The figure was already too close for her to escape by hiding among the boulders, she would have to use magic.

Out of the safety of her warding she watched. The Minither, whoever it was, could be close enough to feel her breath now and would see nothing, would not even notice the cut heather. The haze was still playing tricks. Zanne squinted up her eyes — and suddenly exclaimed: "Siri! What are you doing up here!"

It was Sirato, certainly. But the girl was behaving very oddly. Her face lifted when Zanne cried out, turning from side to side as if she was sniffing the air. She dropped onto all fours and scurried, scrambled to her feet and tried to run upright: but dropped again after a few steps. She seemed to be in pain, Zanne could hear her crying. But the sound that reached her was not the sobbing of a child. It was a high-pitched animal whimpering, a noise somehow so horrible that it made the hair on Zanne's neck rise up.

She realised that she was still invisible, broke the warding and cried again — "Siri! I'm here — "

Sirato hopped and scrambled, whining through her teeth. She fell on her knees in front of Zanne. But when Zanne tried to touch her she flinched away, her eyes flashing bright and wary. She was clutching something in her two hands, it made her very clumsy on all fours. It was Dimen's moonlamp.

"Sirato, what is it? What's happened to you?"

Siri wouldn't let herself be touched. She couldn't speak. She was afraid like an animal: and desperate like an animal to go to the place where Holne had gone, where the change that hurt her so much would be complete. The moonlamp had brought her here but Rat didn't want to be near Zanne. Rat wanted to bite, to use her claws. Sirato was not fighting anymore. She thought she'd lost the fight, and watched from inside helplessly as the creature she was becoming squealed and snapped at her friend. But some small part of her managed not to let the Rat fly at Zanne's throat: the same part that kept hold of the covenanted silver.

"What's wrong — ? Siri, you'll have to tell me, or how can I help you — "

The girl crouched in the heather, staring with bright eyes that showed no human expression at all. Suddenly she jumped up and began to run away. She moved very fast, even though she kept falling and scrabbling along on elbows and knees. Every so often she looked over her shoulder and all the while that horrible whining went on. Zanne couldn't tell if Sirato meant to lead her or was just trying to escape, but she followed anyway.

The vivid heath was soon left behind. They climbed over rocks where the tall white columbine and blue lupins were parched into dry ghosts by the drought, and the matted soil around their roots fell into dust under hands and feet. Away in the east Zanne saw the route she had taken when she was exploring, where the valley of the wild ponies opened underfoot and the steel lake lay between its cold screes. Siri didn't go on that way. She turned back towards Minith, into the clefts and broken stones of the wrong side of the mountain. The blue sky was so bright it hurt Zanne's eyes: the figure ahead kept dropping and growing blurred. It was not a girl anymore, it was an animal running on clawed feet and dragging a scaly tail. Zanne scrubbed her eyes. It wasn't only Sirato. The rocks themselves were trembling. The whole of the mountain was shaking, shivering and dissolving to reveal what lay deep inside. *Deep inside* ...

The monster was rising to the surface of the pool. As Zanne followed across the mountainside, realisation and understanding began to dawn. At last she saw the connection between her quest, and the horrors that had fallen on Minith. The power like the power of a great Maker, hidden deep in the ancient wilderness. The plague of unnatural beasts ... *Your poisoned mountains* ... She had guessed the secret without knowing it. The thing ahead of her now looked like a rat the size of an eleven-year-old girl. But that was illusion. It was nothing so reasonable.

It led her up towards the peak of the mountain, onto a little plateau of small pebbles. Zanne's sense of perspective came back to her. She saw that Sirato, or what had been Sirato, was standing on the edge of this plateau, on what seemed to be the edge of a cliff.

"Siri!"

Abandoning caution Zanne began to run, sending out Link power ahead of her to hold Sirato with her mind. She stopped a few paces away, and spoke in her normal voice, as calmly as she could.

"*Sirato* — "

The thing keened. It shook and trembled, its outline shifting every instant: Sirato with a beast's face, a child with claws and fur, a patchwork abomination where the two were so mingled they could not be distinguished. A small sobbing voice cried, rising out of the beast's mouth.

"It hurts. Oh, it hurts me so."

Zanne came forward steadily, refusing to be afraid of the power that she felt. Which could do this to her as well, and was running off the girl in waves. She laid her covener's hands on the changed and changing flesh of her young friend, and gripped tightly. "Child of Inland, I know you. Under the Covenant, come back to me. Be still."

For a moment she couldn't tell if she'd succeeded or if she was being pulled into the vortex herself. Then it was over. She and Sirato were standing together in the hot sunlight, and Sirato was staring at her dazedly like a child woken out of a nightmare.

"Zanne? I was in the slack yard . . . How did I get here?"

Then Siri remembered. She opened her mouth to scream —

"Don't do that," said Zanne sharply. "You're better now. You're a brave, brave girl: you were fighting it very hard."

"It was the moonlamp. It brought me to you, the way you said it would."

The silver trinket was still clutched in Sirato's hand. She remembered that she had felt it burning her — the only thing that didn't change and holding it had hurt her changing self horribly. She didn't know how she had managed to cling on.

"I'll never say anything bad about the Covenant again!"

Zanne laughed shakily. "Oh, I think you will. The next time you're bored at pensioner school."

She held Sirato's skinny arms, smooth and human once more but still hiding in their flesh, like buried poison, the threat of that horrible transformation. She remembered how puzzled and shamed she'd been, by the distaste she felt whenever she touched this child. Oh, how stupid she had been. If she had only listened to Siri, who did not know the secret and told it without understanding what she was saying: ... *the bad children, they get sick, they die* ...

"Siri, don't be afraid. You're safe. Try to tell me what happened. Why did you come up to the mountain? Was it just to find me?"

Sirato wasn't listening. Free of the change she was no longer aware of how she had been pulled to this spot: but she looked over the edge of the drop and her whole body stiffened.

"Oh Zanne — look!"

She grabbed at her friend frantically. "Get down! Get down, they'll see us — "

They were standing on the edge of a deep narrow corrie. Directly below Zanne and Sirato the first sheer face gave way after about twice Zanne's height to a gradual slope of scree. Opposite rose a wall of slate blue slabs, climbing up unbroken towards the distant peak. There had been growing things in the bottom of the corrie before the drought killed them, but the dead shapes had a strange look; the skeletons of plants such as Zanne had never seen alive. At the foot of the blue slab wall there had been a rockfall long ago. A shaft of stone jutted out of it, like a finger beckoning from inside the mountain. From this shaft, to Zanne's eyes, there was rising a strong unnatural glow. She could not tell what colour the light was. Was it light or sound? Pulled by Siri's hands she dropped on her hands and knees, staring. She was so fascinated by that rockfall that at first she barely noticed the young people.

Some had already arrived. Some were coming up from the foot of the corrie, where a dry stream bed sloped into a kind of funnel. Siri dragged Zanne down below the rim out of sight and together they watched the guardians of Minith as they assembled. Siri saw girls and boys whom she had known all her life, hopping and scrabbling and loping up from the rock funnel. What were they doing? Why were they here? She put the side of her wrist in her mouth and bit it hard. She knew, she knew...

Zanne counted: fifteen, twenty; more. There were mostly boys but a few girls too. The young people wore masks and hoods, they turned their faces away from each other. Nobody wanted to see who else was here. They must know each other but they would try not to admit it. Zanne saw a flag of bright red hair and remembered Karin Silvermines who had danced outside the meeting house. These were Minith's unruly children, the ones who could not learn the harsh restraining way of life that the mountain people had devised. The ones who could not be saved.

Bending and stooping, wincing as if in pain, they began to strip off their clothes. "That's what I saw," whispered Zanne. "That's what the shadows were doing."

She had guessed the meaning of the fragments of cloth that she had found by the token tree. The wild gang would gather there to undress before they went sheep killing. It was a practical arrangement, so they would not betray themselves by coming home in torn and bloody clothes. Zanne had imagined the young Minithers racing off naked into the darkness, knives in their hands, with anger and repugnance. The concealment provided by that nakedness was so typical of Minith as she understood it. For of course their families must strongly suspect who the night marauders were. But as long as the culprits turned up at the breakfast table neat and sober, Minith hypocrisy would protect them.

Now she saw how different the truth was from her imagining. There was no need for the creatures in the corrie to undress. The force that was breaking into them was doubled magic. It changed their outward appearance as illusion might, and changed the substance too. The doomed flores of Minith stripped themselves in shame. For some of them it was already hard to make normal movements. They pulled and scrabbled clumsily, with leg joints turned backwards and thickened hands: taking off their humanity.

Under the bright sun in the hot eerie stillness the transformation gathered speed. The young woman with red curling hair struggled from rock to rock as if she had no limbs at all, moving even more clumsily than Sirato when she had arrived at Zanne's camp. She wrapped her arms around her naked body as if trying to hide it or hold it together. But her human skin peeled away like the petals of a hideous flower, opening and bursting before it melted into scaly hide, her ribcage swallowing her arms, her legs dissolving into one writhing coil of muscle. Like that, she joined the jostling crowd around the glowing shaft. And still stragglers were arriving. A boy of about sixteen came up through the rock funnel with his upper body hunched over, hands huddled against his chest. He hopped, he skipped: his eyes were bright as blackberries. He cried like a rabbit in a snare. He had not been one of the killers. But he had to follow, to come with the others, even though they terrified his timid beast-form.

At last the gathering seemed to be complete. It was hard to tell the exact number because of the way the shape-shifting happened. It wasn't only the bodies of the sufferers, the whole corrie seemed to be running like hot wax. The changed were not animals. If Zanne didn't make an effort against it she saw, it was true, a weirdly varied pack of wild beasts down there. But it was her eyes, disgusted at the confusion, that made a bear, a mountain cat, a wolf, out of those monstrosities. In reality they were not so organised, not so whole. Some of them were silent, some of them cried. Some of them seemed to have surrendered to the horror completely and were dancing and jigging round the glowing pillar in gruesome delight. She knew from what she could see of their real forms that they must all be in very great pain: she could only be glad some of them were unable to feel it.

Bile rose in Zanne's throat as she watched, but her mind went on working, putting together the strangest, most terrifying stories of the past with everything she knew of Minith.

"So this is the answer," she whispered. "Oh, Sirato, this explains why the focus of power here so confused me. Your elders didn't lie. There is no great Maker in Minith. It's something far different, but as deadly dangerous. The people of the past were greater than we are, hardly anybody understands how great. They did such beautiful and fearful things. They were able to reach into the depth of being, where all the forms are destroyed and reborn and change into each other. They found there a power that belongs neither to them nor to us. It is what lies *between* our magic world and what they called reality. They took that force and made it work for them, made it heat water and turn wheels. But when they'd taken what they wanted what was left over was poison to them. It terrified them. They could not unmake it so they hid it away, buried it under a mountain in the wilderness where they thought it would be safe forever. There it stayed, until Inland people came too close, looking for metal in the rock.

"Because of its power over the minds of the people of the past the poison survived into our time, and this is the form it has taken in our world: change and fear, bound together. The poor Minithers — the more they tried to struggle against it, the more it overwhelmed them. In the place *between* everything becomes its own opposite. These animals, these weird beasts, are nothing but the other side of Minith's ways of restraint and control . . ."

She guessed that the rockfall must be connected inside the mountain by a fault line that lead straight to the burial vault where the people of the past had hidden their fear. The young Minithers who were most vulnerable to the plague must be impelled here from time to time, drawn horribly to the source of their sickness.

Sirato was holding the moonlamp very tightly. There was a feeling like pins and needles in her arms and legs. Her stomach was churning, she thought she might be sick. She tried to look anywhere but into the corrie. It would be horrible, horrible to be like that.

Not horrible. Rat wants it. Rat wants to bite . . .

Zanne thought of the young names written up on the walls of the meeting house. She imagined what this change, repeated maybe over years, would do to a human body. Sirato's young mother, who was shut away in her room to die . . . She had been so unjust: to Gwil Slack Road, the empty shell of a man who has suffered too much. And to Lecte — and poor Holne himself, who had told her: *none of us can leave, nothing can be done* . . . She had given many names to the spectre that haunted Minith, blighting lives and making her own errand so difficult. She had never thought of calling it courage.

But it was mistaken courage. The Minithers had quarantined themselves for long enough. Now that she understood, she was sure that she could help. However, she could not pull this whole crowd back from the change alone: she was afraid even to try, so near the source of distortion; and Siri should not stay here, not even with a covener's protection.

"Siri — come on. We've seen enough."

Siri cried loudly. "No!"

She threw the moonlamp in Zanne's face, turned her head with lightning speed and sank sharp white teeth into the hand on her arm. Zanne let go for a moment, catching the lamp by reflex. It was enough: Siri darted away.

"I won't go! You're all the same. Anything I have of my own, you take it away from me. I won't be quiet, I won't be good. I want to dance and sing, down there with the others — "

She had drawn blood. She could taste it and she was glad. In the corrie her sisters and brothers were dancing. She couldn't have her fur and claws because the stupid Covenant magic was still holding her, but she could join them.

The change that could not break into her body was reaching her mind instead. Sirato only knew that she didn't feel sick anymore and she hated Zanne. Aghast, Zanne grabbed the girl's arms. The fury that glared out of Siri's eyes was as shocking as the other transformation had been. The child fought like a cornered rat, kicking and clawing and biting. Before Zanne realised that this was no time to be gentle and used her full strength, it was too late. Grappling with her, Siri pitched herself from the rock with complete recklessness. They fell together onto the scree. The girl was undermost: a sharp stone had cut open her forehead, she raised her bloodied face and laughed — then their two bodies were rolling together down the slope, Sirato still howling furiously. "Let me go! Let me go!"

Zanne managed to get to her knees, the rattle and crash of falling scree sounding in her ears like thunder. Pebbles that seemed fluid as water slithered under her and came to rest. But the world was still shaking. At this close range the monsters seemed unreal. The glow from the rockfall was stronger, it seemed to pulse through her vision, confusing everything.

A small cold hand touched her arm. Siri moved closer, giving a little gasp of fear as the pebbles rattled again. Fortunately the changed didn't seem to have noticed the noise.

"I'm all right now. I'm — I'm sorry, Zanne." Her voice trembled. "Can you magic them?"

"No I can't," Zanne answered softly. "There is too much of another kind of 'magic' here. We'll have to creep away very quietly. Keep hold of my hand and at least we will not change, you and I."

The scree was too steep and noisy, they dared not try to climb. Hand in hand they crept towards the far end of the corrie, where the course of the vanished stream showed as a dry waterfall, forming a rocky stairway. Zanne was trying to hold herself and the Minith girl invisible, she thought that much magic was safe. Neither of them stumbled, they made no sound except for their breath. But suddenly, for no reason, the heads of all the beast-things turned at once. Siri cried "Run!" and let go of Zanne's hand. She got between the beasts and her friend, grabbing stones to throw at them. It was a brave move: but now the slight protection of Zanne's warding was broken.

She held up the moonlamp.

"Don't you know this? This is the Covenant. Don't despair, there's always hope. I know what's wrong — I can help you ..."

The lamp was like a candle in daylight. The creatures opened their mouths, crying and snarling in pain and savagery. Change that is greatly feared is called destruction: these things were now destruction given living form. There seemed to be nothing left, nothing human that could be reached. Siri threw a rock.

"Get back! Leave us alone!"

Zanne grabbed her and they ran, flinging themselves on the first foot and handholds of the dead waterfall. Up they scrambled, Siri sobbing tearlessly in sheer terror. "They won't hurt us!" gasped Zanne. "They have only killed animals, not human beings — "

She was not so sure. Whatever had started happening in Minith when Hillen's emissary arrived, was reaching a deadly climax.

Zanne fell at the rim of the corrie, bruising her ribs as she pulled herself clear. Rat would have kept on going: Siri turned and held down her hand. She would rather be torn to pieces than be a sneaking Rat again. They ran together through a jumble of giant boulders. In every direction the horizon was wide and empty, there was not a sign of human life. It was hard to believe that Minith town was sleeping through another hot afternoon just a few vales away. Zanne jumped up on a flat-topped rock and pulled Siri after her. She stared around — they were lost. Zanne could sense where Minith valley lay, but she couldn't tell what hidden crags and gorges lay between.

"Sirato, where are we?"

"I don't know," wailed the girl, helplessly. Poor Siri, the only paths she knew were between one field and another, between Minith and Slack Road.

The changed were close behind. Zanne felt their purpose, their need, beating on her face like the heat of an open furnace. She knew now there had been no plan, or hardly any, behind the plague of death. The creatures killed because they must.

"Change is not destruction!" she shouted to them. "Not in our time!"

But the power buried under the mountain had been named and given its meaning, the same meaning as in the past, by too many generations of Minithers. And in Inland meaning and substance are one and the same. Zanne felt the fear beginning to take hold of her, the same unnatural dread she had suffered before on this mountain. Fear, fear fear —

Sirato shouted, "Go away! Go away!" and flung the pebbles she had stuffed into her pockets as she ran, but the effect was pitiful. She might as well have tried to drive off the mountain. She knew that this was what she'd been dreaming of all her life. Those hideous faces that used to peer over the partition — they were here, real in the sunlight.

Zanne looked up to the bright dome of the sky. No sign of life — but yes there was. A pair of tiny sailing cross marks cut into the emptiness.

"Kee-ah!" cried Zanne. "Kee-ah!"

The buzzards spiralled down.

"Under the Covenant — " Zanne shouted to them. "Help us — please!"

The birds circled lazily as if considering whether they owed these two humans anything. Then she-buzzard dropped like a stone, screaming, her great taloned feet thrust out: her smaller mate plunged after.

Zanne and Sirato jumped down the far side of their refuge and raced away towards a rim of wine colour where the rocks ended and the heather began. Zanne was willing the heather into *safety* in her mind. Reach that margin and we will be hidden, they won't be able to catch us — she made that magic, the most she dared to risk on her own.

But before the heather there was a sunken field of bog

cotton and dry rustling reeds, which had been invisible from the rocks above. The buzzards had tired of mobbing the strange ones. After all, those things killed sheep and left the carcasses for others to pick. Zanne fell on her face, pulling Siri down beside her. She was clutching heather roots and smelling the honey scent. It was so real that she could not believe the grass stems that she found instead. Swiftly she understood her mistake. *The dry bog is our refuge* — she cried aloud. But it was too late. She was exhausted.

"I won't hurt you — " she gasped.

If the creatures facing her could still understand human language they might have laughed. They were Minithers of course, and knew only a garbled and diminished version of the story of Zanne of Garth.

"I won't hurt you — " she repeated stubbornly as she staggered to her feet, putting the girl behind her. The pack all leapt together. Something big and tawny brown came flying through the air and knocked Zanne sprawling. She tried to get up, screaming "Siri! Run! — ", and hit at it with her fists but it just grabbed her and threw her down again. She cried out in horror at seeing that distorted mask so close — then everything was lost in a tumbling confusion of hide and heat and claws and teeth. The tawny thing leapt at the throats and flanks of its fellows. It seemed to have claimed the two humans as its personal prey, or maybe in its mad and pain-wracked mind it did not know friend from foe.

After a long time, the chaos ended.

Zanne sat up slowly. She touched a mess of scratches on her bare arms. They were bleeding, but only slightly. Otherwise she seemed to be unhurt. The dry bog was empty. The pack had disappeared. There was only the sun still high in a blue sky, and the heavy silent heat of a late summer's day in the wilderness.

"Where is it? Where did the big cat go?"

Sirato was close by, crouched down on her heels with her arms wrapped round her knees. Her face was bloody from the cut on her forehead, her smock was ripped down the front, that seemed to be all the damage.

"It wouldn't let them," she whispered. "It wouldn't let the others hurt us. It was ... it was my brother."

She began to cry then, desolately.

CHAPTER EIGHT

THE MAKER'S CAVE

THE TRACK THAT led from Minith town to the waggon road lay like a dusty white snake along the valley floor, winding between low blind ridges of dun and brown. It was about an hour before dusk. A dim haze hung in the air and nothing stirred, not even one lark singing. Two small figures detached themselves from the brown expanse. They climbed from the bed of a dry stream onto the track and stood for a moment looking about them. Then they slowly began to walk back to Minith. It wasn't far. In about half a vale the grey cone of the meeting house came in sight, and the burnhouses and yards down by the river. No smoke or steam rose from the metal works, Minith seemed completely deserted. The yellow-haired girl and the child gazed at everything they passed in tired amazement, as if they had been wandering in the mountains for years and had almost forgotten what a house or a yard wall looked like. At the fork in the track Zanne paused, looking down to the cottage by the meeting house. She shook her head a little and they walked on. A faint sweet sound of running water rose from the irrigation channels behind the pensioners' row, and farther off the Burnhouse murmured drowsily. They stopped outside the last cottage in the row. It was a little larger than the rest, a neat and severe block of silvery bricks with bean rows and currant bushes in the front garden, and a tidily stripped patch where Anarad's raspberry canes had been. This house was as quiet as the rest, but it had an indefinable air of occupation.

"I have been badly mistaken," said Zanne. "We both have, Siri. Your aunt wasn't being cruel. She was trying to save you."

Sirato shook her head. "They ought to have told us," she muttered. "It *is* cruel, not to tell children things."

Zanne went up and knocked on the cottage door. After only a short pause a voice said, "It's open, come in — "

Anarad Pensioner's parlour was a larger room than Zanne had expected and the front door opened straight into it. It was gloomy in there after the late sunlight. There were a lot of people: a lot of sombre Minith faces staring at her. She had the impression that they were all crowded together to shelter from the dry and silent storm she had imagined on the mountain. She saw several faces she knew, but none of the elders seemed to be present. That was good. She had a chance of reaching minds not sealed off completely behind walls of proud despair.

"Zanne Covener!" exclaimed someone, startled. "What are you doing here? We thought you had left the valley."

"And Siri Slack Road — "

Anarad, a little woman with a scraped-back bun of white hair, came forward abruptly. She took Siri by the shoulders — glancing back at her guests to share, silently, her puzzled relief. Zanne smiled a little: the Minith schoolteacher had given herself away.

"I couldn't leave," she said. "I was ashamed to leave, because of the way I behaved at our last meeting. I wanted to find some way to make things right. I stayed up in the mountain. I was there today when Siri came to me for help. She was very ill, then. I think you know how ill. But as you see *she is herself again*. She is a brave girl and a good fighter."

Siri hung her head, blushing.

Zanne drew a deep breath. "And then we saw the sheep killers. It was as I told you: a gang of your own flores. But I understand now why you all pretended that you didn't believe me. We saw them, in that corrie with the rockfall where the glowing shaft of stone comes out of the mountain. We saw them change."

The Minithers were listening the way they listened at the meeting: blank faced, refusing to admit anything. At Zanne's last words there were murmurs, but even now the majority were trying to hush the weaker ones.

"Oh, don't you see — " she cried. "You don't have to keep your secret anymore. *I understand.* I know how I have misjudged you." Her eyes filled with tears, to think of so much grief, hidden in the heart of Inland. "For generations you have suffered this plague alone. You have kept it out of the web, shutting away part of yourselves from the community of magic, so even Hillen did not know what was wrong. Every year watching your children, knowing that some of them were doomed. You've never let anyone infected leave the valley, you have lived in misery to protect the rest of Inland from contamination ... I – I honour your courage."

This was not the moment to tell them how that mistaken courage and isolation had distorted their lives, as much as the plague itself.

"But it isn't necessary. You don't have to go on carrying this burden. There need be no more monsters, and you can give up your 'restraint'."

Anarad Pensioner got up from her place again. She marched to the door and opened it.

"Out! This is my house and I won't have such talk in it. You insult everyone in Minith. You don't know what you are saying."

Zanne stayed where she was. "No. I won't leave. I will *make* you listen. I know where your plague comes from. There is a store of poison buried under your mountain, poison from the past: that's what is causing these terrible effects."

The whole room seemed to stiffen in shock.

"We know that," said Anarad at last. "What can we do? We cannot leave, the poison is in us now — and Inland must have its metal."

"Ah. So *that's* it."

Since she had seen the changed, there had been only one mystery left for Zanne. Looking back, it was obvious that the Minithers had known the truth all along: the identity of those they called the guardians; and that there was no great Maker but something worse buried under their mountain. The puzzle had been why did they stay? If they were afraid the infection would travel with them, they could have kept themselves apart elsewhere.

"Well, you have been very brave. The whole of Inland is in your debt. But it is over now. I'm here to set you free. You know who I am. I suppose you thought I couldn't help unless there was a Maker involved. It isn't so. If you will let me, I can give this old poison the death it needs. Minith's sickness can be cured, I promise you."

There was a long silence. Zanne waited for some kind of outburst, but it didn't come. Minith's code of restraint made it easy for people to hide their feelings. It was hard to tell what was going on behind those stolid masks.

At last someone spoke. "You say you will stop the changes?"

Zanne felt her knees give way with relief. She had broken through.

"I, by myself? Of course not. But under the Covenant, I can help Minith to heal itself."

Another silence.

"There will be no guardians anymore?"

Zanne nodded. Obviously, it was hard for them to take in the good news. She stood smiling hopefully, watching the eyes that met and glanced and looked away from each other; almost as if ashamed.

Sirato was watching the faces too. Suddenly she took a step closer to Zanne, and tugged at her arm.

"Zanne," she hissed " — I think we should go now. Let's go . . . "

Zanne looked round, puzzled. "Go? Go where — ?"

"Under the Covenant," said a woman's voice quietly. "We have never been afraid to do what must be done."

There was another silence, more slow glances exchanged. Then suddenly the Minithers all began to come to life.

"Give her a chair, someone. And a stool for little Siri. Look — you are dropping both of you."

Zanne and Sirato were settled by the tea table. Anarad brought water and towels so they could wash the sweat and grime and blood from their hands and faces. Someone else poured beakers of herb tea sweetened with honey: a plate of plum bread appeared, spread with more honey and white butter. The water was cold, the towels were rough, the chair extremely hard to Zanne's bruised bones. This was still Minith . . . the rock people were almost funny, in their clumsy attempts to be gentle. Zanne smiled and smiled at them all, dizzy with relief. The bread was the best food she had ever tasted.

She couldn't understand why Sirato, who was eating diligently nevertheless, still looked so fierce and wary. Poor little rat, she wasn't quite human even now. It would be years maybe before she learned to trust again.

"Before I can work," began Zanne, "we will have to penetrate the poison vault itself. But before that I think we should call another meeting. Where are your elders by the way? I don't see any of them here."

Mab and Truc from Slack Road had appeared out of the crowd of acquaintances and strangers. They sat on either side of Zanne and Sirato.

"No need for that," declared Mab. "There is a meeting called already. Because of the guardians, you know. We have to find a way to quiet them. All of us here will join it soon. But you don't need to see the elders. We know where the vault is. We can take you to it."

Zanne looked up from her bread and tea in astonishment. "You can *take* me there?"

"Oh yes." Mab nodded confidently. "We Miners, we know our way around inside that old mountain."

She patted Zanne's shoulder. "We'll take you there right now so you can see . . . see if it's the right place, you know."

Zanne was startled. "But this is Covenant business. It concerns the whole meeting."

The eyes of the old beast-tender and his workmate met over Zanne's head. "Don't you worry about that," said Truc. "There's enough of us here. We know what the elders would want us to do. And our covener too."

"But — it must be a long way. I suppose it is somewhere below that corrie with the rockfall. Besides, it will be dark soon."

"Oh no, it's not so far by the way we will go. And then underground, you know, night doesn't make any difference."

Zanne guessed that these people wanted her to know everything tonight, before the stubborn elders had a chance to interfere. That worried her, although she couldn't imagine why Lecte, Carad and the others should need any more persuasion now. Maybe it would be better to wait. But the expedition to the mountain was already under way. It seemed she couldn't do anything to stop it. Anarad Pensioner was to be her guide: the old lady had been a famous miner once, and still knew the inside of the mountain better than any Minither alive. Mab and Truc were coming too. "Because Slack Road, our farm, took you in, Sunny," explained Truc solemnly. "So it's only right that we should take this responsibility."

Zanne and Sirato were not allowed to help with the preparations. They were told to sit and rest, while more fruit bread was brought out for them, and tea and cheese and a jug of tart, refreshing sour milk. The Minith people clustered around, as if trying to make up in one burst of hospitality for all the harsh treatment they'd given to Zanne of Garth. Zanne glimpsed Anarad and Mab stowing a remarkable amount of equipment into a bulky pack: rope and torches and other things she didn't even recognise.

"I'll be well looked after this time," she joked. "No more meddling about and 'prying' on my own."

The Minithers looked ashamed. No more of that, they agreed.

The party set out. Zanne was half-afraid Lecte Slack Road would be waiting for them in the street, demanding to know what was going on. There was no one. The meeting house cone looked gloomy and deserted: the meeting clearly had not begun to gather yet.

"Oh, wait a moment," cried Zanne, suddenly remembering. "Sirato — can somebody take her home? Or could she stay at your house, Anarad? I don't think she should be out on her own."

They all knew why. But Anarad shook her head.

"Sirato is coming with us. It is safer that she should."

"I don't think so. She is protected by my magic, but even so she shouldn't be near the poison."

"It's safer for her to come along," repeated Anarad.

"Safer — " echoed Mab, heavily.

Siri had come out of the house with Zanne, and was sticking close to her side. She looked up at her friend unhappily. She hoped she was wrong, she hoped she was just being a mean little Rat. But still, even now ... Siri knew Minith, as Sunny — Zanne — never could know it.

You don't understand them, she wanted to say. Not even now. But that seemed wicked, after Anarad had given them plum bread ... Siri didn't want to be Rat again. So all she said was: "I'm coming with you."

They went on up the track towards Slack Road, but soon turned right on a steep path so well worn its stones were as smooth and even as craft-laid cobbles.

"This is the way to the mines."

"Yes," agreed Anarad. "The way to the poison vault is through our mines."

Zanne fell silent. It was grey dusk. As they climbed, heads down, with the last of a dull sunset fading away behind them, she was puzzling over this newest information. It was almost beyond belief that the miners had actually worked close to the source of poison, knowing that it was there. Perhaps when Anarad said "through" the mines, she meant the actual vault was a long way beyond.

Siri slipped closer. "Don't trust them — " she whispered.

"Oh Siri, don't be silly. Mab and Truc? We know them, they're our friends."

"That's exactly why," muttered the girl, mysteriously.

And said no more, because then Mab caught up with them.

"Mab," asked Zanne, "how do you tell, if someone is going to be affected? Does it start when a child won't learn your 'restraint'?"

"Most people would say so. When a child has the signs, we

don't try to keep them from their natural fate. At least we should not, that would be defying the Covenant." She broke off, frowning. "And then, once a young girl or a lad is sick and knows it how can you expect them to work and be sober? It would be too cruel. And we are not cruel to them, never that — "

Zanne nodded sadly, thinking of Holne. No wonder everyone at Slack Road had been so gentle with that idle, insolent young man.

"Sometimes a whole family has the mark on them from very young. But it can break out in a grown woman or man too. We can never be sure. We keep the secret from children and the young people — those who don't learn the hard way. At their first meeting they are told everything. They're old enough then to bear it, and to understand how they will have to live."

"In fear."

Mab touched Zanne's arm. "Sunny — I mean, Zanne — suppose you're wrong. Maybe you cannot stop the changes. You could still leave. Go back to Hillen and just tell them you failed and that Minith must be left alone."

Zanne shook her head, feeling the woman's concern and touched by it. "Thank you, Mab, but it's no use. Whatever the danger — and there is danger — I have to try." She bent her back to the steepness of the hill: it was a tiring climb after a long and exhausting day. "Remember this, Mab. What Is brought me here. And the power of the past recognises me. That's clear from the way your changed have been behaving. They can't help themselves. All the killings — that seems to me now like the poison shouting to me: Here I am! Here I am! These dead things you know, they *want* to be at peace ... Yes, Mab, I do believe I will be able to end Minith's sufferings — "

The Minither sighed. "Not many coveners have power

over the old things, do they? If you were to fail, no one else would come."

"Probably not," agreed Zanne.

Mab sighed again.

On the flat ground in front of the workings, hummocks of tailings and the round dome of the stone crusher loomed in the twilight. Mab and Anarad gave out lamps. Truc uncoiled the rope and rather clumsily fastened it around Zanne's waist and Siri's.

"That's right," grinned Zanne. "Tie me up, then I'll be no trouble." The old shepherd frowned. He obviously felt this was no time for joking.

They went into the dark. The floor of the tunnel was flat as the floor of a room, its walls were neatly squared. Their lamps caught silver flickers everywhere.

"You miners are very tidy people," remarked Zanne cheerfully.

No one answered.

After that, Zanne gave up trying to lighten the mood of her companions. From one tunnel to another they moved deeper into the rock. Sirato could feel the whole weight of the mountain. But she wasn't going to let that fear bother her. She was here to look after her friend.

Zanne was reaching out, to trace the focus of the power. Somewhere, somewhere close the fabric of rock and air was shaking, was breaking, as she had seen it in the corrie. Too close! She saw that the tunnel they were in now was much older, and showed no signs of recent workings. It was opening out, there was a big cavern ahead. The blue flames of four spirit lamps lifted and wandered in a huge space too clear cut to be natural, too vast to have been blasted by Inland people.

"Why — this is ancient! Are we there? Is the vault near?"

"Not just yet," said Mab, who was leading. "There's something in here we want you to see first."

Her voice sounded odd, distorted by the echoing cavern. She had stepped into a dark hole in the wall of their tunnel. Zanne and Siri followed, Anarad and Truc stayed outside. Anarad at once began to shrug her big pack from her shoulders, and Truc took it from her with great care.

Zanne wondered what they were doing, but she was distracted. Mab had taken a work flare from her belt: a fire-hardened wooden stake with a head of bog cotton and tallow, dusted in a bright-burning mineral that the Minithers used for this purpose. She lit it and raised it high. Zanne and Siri saw an oval cave not so big as the one outside but still large. Its walls and floor were broken: Zanne remembered the rockfall up above. Something had happened to this mountain between the fall of the past and the birth of Inland, and the tomb which was meant to be so safe had been shattered . . . Her calculations ended when she saw what else Mab was showing her. Around the walls of the cave loomed big ungainly shapes, shrouded in murk and debris.

Zanne gasped in astonishment. "Makers!"

"Yes. We call it the Makers' cave."

"But no one ever mentioned this!"

"We don't talk about such things in Minith."

The dead servants of the past lay where they had fallen, most of them no more than rotting heaps of rusted metal and of stranger materials. The makers must have been abandoned here when the poison vault was finished: considered too contaminated for further use. The air in here must be very dry, or there would have been nothing left. The strange shapes were too alluring to be resisted. Zanne quickly loosed herself from the rope and started towards the nearest.

"Why, I've never seen or heard of such makers before.

What did they do? Does anyone know? Did they use emf or some other power?"

She stopped herself. Normal Inlanders would find this excitement very shocking, though in fact they had nothing to fear. Zanne of Garth had learned her lesson. She sighed: but then a small frown gathered between her brows. It was odd that her guides had chosen to bring her here tonight. Didn't they trust her yet?—was this some kind of test for the "maker-lover"?

"Mab—?"

The farmworker's kindly face was very sad. Perhaps it was the blue lamp light that made her look so doleful.

"Look over there, Zanne—"

Zanne looked. At once something hit her hard, on the back of her head.

She regained consciousness thinking urgently of rockfalls, bad air: and sat up hurriedly, feeling herself unharmed and anxious for her companions. That was when she found that her hands had been tied behind her. Siri was sitting beside her on the floor of the Makers' cave, wriggling furiously. She was tied too. Mab and Truc stood shoulder to shoulder, looking down with identical expressions of righteous regret.

Zanne was astonished.

"What d'you think you're doing!" she demanded.

"We tried every way we could to stop you," explained Mab. "But you wouldn't be told. You won't give up until you have destroyed our Covenant."

"Your *Covenant*?"

Truc shook his head gloomily. "Ah, you're a clever young woman and handy with the animals. But you outsiders live too soft. You don't know how hard the Covenant is."

"You don't have to know," added Mab gently. "We can bear it for you. We are strong enough."

"You beasts!" cried Sirato. "Let her go! If you don't, the Covenant will get you. It will! It will!"

The two paid no attention. They were picking up the lamps and the remains of the rope coil: tidy and methodical as Minithers must always be. Anarad's white head poked in through the entrance behind them.

"Thirty measures of slow," she remarked enigmatically, with a last glance of pity for her naughtiest pupil.

"Ssh, Siri, don't worry." Zanne was testing knots behind her back. These people were quite mad, argument was pointless. "This is just a silly trick. We'll soon get out of it."

But Sirato was wiser.

"What are you doing?" she shouted, terrified.

Truc and Mab paused on their way out.

"We're not coveners," said Truc. "We have no right to kill. We'd have taken you to Anlys, but the poor woman has enough to do tonight."

"The air's good in here," Mab assured them. "There'll be time for whatever's proper. You must see to it yourself, covener ... And the child. Don't — don't let our little Rat suffer, will you?"

Then Zanne knew, as the child had known all along. In a moment the stupidity of her mistake flashed over her. She had seen the hideous effects of the poison, and straight away handed herself and the child over to people who had breathed the same air, drunk the same water as those hideously transformed things....

The short-lived torch that Mab had left poked into a crack in the floor flickered and went out. Somewhere in the dark footsteps retreated, briskly but without any unrestrained hurry or confusion. Sirato lunged to her feet.

"Quickly — out of here!" she screamed.

Thirty measures ... twenty ... ten ...

The rockfall came.

Almost before the echoes had died Sirato began to fight with the rope that tied her. The darkness was painted black against her eyes, she could taste it like fur in her mouth. When Aunt Lecte had locked her in the cupboard she had been afraid she would suffocate, but it was nothing like this. The closet in the counting room was filled with fresh air, smelling of beeswax polish and herbs from the kitchen garden. There were no scents here, only an old, old staleness. No one could keep little Rat tied up for long. She squirmed until she had pulled her arms over her head and set her teeth to the rope. In a very short time she was free. Then for the first time she thought of Zanne. She could hear her own breath coming in short sharp gasps: there was no other sound.

"Zanne?"

No answer, no movement. She began to grope about in the darkness. Within an arm's length she found herself grappling the sharp edges of the new rockfall, a pile as high and deep as she could reach.

"Zanne! Zanne!"

With a sob of relief she found something softer than stone: Zanne's knee. By touch she discovered that her friend was still sitting beside her. She reached up and found Zanne's face. It was cold and still, she didn't seem to be breathing. Sirato shuffled a pace backwards, staring at the slumped body that she could not see. Zanne must have been knocked unconscious by the explosion, when Anarad blasted the entrance shut. Or else ... or else ... Sirato whimpered faintly. She had heard what Mab said. She wasn't a baby, she guessed what it was that Zanne the covener must "see to". There was only one way out of this cavern now.

"Oh Zanne, don't go without me!" she cried, "Don't leave me here alone — "

Sirato had never been underground in her life, except in

the dreams. Still she remembered something of Anarad Pensioner's lessons. If you are trapped by a fall dowse your lamp and don't strike a light. Wildfire eats air the same as you do. Find a moving draught and go to it. Go on your hands and knees — there may be a break in the floor. If there is no moving air, then stay still. Under the Covenant you can be sure the other miners know your danger: help will come.

There was no moving air, and no help would come. It was a big cave. Siri wondered how long it would take before she began to die. Long enough to get very hungry and thirsty, certainly. She wished she had not bitten that rope. Human girls don't use their teeth like that. She thought she could feel the change beginning again: and that convinced her, more than anything, that Zanne was really gone.

She was under the mountain. It had eaten her at last. She could see nothing but she knew that all around her the rock was stirring. Little tiny sparks were dancing out of it, dancing into Sirato and pulling her skin apart — letting out the teeth and claws and greasy fur.

Rat was already getting hungry.

She jumped up. She had had a hideous thought. She ran and fell, scrambled and fell again: crashed into one of the dead makers and collapsed on the floor with her head ringing. She was not trying to find a way out. She only wanted to be far away from Zanne's body when the change came. Rat, trapped Rat: what would it do when it was scrabbling and starving?

The collision had frightened her. She went a few paces on her hands and knees, and then her fingers slipped into nothingness. She found the edge of the break and felt along it, leant across and tried to reach the other side. The crevasse was wide and long. She found a scrap of stone on the floor and dropped it, invisible, into the invisible abyss: she did not hear it land.

Siri crouched on the edge of the pit. Little Rat had found a place to hide. In a moment, just a moment, she would be safe —

"Sirato."

A light sprang up. The Makers' cave was visible again, from its shadowy roof to the dead ancient monsters ranged around its walls. Siri turned and saw her friend sitting cross-legged and wide awake with the silver moonlamp on the floor in front of her.

"Come away from there, Siri," said Zanne very calmly.

The crevasse was a jagged splash of black paint on the grey floor.

"I can't, I can't. I'm changing. I don't want to die like that."

"You won't change. Not while I am with you. And who said anything about dying? Come here."

Zanne didn't move until the girl was well within reach. Then she reached out, with a speed that told she had not been as calm as she seemed, and grabbed Siri's wrist.

"Good girl. Now don't you be so silly. We're not finished yet. And Siri — if you get to feel like that again *tell me*. I can help. It's the poison, you know: the same stuff that changed your body, working another way."

Siri felt confused. Had she really meant to throw herself down the hole? She must have been crazy.

"Zanne, what happened to you? I thought you were — gone."

Zanne smiled. "Gone? Well — I was thinking, I suppose. Still, you might say I have been away. I have been to Hillen."

Siri couldn't see how. It must be Covenant magic.

"To Hillen? Oh, Zanne, you went to fetch help. What did they say? How long will it take them to get here?"

Zanne was silent for a moment. Then she shook her head.

"What did they say? Very little — as usual. No, I'm sorry

Siri. Hillen Coven is here now, as much as it can be. And we're going to have to help ourselves."

"But they've left us to die! They were all in it, not just Mab and Truc and Anarad. They made Mab and Truc do the worst bit because we would trust them. They're horrible and wicked. They ought to be punished — !"

Sharp-witted little rat, thought Zanne. She wasn't fooled for a minute. I was. I have never had to learn what Siri has learned: I've lived soft, Mab was right. She knew the worst now. She looked down at the silver moonlamp and heard Anarad Pensioner say again: *Inland must have its metal.* Her hands closed over the polluted silver, tenderly.

"Perhaps so. But who has the right to do the punishing, Siri? You're a Minither yourself. And so am I, and so is every covener at Hillen. Do you see?"

Sirato had only just begun to believe in the Covenant and she wanted vengeance, not riddles. "I suppose you know best. But it doesn't seem fair."

Zanne chuckled. "Always fair," she corrected. "Magic isn't easy but it always plays fair, that's what my old teachers used to tell me."

She stood up, in one neat movement. "Come on, Siri. It's time we joined the meeting."

"The meeting? But how can we — ?"

"Watch and see. I suppose our friends thought it was very appropriate, shutting me up to die with the wicked makers. They don't know how right they were about Zanne of Garth and her shocking habits."

By the moonlamp's light the rockfall was even worse than Siri had pictured it. A huge pile of broken rock had pushed into the cave and shattered the wall for a long way on either side of what had been the entrance. The Minithers had come very near to killing their helpless prisoners quickly instead of slowly. Siri tried a few of the stones, without much hope. She was afraid of starting a further fall — and even if they avoided that disaster it might take days to dig through. She had seen her friend split a river pebble with a blade of grass, but this would need a different scale of magic.

The moonlamp had moved away. Zanne was walking round the cave. Skirting that gaping crack in the floor she stopped beside each of the dead makers.

"What are you doing? Are you looking for tools so we can dig?"

"That's right."

Zanne sounded more confident than she felt. Once when she was a young girl she had found a cave like this one, where relics of the past had been preserved. She had been able to wake those great tools and make them move again because unlike most coveners of Inland she did not see them as alien to her magic. Her particular talent showed her the identity between the powers that the people of the past had harnessed, and the forces of nature. But there had been another factor. Zanne loved all kinds of tools, and she had been able to feel in those Mid-Inland makers the familiar ones used by tradespeople of her own village, built larger than life: the water wheel, the cider press, the lathe. It was not like that here. Zanne knew nothing whatever about mining.

But she did know that somewhere close to this sealed cavern, the evil that she had disturbed by coming to Minith was reaching its final climax. Something was happening which must be prevented. There must be a way, there must be a way to reach that terrible place in time...

"Magic depends on likeness," she murmured, half to herself. "Find me something that was built to do the work of a hundred picks and shovels."

"I can't see any shovels," said Siri. She had followed the lamp, keeping well back from the dead horrors. She spoke soothingly, for Zanne's mind seemed to be wandering.

"That one's a bit like a big hummocky I s'ppose."

"A what?"

"A hummocky. The little red garden miner — you know it."

"A mole?" hazarded Zanne — though she had never seen a red one.

"No, no. A worm. We call them hummockys because of the little heaps of tailing they push out, from their tunnels in the soil."

An earthworm. A giant earthworm, meant to eat rock instead of soil: chewing it up in front and pushing it out behind. Zanne gazed at the maker that Sirato had picked out. The moonlamp flamed white, showing every line as clearly as if in bright daylight. Sirato, hovering nervously, thought that Zanne had "gone away" again. The figure holding the lamp looked empty, and as thin as its own shadow. Then she gasped, and almost screamed. The dead thing began to move. It raised its long segmented snout, which had been lying tumbled on the ground. The things it walked on, neither wheels nor feet but something like sled runners, gathered themselves out of the blur of decay. At the end of the snout a whorled mouth opened. There were meshing wheels or blades inside, which began to move with a clashing, unearthly sound.

"Ah — "

Zanne came out of her stillness laughing in delight. She had not heard that music for many years.

"Isn't it magnificent!"

The maker was far worse decayed than the ones she had raised from the dead in Garth: but Zanne's talent was better trained than it had been, and it was still growing. Perched on the worm's back, behind the grinding mouthparts, there was a kind of bubble with immensely thick walls, like the shell of a snail. By Zanne's magic it was whole again and ready to protect the worm's riders.

"Quickly now. See, there are some little steps. We have to get inside."

"Nooo!"

The giant worm snarled. Its mouth moved questingly. Poor Sirato dared not leave the circle of light but she had backed away as far as she could. She did not see anything beautiful at all. The magic presence that Zanne had given to the maker made it only more hideous. It ought to be dead and it was alive. Siri's vision was sharpened by the poison that was everywhere in the air and rock under this mountain. Normally any Inlander would have felt disgust at this thing's existence without knowing why. Sirato could actually see how the alien thing shuddered and reformed itself every instant, fighting with the different reality of Inland.

"I can't!" she cried. "I feel sick, my head hurts. It's like — it's like the changed!"

Zanne was already in the cab. She got down on her knees by the door. She was itching to grab Sirato and bundle her inside — there was no time to lose. But she forced herself to behave like a covener.

"You're right. It is like the changed. It doesn't belong in this world. I think what upsets you is the feeling of *crowdedness*, the feeling of two things trying to be in the same place: our world and theirs. You can't help that. But you can choose whether or not to call your upset, fear. All you have to do is decide not to be afraid. Does that help?"

If Zanne had tried to bully Sirato out of her panic, she would have failed. But the calm voice roused Siri. She remembered throwing stones at the terrible beast creatures. She had been proud of that bravery. She saw that there could be more, things even more impossible for a sneaking little Rat. Not to throw stones at the unknown, the terrible thing: but to trust it, to accept it. Her eyes kindled. She couldn't be like Zanne, not really, but perhaps she could pretend.

"*Not to be afraid* — " she whispered, as if the words were magic, and put her hand on the grip beside the little steps. The touch of it almost had her screaming again: it was not metal or wood or stone — it was not anything. Sirato climbed up, into the belly of the monstrous un-thing.

She collapsed on the floor.

"Now the door is going to close," said Zanne firmly.

Something hissed. They were locked inside. Sirato bit her tongue to hold back a wail. Forgetting how proud and brave she was she doubled over, clutching her head with both hands.

"Oh, oh, oh — "

The worm moved. Sirato had never felt anything like such a sensation. It was like being carried over a huge weir, by a thrust of water more massive than a hundred Burnhouse streams together. She was lifted up in the middle of a shuddering mass, and carried; and then a terrible noise began, a crashing grinding whining smashing...

Sirato cautiously uncovered her face. The windows of the bubble were dark and moving. She thought they were somehow underwater, then she realised that the dark was rock. She was looking at the inside of the worm's burrow as it chewed its way through the rockfall. She cried Oh! again, this time on a long drawn-out breath of wonder. The huge grinding noise went on but it was like a storm out of doors. She sat up and stared. In front of her there was a shelf covered with bumps and whorls and little dead eyes. She leaned closer to see, fascinated.

"Neither wood nor skin nor stone, nor metal out of the rock," said Zanne's voice beside her. She sounded as if she was smiling. "Don't touch, Sirato. Those were the controls but we can't use them. This ghost is running on pure magic."

Everything was confused. They were inside an earthworm, watching it chew up tiny lumps of soil. Siri almost expected the worm's pointed head to burst through into a world of shiny green blades, tall as houses and sharp as knives. But that wouldn't happen. She felt a surge of fierce delight, thinking of the real size of this thing.

"Now they'll get a surprise, Aunt Lecte and Carad Breakwater and all those others. When we come riding down to Minith town in this they're going to be sorry!"

Her last words became a high-pitched shout, loud and shrill in an unexpected silence. The worm had come to a halt.

"We're free," said Zanne. She opened the cab door and climbed down. Siri followed, finding her legs rather wobbly. The underground darkness was a shock, she had forgotten that escaping from their prison did not mean escape from the mountain.

"That's something to remember for your grandchildren," said Zanne grinning. "Let me tell you, Siri Slack Road, there are not many Inlanders who would have ridden in the belly of that monster with me. You think you're weak, but inside you are like a rock. Just like your aunt Lecte."

She held up the moonlamp. They were in the tunnel along which Mab and the others had led them, supposedly towards the poison vault. But there was no cavern mouth in that direction now, only an unbroken wall of rocky wreckage. Anarad's blasting had blocked the way completely. Zanne looked around her. She knew now where she would find the people of Minith. But she could not tell how to reach them. The presence she had been hunting for so long was too close. She was inside Minith's disease, she couldn't find it.

"Sirato," said Zanne softly. "Tell me, child of Minith, are you being called to a Covenant meeting?"

There was so much going on in Sirato's mind that it was

hard to tell. But when Zanne asked, she knew the summons was there.

"Why yes — " She broke off in surprise. "But not to Anarad Pensioner's house. The call — it comes from there." She pointed blankly at the rockfall. "Zanne, I don't understand."

"I think I do."

Zanne's voice was grim. "I made a mistake, Siri — I mean, another of my many. When I found out about the changed, I thought I understood everything. I thought that horrible secret was to blame for all that seemed to me wrong and twisted about Minith's Covenant. I was very wrong. I should have realised, this plague doesn't change only bodies, it does not affect only a few. Minith is poisoned all the way through: and in a way your brother and his companions are not the ones who have suffered worst. At least they know that they are sick. Siri, we have to reach your people at their secret meeting place. There must be other ways. I can feel that this mountain is riddled with passages. Can you be my guide?"

Sirato didn't ask for more explanation. Fired by Zanne's urgency, she turned eagerly to the giant worm.

"There's no need. The maker will take us through — "

But the monster had changed. It had laid its head down on the rock as if it was tired. As she watched, it sank further into itself like a snake's discarded skin or the chrysalis when a butterfly has left it. It was Zanne's magic that had slipped out of the shell, leaving it dead and empty as before.

Sirato stood uncertainly.

"Oh — the poor thing."

Zanne almost laughed. That was the first time any other Inlander had ever pitied one of her beloved makers.

"It's no use, Siri. I can't keep the worm alive anymore. It's too dangerous, there is too much of that poison in the air here. And if I could it would not solve anything if we charged on the Minithers roaring and snarling in that thing. Fighting force with force is like trying to put out a fire with lamp oil."

Sirato looked around her, shivering. So much blackness, so many dark holes.

"I'll try," she quavered. "I'll try — "

So they walked. Every time they came to a choice of ways, Siri said yes, or no: or more often, I can't tell! The light of the moonlamp bobbed on wet rock and dry rock, and on a roof sometimes so low they had to crawl. Zanne found that her pace was quickening. From a brisk walk she had progressed to a stumbling trot, so that Sirato was struggling to keep up. And still something urged her — *hurry, hurry* . . .

"Zanne — Zanne! I don't know what to do! I'm lost!"

"Lost — " gasped Zanne. "All lost, all of them. I can't bear it!"

She stopped dead.

Siri ran into her back: her "guide" had been leading from behind for some time.

"Zanne?"

"Hush."

Zanne suddenly knew that there was more in her mind than the new understanding and urgency that she had gained from her vision of the Thirteen. As once before, in that cave where the wild cat was about to attack, someone was trying to speak to her: in the way Inland magic called *forbidden.*

She stood very still, dowsed the moonlamp and put it in her pocket. The moonless night of earth flooded over her and the Minith girl. Siri groped for her hand. And there, almost at once in that cool blackness she found a voice.

She recognised it, at last. But there was no time to think about that revelation.

"I'm coming!" Zanne cried silently. "Hold on!"

She began to run again, without a light, pulling Siri along behind her through the black, blind veins of the mountain.

CHAPTER NINE

THE GOOD SHEPHERD

ZANNE KEPT ON running, her bare feet meeting and leaving the cool unseen rock without hesitation, trusting completely in the voice that called her. Through a maze of twists and turns she and Siri hurried, until at last there was a spark of light ahead. It grew into a yellow flower petal and then into a ragged oval opening. They stopped together, standing in a hole in the wall of a big brightly lit chamber. They could see other entrances, the main one large and wide and well-used. No one seemed to have noticed their arrival.

The chamber was full of people. Some were carrying mine flares and wildfire torches, more torches were fixed around the walls. Everybody seemed to be moving, jostling and pushing to and fro in an unruly dance. But as Zanne's eyes adjusted to the smoky flamelight she saw that the people were standing still. She felt sick. Only one group in the crowd — the guardians — had made the full change. But it was working in them all: a hideous fluid stirring in faces and limbs and bodies.

The cave was partly natural and partly makers' work. There were signs that the big entrance had once been sealed, and there were cracks and fissures in the walls that must have been caused by the same violence that split the floor of the makers' cave and caused that rockfall above. Zanne wondered if the first Minithers who chipped and burrowed their way in here had known what they were doing. Was the seeping poison already drawing them to itself, or did they come here innocently, looking for metal? It hardly mattered, the result was the same. In the wall opposite to Zanne and Sirato's window there was a huge square block of the ancient building material Inland people called 'powder stone'. It had been fitted tight once, like a stopper in a bottle. It was cracked and ominously discoloured now. Zanne swallowed hard. She had told Sirato not to be afraid. But it wasn't so easy, in the very presence of the terror from the past.

The Minithers were beyond fear tonight. They had relaxed their rule, there were children and flores here. She saw even babies in their father's or their mother's arms. What was it they were going to do or suffer that everyone had to see? The beast-creatures were penned in the middle of the crowd by the walls of bodies. They ran about and danced, shuddering and snarling in the pain of their transformation. The crowd was like a mind holding a nightmare ... the bad dreams of the past.

"We are their dreams!" cried Zanne. "Magic was a dream in their world, just as the makers are ghosts in ours. But there are nightmares too. The people of the past were terrified of that poison: if the poisoned waste had escaped from containment it would have caused horrible sickness in their time too. But nothing like this. In our magic world things can happen that could never be more than bad dreams and fireside stories in the past ... Oh Siri, Inland is a terrible place! Siri — ?"

The girl was gone.

Zanne stared into the seething pit. She could not see anywhere the wiry, dark-haired child in a torn smock. She could not remember when she had let go of Sirato's hand. She had lost the only Minither she had managed to save. Calling the girl's name frantically she scrambled down the rockface and plunged into the melée, forgetful of everything but Sirato's horrible danger. The Minithers had not set guards. They believed there was no more danger of meddling intrusion into their secrets. But as Zanne thrust her way through the packed bodies she was soon recognised. Hands grabbed at her, voices exclaimed. She was handed over to a pair of burly miners.

"What shall we do with her?"

"Take her to the elders, they will decide."

They did not seem to know how they were changed. The combination of those serious, restrained Minith voices and the oozing shuddering flesh was horrible.

In the centre of the chamber three of the elders — Carad Breakwater, Lecte Slack Road and Trevi Burnhouse the miner — were gathered with their covener. A passage had been left clear from the place where they stood to the cracked block of powder stone.

Zanne could see now why Anlys believed she must never leave Minith.

"So," said Carad, her broad ruddy face moving strangely. "Mab told us you were sealed in the Makers' cave. Hillen magic is something to reckon with after all." She glanced contemptuously at her covener. "We never found it so before, I must say."

Lecte Slack Road looked at her truant dayworker with bleak pity. "You should have stayed with your makers," she said. "You are the most to blame for what happens here tonight: still, I would have spared you what you will see."

Zanne noticed that there was a kind of rope harness hanging from the powder stone block. A cold thrill went through her.

"What is that for? What are you going to do?"

Anlys Covener gave a kind of sob. She was clutching in both hands a roll of heavy canvas, the bag that held a covener's tools — tools she had never used in Minith, where the people ate no meat.

"Generation after generation," said Lecte, "we Minithers have suffered for Inland. Most of Inland's metal comes from our fertile mines, and that is a fact. Now even Zanne of Garth the maker-lover knows how dangerous the past is to our world. Even you, at the end, changed your mind and gave up what you most loved, isn't that so? The evil life of those days was built on metal: the towers of light and the makers and all the other abominations. Therefore, when Inland takes metal from the rock, there is a price to be paid. When the miners, our ancestors, first discovered the poison, they understood how things were meant to be. They accepted the Covenant that we accept still, for Inland's sake. Because we are weak and human each of us tries to keep our children safe: tamed and quiet and restrained by constant wholesome work. Because we are Covenanters and strong, when the final choice comes ..."

Her voice shook. "I have been at fault. I tried to evade the punishment, and I thank my fellow Minithers for reproving me. It is right that I sacrifice, tonight, what I love best."

"It is because of you, Zanne," declared Carad, "that the poison is working more strongly than ever before, and making us pay a higher price than ever. But we can bear this too, under our Covenant."

A silence had grown. All eyes were turned towards Zanne and the elders: hundreds of crazy Minith eyes. They were not ashamed. They wanted, they even expected Zanne's approval. She looked at the serious proud faces of the three elders. It seemed impossible that these were Inland people. If they had all been changed into savage monsters with blood dripping from their fangs it would have been less horrible. But they thought that they were good. They were as righteous and self-satisfied here, as at one of those long-winded daytelling sessions around the supper table.

"What do you mean?" she cried. "What 'sacrifice', Lecte?"

No one answered. Zanne stared at the harness on the powder stone, and Anlys with her butcher's tools. The sacrifice of Lecte's dearest treasure —

"You are mad!" she whispered. "All of you — " This time she intended no insult or accusation, she just could not contain her horror at the extent of the damage Minith had suffered.

Siri knew what she had to do the moment she saw Holne. She was very frightened. If she plunged into that crowd the change would get her again, and she didn't have the moon-lamp this time. But Holne, when he was a wild beast, had remembered her and Zanne and driven the other beasts away. She couldn't desert him. Sirato didn't know what Zanne was going to do. All that business about Hillen Coven being here and not here was too confusing. Nor did she understand what this meeting was about. It was hard to think at all: the smoke and flames got into her head and made her mind buzz, disturbed her vision. But she felt the threat to Holne. He was going to be punished, punished for something that wasn't his fault —

Knowing that Zanne wouldn't let her go she said nothing; just climbed down silently while Zanne was busy with more of her riddles. It was easy for a little girl to dart between the arms and legs without being spotted.

There was Holne. He wasn't with the other monsters. The people around him were normal young Minithers. He was half changed and half not changed, a mountain cat on its hind legs with a hairless muzzle and red-rimmed human eyes. They had put clothes on him over the animal hide: a sort of long dark blue smock that she didn't recognise, sewn all over with white embroidered stars. The effect was horrible. Only yesterday she would have run screaming from such a vision. But things had been happening to Siri so fast that she had learned not to trouble with inessentials. It was her brother she saw, not the monster.

"Holne — " she hissed. "Holne — come quickly. Zanne's here. There's going to be big trouble. Come on, I'll show you the way out."

He heard her, she was sure of that. She danced from foot to foot trying to see between the shoulders. Now the flores on either side seemed to be leading him off somewhere.

"*Holne*!"

The beast's eyes turned on her. Its thin dark lips writhed back from its teeth. There was a bubbling sound from the throat and mouth no longer meant to make words. "*Get away* — " snarled a terrible voice. "Little Rat — get away from me!"

Zanne was trying desperately to think of some argument that would break through the insanity. It was no use telling them they could be free. They loved their bondage. It was no use telling them metal could be had without this suffering. They wouldn't want such paltry stuff . . . In their twisted way Minithers actually enjoyed their life of pain and fear, and hated Zanne for threatening to take it away from them. It wasn't for nothing that they called the monsters "the guardians". The only way to argue with crazy people is on their own terms. What were those terms? Nothing was more important to Minithers than their good opinion of themselves.

"It is not true," she cried at last, "that you have saved Inland. You cannot cut yourselves off from us. You've kept your secret from the web of Covenant meetings, but still the poison has escaped. If we had known, do you think we would have shared your harvest? We are all to blame, for leaving you in your isolation: but we have all suffered too."

"That's a lie." Carad stated flatly. "Never a one of the changed or partly changed has left these valleys."

"No, but we all use your metal and it is polluted. There is not enough good magic, everyone knows that. Inland isn't all powerful. It is a struggling new growth trying to spread out over a dead world. In magic everything affects everything else. You think you are paying for our knives and ploughshares. It isn't so, good can't come from evil in our world. Instead all Inland has to pay for your 'brave suffering'. You are not strong. You are weak. You have been a secret drain on the strength of the Covenant: and who can tell what has been lost because of you? Maybe there are great tracts of desolation that could have been green fields. The fact is, Minith has been sending out imperfect goods — "

She had reached them. In their pride at least, the Minithers were sincere. They were listening.

Why, this is their meeting house after all, she thought. No wonder that other place felt like an empty barn. Mad and wicked as this gathering was at least it was real to the people, not a pretence acted out just for show. There was a chance.

Then someone, she recognised one of the old lamp tenders from that other meeting house, touched Carad on the shoulder.

"He's ready."

The crowd stirred all together, like one animal in pain.

Sirato wasn't going to be put off. Many hands, indistinct figures, pulled her back. A way opened for her brother and his escort. She dived into the space behind them and jumped to snatch a fold of that strange gown.

"Holne — don't go with them! The Covenant will get you — "

But as she touched the cloth something invisible slapped her hand away and pushed her violently to the ground.

Four young women and four young men led Holne of Slack Road through the chamber. Lecte Slack Road was at fault. She had taken in the outsider, and she had tried to keep first Holne and then Sirato from the changing disease. Therefore her nephew must be the one. It would do Lecte good to see him die. Nobody knew if this thing had been done before. Records were not kept of the meetings under the mountain. But the Minith Covenant was based on self-sacrifice, and what could they do to themselves that was worse than wilfully taking on the guilt of murder? It had been decided that this was the way to appease the poisoned mountain, so that the young people it changed would only suffer and die, they would no longer be compelled to kill.

Zanne saw Holne led towards her, dressed in a mockery of Hillen Coven's robes. Anlys Covener was fumbling with terribly clumsy hands, trying to open her butcher's bag. Zanne saw the furred, clawed paws of a bear . . . that shook and writhed and became hands again from one moment to another. Anlys was whimpering faintly.

All around the crowd pushed close. The smoky wildfire flickered in red and orange overhead, painting weird shadows on distant rocky walls. Holne did not struggle. His distorted face seemed peaceful as they strapped him up against the block. After all, he was only exchanging a slow death for a quick one.

Anlys had taken out a long knife. That was not what a covener would use to kill meat, there were kinder ways. Apparently this death must be as brutal as possible. One of the young guards was lifting Holne's head to bare his throat. Her eyes were terrified, as if what her hands were doing was out of her control.

In that moment, it came to Zanne with strange clarity that whatever happened here Inland would survive. Anlys, and others before her, had fallen and vanished into this pit of horrors in the heart of the magic web. But one day a stronger covener would come, and the pit would be cleansed. Even if Zanne failed, even if she died here, in the end all would be well.

It was quite possible that she might die. For she was not going to let them kill Holne, she was sure of that. Zanne had been sent to help these people, these individual human creatures here, not their children or their children's children. It was Holne who mattered to her; and Lecte and Truc and Mab and Carad Breakwater: the people who would be destroyed by the murder just as surely as their victim. She remembered the voice that had cried in her mind, sobbing *all lost, all of them ...*

But there was no voice now.

She could still feel the presence of Minith meeting. She had made them doubt the value of their suffering and that had woken them up, on the brink of destruction. If only she could gather the wavering minds and hearts, draw them into herself. But Zanne was only a killer of dead makers, she could not lead a meeting.

"Anlys — put that knife down! I need you!"

"She is our covener. She will do the will of the meeting."

It was Carad who spoke: and now even Carad had lost her dignity. She sounded terrified and helpless, like someone who has been acting a part in a horrible game, and suddenly finds that the game is real.

Suddenly Lecte Slack Road, who had been watching in silence, cried out, "Zanne, can't you see? We want to draw back but we can't, it's too late. Do what you came to do. Use your magic, if you really have such power. Don't wait for our consent."

The buzzing silence had thickened to a hum of discordant sound, of many voices softly crying, whining, whimpering. A hand or face or patch of sober clothing showed here and there, but the ugly confusion would soon swallow these last traces. It was as if Zanne and Lecte stood alone, the only human creatures left. But Lecte's power of resistance, strong though it was, was not enough. Zanne needed something more: a magic mind to link with her own.

"I cannot," she cried. "I cannot use my magic here, without the will of the meeting. You know that, Lecte. There must be a covener. Is there no one? No one in all of Minith?"

Then Lecte Slack Road, at last, gave up the fight. "There is no one," she whispered. "It's no use, Zanne. Minith rock doesn't breed magic talent. That has always been the way, part of the price we paid." She turned her face, set and still, to watch without flinching the final horror.

The thing that had been Anlys Covener snuffled and moaned as it shuffled towards the block where Holne stood.

If she made a sudden rush and tackled the bear woman physically, without magic, what would the rest of this mad hideous crowd do? Zanne shuddered. Well, she could soon find out the answer to that.

"No," whispered Zanne. "I won't give up, I won't ..."

Running towards this chamber in the black night of the mountain, she had been certain that another magic mind was calling to hers. That contact had vanished before she and Siri reached their window in the rock wall. Where was it now? Where was that mind, and how could she reach it again?

She could not see the creature tied to the powder block as a wild cat any longer. It was nothing more than a mass of writhing flesh, that seemed to scream silently as it cringed from the touch of the poisoned stone.

The power of magic is in likeness, in identity ...

Oh, no.

Zanne drew a breath. "Very well," she said calmly, clearly. "*I am a Minither.* I told you that before, in your other meeting house. Now I suppose I'll have to prove it."

She closed her eyes. Ever since she had arrived in Minith, she had been lecturing herself: don't think yourself better than these people, don't judge them. When at last she knew the whole truth about the Minith plague she had believed what she told Siri: this madness is part of Inland, and therefore part of me as well. But to say *I am a Minither* was not enough anymore. She had to make that real. Deliberately she released all her defences, all the barriers that she had built up, half-unconsciously, against what happened to people here: and fell into that vortex from which she had rescued Sirato, out on the mountainside in the sunlight. At once the change, which she had been watching as a shocked spectator, was outside her no longer. It was in her flesh, in her mind: breaking, bursting. The power of the past flooded through her, not as Zanne of Garth could comprehend it but as Minith felt it: fear and destruction tearing her apart. She had known that magic talent in itself offered no protection. She found out it was much worse than that. Her magic intensified the effect of the poison. She could hear somebody screaming, and knew it was herself. In the rock chamber she thought she saw her own body, a thing with tufts of yellow hair, falling on its knees and writhing, splitting open ...

"Help me!" she screamed — and half saw, half sensed the staring Minithers draw back. They could do nothing.

Help me —

And she was there, in the same reality as that other magic mind. It could hear her now, even through the wild tumult of its own pain ... It could answer her desperate call.

Zanne opened her eyes. She was smiling. The stilled and hopeful Minithers all knew why. None of them (but one) understood how: but at the last moment, the flock had found a shepherd. Zanne looked down at her whole and painfree body and wondered if that other thing she had seen had been real. Had she and all these people really fallen — right over the brink of worse than death? Whether or not, it didn't matter anymore. They were safe now. No one spoke. There was no need to announce what had happened. The meeting was joined and had work to do, that was all.

She stepped forward to the block of powder stone, aware of the mixed reactions of the Minithers: how some were quite bemused and some still almost resentful as if something precious was being taken from them. Others were already beginning to wipe this night from their memories. But the balance had fallen. The underlying will to accept Zanne's intervention was there, and channelled so that she could use it. She was aware of Sirato somewhere nearby, excited and delighted because the good Covenant had "won". And poor Anlys ... The young guards had melted into the crowd. Holne and Zanne exchanged one glance, then the grotesque half-monster too slipped away and hid himself in the shadows.

Zanne laid her hands on the ancient stone. She reached into herself, and into what lay beyond the forms of rock and stone and earth and flesh and even mind itself.

"The people of the past were right to be afraid," said Zanne. "They took a terrible power and tried to use it and not use it, to take one part and ignore others. The great forces of being deserve more respect than that: and they have ways of taking what's owed to them. But the fear has outlived its time. In Inland, though we sometimes make mistakes, we do understand that everything moves together, that there is no separation. And we have opened another path from the deeps of *between* into the world. We call it magic."

"In our reality, there is nothing behind this stone. There is no secret under Minith mountain, only rock and air and water ..."

Those who were nearest heard the young covener speak but none of them troubled to follow her words. All they wanted was to have the thing done, they didn't need explanations. They saw that she had tears in her eyes, and wondered why. But once again the child who had longed to see the shining makers dance their dance of power and hear them sing, found herself face to face with the lost past. Once again she brought to the things she loved the only gift she had to give: death, the greatest transformation.

Don't blame me, whispered the covener. *I will die too ...* And softer still, she promised: we will be back, power of the between. We will call on you again one day, and no one will be poisoned then.

In the antechamber, all was still. Then someone laughed, and someone cried — "The changed — look, they have come back!" A girl with red hair ran up out of the crowd: the elders gasped when they saw her. She clutched Zanne's hand, sobbing.

Carad Breakwater was blinking as if she'd just woken from a heavy and troubled sleep. Rapidly, she recovered herself.

"So it worked. Very good. Zanne of Garth, Minith thanks you. If you did harm, you have undone it. Of course our trouble will return — " she went on proudly. "It will always be with us. But at least we may have peace for a while."

The small grey-eyed girl with the ragged yellow hair looked up at the broad imposing Minither farmer. She smiled a little, but said nothing.

"A respite," agreed Lecte Slack Road. "And a chance, let's hope, to change in other ways — "

The powder stone block behind Zanne began to crumble.

The whole crowd leapt backwards together, parents grabbing children and covering their faces in a futile gesture. There was no chance to get away. So swiftly that no one could see how, the block was gone. The gap in the antechamber wall stood open and the people of Minith looked into the inner vault. The source of all their terror had become an empty cave. Torchlight gleamed on its bare rock walls. As they watched, a little grey dust that had drifted on the floor rose into the air and vanished. Through a split in the roof far above they could feel the cool air, and see the blue sky and starlight of a quiet summer's night.

EPILOGUE

A LITTLE BIT OF DARK

THE MINERS HEARD the rain as they came out into daylight. They walked the last stretch of tunnel in a dim mobile brightness, dowsing lamps and unstrapping the baskets from their backs. Outside the stone crusher groaned monotonously. The pair who were turning it trudged with their heads down, water streaming from their oilskins and hat brims. In a few hours the mountain had been completely transfigured. Yesterday, as the last of the grain was brought in, it had been burning summer. Miners had climbed up to work through scorched grass and shrivelled thorns into a high desert of sharp-edged horizons and violent colour: ochre and black, steel-blue and rust-red. Now everything was soft, the world was painted like a dove's breast in a thousand different shades of grey.

In the sorting hall, an open cave from which many passages led away into the workings, the miners turned over the contents of their own and several other basketloads while the rain sang and streamed outside.

"A poor harvest this year," remarked one woman gloomily.

"Indeed yes, and for many years to come," agreed another.

It stood to reason, whatever that strange covener girl said, that the loss of a burden must be paid for.

"But that's the way things are. Life's hard, like the rock. And we were in the wrong. We have to thank Hillen for reproving us."

"That's right. It always does people good to have their faults shown up."

The miners sighed in unison. Then Trevi Burnhouse, one of the best judges of the ore in Minith, took up the samples he had chosen. While the others put on their waterproofs he went to one of the newer tunnels. Inside, just within reach of daylight, he eased the promising chunks of quartz into a seed groove, chipping the grafts into place with a few expert blows of a small hammer. The greedy past had left so little metal in the rock, anywhere. It was fortunate that Covenant magic could bring the seed to life.

Trevi sighed heavily. "I doubt if more than one of those will take," he muttered, rubbing one hand over the bed before it. The grafts there had amalgamated beautifully: but of course you couldn't tell, not for a long time yet. Might not propagate at all, with all this fuss and bother.

He said as much to the others, and they all agreed. Contentedly, gloomily, they shouldered their tackle and set off into the rain, each heading for an identical silver-grey homestead, a frugal meal and the sober recreation of the daytelling.

Sirato and Zanne came down to the token tree. It was over a month since the night under the mountain. Zanne had been travelling around the valleys: to bleak Crags and the other high farms, to Breakwater down among its huge ancient pines. She had returned to Slack Road to say goodbye, and to complete one last task before she left Minith. She and Sirato had been into the mountain again. Siri had waited outside while Zanne went alone into the Makers' cave, to do what must be done. When she came out again the old makers, like the poison, were gone: nothing left but harmless dust.

Zanne was wrapped in her waggon cloak but the Minither girl was bareheaded, and danced about joyfully with her mouth open to catch the splashing drops.

"Isn't it lovely, Zanne!"

Zanne had been quiet and sad since they left the tunnels, but now she smiled.

"Beautiful. But I will have plenty of chances to get wet between here and Hillen."

They were ambushed by a pair of soaking overgrown lambs, who seemed as delighted as Siri at the breaking of the drought and wanted to celebrate by playing head-butting with all comers. Sirato kicked them with her hard little feet and chased them until they vanished over the rocks.

Laughing, she came back to Zanne. They stood looking down into the cloud-filled valley: even the roofs of Slack Road were invisible.

"What did you mean, that night in the tunnels," asked Siri at last. "When you said Hillen Coven was with us 'as much as it could be'. Are they still here now?"

She imagined thirteen dark-robed figures, visible to Zanne's magically trained eyes: perhaps hovering in the rainy sky.

Zanne shook her head. "No, it isn't like that. You know, Siri, we always say the Covenant is in everyone, and the whole of Inland is held in every person's mind and heart. I thought I believed that but I didn't really, before Minith taught me. When I came here I thought I was 'under orders', just like one of those guardians of Minith Covenant. When things went wrong I was expecting some higher authority to tell me what to do. But Inland doesn't work that way." She grinned. "When I was a horrible conceited little girl, I used to say 'I am Hillen Coven'. The frightening thing is, in the end that's true. And so are you, Siri."

"I will remember too," she added thoughtfully. "That I would have lost Minith — not to mention my life — if I hadn't given up my safe separation from your trouble. Things only came right when I, the rescuer, had to ask for help."

Sirato nodded seriously. "What will happen to Anlys?"

She believed, like everyone else, that at that last desperate moment the covener had overcome her shameful weakness, and Anlys had been the channel for Zanne's magic. Minith memories of that night were confused and always would be.

"She has gone back to Hillen. The rest's none of our business." Zanne looked grave. She was thinking of all the harm done: of Rian Mountainside and so many others, of all the pain and shame that could not be made to disappear by this happy ending. But then she turned to the clear-eyed, lively girl beside her, and suddenly laughed.

"Siri, I have a goodbye present for you. Hold out your hand and close your eyes."

"Oh! Zanne — is it a moonlamp?"

"No, I'm afraid not. Quite the opposite."

Siri did as she was told, looking puzzled. Her fingers closed automatically over something cool, flat and hard.

"Open your eyes."

She looked down. Lying in her palm was a fragment of silvered glass, smoothed into a round shape. Zanne must have rescued one of the broken pieces of her mother's mirror. The girl smiled. She didn't need that consolation so much anymore, but it was a nice thought. She was about to thank Zanne politely, when she saw that the small reflection of her face (her mother's face) had vanished. She was looking through her own hand into an abyss of utter darkness. She could no longer feel the glass. Her eyes were drawn deeper, deeper . . .

"Oh, Zanne — it's — it's magic . . ."

"Put it in your pocket," suggested her friend. "Keep it there. Then perhaps you won't be frightened of it anymore."

At the door of Slack Road kitchen Lecte stood waiting with Zanne's pack and staff.

"Go indoors," she said to Siri, "and see what your father has brought for you."

Sirato's bright face went white, then red in two burning spots in the middle of her thin cheeks. She dashed into the house.

Lecte shook her head grimly.

"That child is far too excitable."

"Is it the violin?"

She knew that Gwil had been away for several days on a perilous voyage to the nearest tradestown: an act of great love. The shy brickmaker must have been terrified, he'd never been in a town before in his life.

"Yes it is, and a good one. I hope she will take proper care of it."

Lecte Slack Road was the same, nothing would alter her stern character. But some of the bleak lines had gone from her beautiful proud face. As they both listened to Sirato's cries of excitement from indoors, she almost smiled.

Zanne settled her pack and hesitated, looking out at the wet yard.

"Lecte," she asked softly, "why did you leave Hillen?"

The older woman was silent for a moment. But she did not seem offended, at the uncovering of that old disappointment.

"Nothing very terrible, Zanne of Garth. My magic tricks faded with my childhood. So I came home. Minith has always been stony ground for covening talent. Perhaps, who knows, that will change now: and we will have magic-makers of our own."

"Perhaps it will." Zanne nodded to herself. "You know, I always felt there must be magic in your family somewhere."

With a brisk gesture she dismissed the subject. "I am sorry I have not been able to say goodbye to Holne."

Lecte flinched a little. "He isn't coming back, Zanne. He left us days ago. He cannot bear to stay in Minith. Some of the others are the same. They think people will always see them — as they were."

"Don't give him up, Lecte. Call it his choice journey, for that's what it is."

The farmer looked at the young covener with sudden hope: but if Zanne knew more, clearly she wasn't going to tell. She just stood smiling faintly, fingering some newish scratch marks on the smooth ash wood of her staff.

Outside the porch the rain splashed down with unrelenting vigour. Lecte turned and produced from a shelf inside the door a small package.

"Well, Zanne, no one can pay you for what you have done for Minith. However we at Slack Road would like to give something to Sunny the roadwalker, a little memento. Think of us when you use it — if you do."

Zanne unfastened the package. Next moment she burst out laughing. Lecte Slack Road laughed too, and the laughter made her look quite a different woman.

The present was a hair-comb, of plain bright Minith steel.

Then Gwil came out, with Siri and her new treasure, and Truc, Mab and Danno came from their work in the yards. All the household of Slack Road stood together to wish Zanne well, and wave until her small, sturdy figure, humpbacked from the pack under her cloak, had passed out of sight.

Zanne tramped through the empty valley towards the waggon road. Rain was beating on the hood of her cloak. With her leggings rolled above the knee she splashed cheerfully through the ochre puddles. Left and right the mountains were invisible. The soaked dead grass by the path side streamed water, water filled every runnel of the thirsty ground. Zanne was thinking of the child Sirato, safe and happy with her music: of how all Minith would be restored to health now that the old poison no longer twisted hearts and lives. The mountain people would never lose their dour ways entirely. But they would learn, grudgingly and slowly, how to be happy as well as hardworking and proud.

And what had Zanne of Garth learned? How had she been changed? She had told Siri something about it, but not all. She had learned that there was terror, even in Inland. That the magic world she lived in was fearful as well as beautiful, not only when things went wrong *but in itself*...

Zanne stopped, and turned to look behind her. The mountain was there, invisible in its rain cloud. It was watching her still. She walked on: but after a few paces stopped and stared back again. There was no sound except the beating rain. But she knew that something followed her. *Fear that not even Covenant magic can wholly drive away*... She walked on and looked back twice again: and at last it seemed she could tolerate the invisible presence no longer. At a bend in the track where a battered thorn bush offered an apology for shelter, she sat down by the side of the track and waited.

He came out of the murk and stood a few paces away. Every trace of the self-confidence and bravado that had so irritated Zanne in Lecte Slack Road's favourite had vanished. His shoulders were hunched, his head bowed in shame as if the waterproof cloak huddled closely round his shoulders still hid something horrible. His eyes met Zanne's, and quickly winced away.

"Holne," Zanne welcomed him evenly. "I thought we might meet on this road. I am glad. I was hoping that you would give me a chance to apologise."

The young man shuddered. He came a step nearer.

"But you must admit, you behaved very suspiciously right from the beginning. And then, when I saw you breaking Siri's violin ..."

"That was the cruellest thing." Holne's voice no longer had the ring and assurance that it used to have. "But people always said that was the way it started, with unrestrained ways. And she was turning, I could see it. I didn't know any better — I thought I was helping her."

He crouched down on the wet grass, still keeping at a distance as if he thought he was infectious.

"I tried to tell you, Zanne — what was really happening."

"Yes, and I kept on ignoring you and taking offence: I was to blame."

Holne didn't seem to notice her last words. "But you don't know ... you think, maybe, I was helpless. I wasn't. *I was the beast* ... Even when I tried to warn you and protect you it was there too: smiling, sneering, spying ..."

"Hush, Holne. It is over. Whatever wrong you did, I think you saved my life more than once. And in the end, as we both know, you paid all your debts."

Silence.

"Don't," whispered Holne at last. "Don't speak of that. I know what I am. I was a — a freak, long before the plague began to affect me. I know what they call what I did to you those times at Hillen — *the forbidden magic.* I've always hidden my talent, I will go on hiding it. Boys who meddle in magic ought to be whipped."

The rain splashed noisily. A curlew began to cry, somewhere above them on the lost flank of the mountain.

Zanne sighed. The young man's hope and hunger sounded so clearly through his despairing words that she felt more like laughing, but it wouldn't be kind.

"Boys who meddle in magic usually confine themselves to

a few showy illusions. I don't believe you would know how to produce an illusion at all, would you, Holne of Minith? You go straight for the hard, serious work. Believe me, there are very few students at Hillen at present who could have hidden from me the way you did so often: or spoken to my mind without my invitation."

Holne looked up at last. His face was drawn and wan, but it was no longer the handsome and slightly brutal mask that Zanne had known. She could see the real person now: Siri's brother yet so unlike her, as neat and precise by nature as Siri was wild and careless. She saw what a covener he would make — clever and delicate, surefooted as a cat in all his shiftings and holdings.

She grinned in amusement. She had always wanted to bring a new magic-maker back to Hillen. It was just like the awkwardness of Minith, to be different from the rest of Inland in this way as well.

"I admit," she said, "that I can't see any easy way out. It is going to be hard for you at Hillen. For one thing, most coveners start their training when they are six or seven years younger than you. And then some of the teachers will be prejudiced, and the other students will give you a horrible time, for sure. What's more, who knows, maybe there is a core of truth in the prejudice. I don't know of any other men who are coveners — maybe you will fail in the end. But if you spend your life trying to hide your talent that won't be easy either. You could, of course, ask the Holder to take your magic away, and then you would be free. But could you really give up that part of yourself? Would you ever be happy afterwards? I don't think so."

He stared at her: longing to believe in what she promised, but still clinging to his shame.

"Zanne — *I have been a monster!* I cannot, I cannot come to Hillen."

Then she did laugh. "If that's what you really think, Holne Slack Road, I wonder why you followed me out here. Well, never mind. It is a big choice, I know that. Take your time, go wandering as long as you please. I leave you one thought. Minith needs a covener. Oh, someone will come: but she won't be a Minither. I don't think things will really be right here until the meeting has someone who understands. Someone who can love these rock people and laugh at them, and teach them to laugh at themselves. The question is, Holne, how long are you going to keep them waiting?"

The young man stood by the side of the track until Zanne's small figure had vanished into the white cloud. He stared at the raindrops splashing in violent small fountains in the puddle at his feet. Then suddenly he raised his head.

"Zanne!" he shouted, setting off at a run. "Zanne — wait for me! I've changed — I've changed my mind!"

At the end of the day the rain stopped. Sirato knelt up on a settle at the kitchen window watching the dregs of a wet sunset. Tiring of that, she took out of her pocket the little bit of dark and gazed and gazed. Through her hand, through the kitchen floor: through the earth and right out the other side of things. If she looked long enough, she began to see the stars . . .

"He'll be back," she murmured dreamily. "I know he will."

In another year or two she would be leaving home herself, to learn her trade with a real music-maker. That was what she'd always wanted. But this evening, with such a wet cold world outside, she was secretly a little glad that she didn't have to set out at once. She thought how strange it was that life could become so completely different: in a night, in an hour, like waking up from a dream. Already she could hardly remember what it had been like before. It was as if when

Zanne's magic had changed Minith's fear into harmless dust, it had even changed the past as well...

Aunt Lecte came in from the brickyard, shaking out her waterproof in the porch. Siri jumped up guiltily, wondering what she was supposed to be doing just now.

"Sirato!" exclaimed her aunt. "I thought you were going to practise. Get upstairs at once. And mind, I am listening, so don't sit there dreaming. Let me hear some music."